THE
YOUNGER WIFE

THE
YOUNGER WIFE

SALLY HEPWORTH

HODDER &
STOUGHTON

First published in Great Britain in 2022 by Hodder & Stoughton
An Hachette UK company

1

Copyright © Sally Hepworth 2022

A CIP catalogue record for this title is available from the British Library

Hardback ISBN 978 1 529 39235 7
Paperback ISBN 978 1 529 33094 6
eBook ISBN 978 1 529 33095 3

Printed and bound in Great Britain by Clays Ltd, Elcograf S.p.A.

Hodder & Stoughton policy is to use papers that are natural, renewable and recyclable
products and made from wood grown in sustainable forests. The logging and manufacturing
processes are expected to conform to the environmental regulations of the country of origin.

Hodder & Stoughton Ltd
Carmelite House
50 Victoria Embankment
London EC4Y 0DZ

www.hodder.co.uk

Author's Note

In this novel, you'll meet a character by the name of Heather Wisher. Heather Wisher is, in fact, the name of a real person—specifically, the winner of my Instagram competition to have a book character named after yourself. I want to be clear that while I used Heather's name, the character of Heather Wisher as created in *The Younger Wife* is entirely fictional and not representative of her real-life namesake. (Unless there are any flattering comparisons that Heather would like to draw, in which case, she definitely inspired those parts.)

Prologue

always cry at weddings. Nothing original there, I know—except, perhaps, the reason. Most people cry for joy apparently, or because they've been catapulted back to their own wedding day and are overwhelmed by the emotion of it all. I cry because I am sad. Sad for me, sad for the bride, sad for the institution of marriage. Sad enough that it makes me cry. I'm especially sad at this wedding.

When I arrived, half an hour early, the surrounding streets were already jam-packed with shiny black Range Rovers, Mercedes, and Porsches. I suppose Stephen Aston's wedding was always going to be a fancy affair. It's a warm day and I'm sandwiched into a pew in the nondenominational chapel, surrounded by bunches of freesias, hyacinth, and snapdragons. The venue is entirely too small for the number of guests. The altar barely has space for the groom and celebrant—Lord knows where the bride will stand when she decides to show up.

I am seated toward the back and no one pays me any mind. Why would they? I'm a woman of a certain age; for years I've been bland

and forgettable. People around me—the young, primarily—are always happy to take center stage. My friend Miriam often laments how we have disappeared now that we are older. *No one sees me anymore*, Miriam says. (*Hello!* she shouts aggressively at the deli server who has chosen to serve the pretty young woman in the yoga pants, even though Miriam has been there longer. I suspect Miriam is not as invisible as she believes.)

Stephen is at the front, and it has to be said that, even now, he still takes my breath away. He is flanked by two tiny boys in dinner suits—his grandsons, I expect. It's ridiculous; the little one isn't much more than a toddler and the other is five, tops. They should be at home napping or playing in the mud, not standing in a chapel! Still, it doesn't surprise me that Stephen would want this. And the guests, judging by their cooing, think it's adorable. Stephen's adult daughters, Rachel and Tully, are bridesmaids, no doubt at their father's insistence. Their dresses are navy and flatter them both—no mean feat given Tully is as slim as a whippet while Rachel is what my mother used to describe as "porcine." Their smiles are painted on, unconvincing, but then who would be pleased to see their father marry a woman young enough to be their sister? And while their mother looks on to boot.

I was shocked to see Pamela here. Guests had exchanged worried looks as she entered on her daughter's arm, smiling and waving as if arriving at a red-carpet event. I'd wonder why she was invited, if I didn't know Stephen. Despite what happened, Pamela is family, and to Stephen, family is everything. Pamela takes her seat in the front row, then immediately rises to her feet again, walking purposefully toward Stephen.

The music changes and everyone turns to face the back of the room. The bride is fresh-faced, fake-tanned, and strapped into a dress that likely cost more than the deposit for my first home. She is very attractive—slim and brunette and thirtysomething. I sneak a look at Stephen. He looks proud as punch, and why wouldn't he? Stephen may be a handsome man, but if you're marrying a woman in her thirties when you're in your early sixties, it has to be said you're batting above your average.

The bride arrives at the front to find Stephen and his ex-wife standing there, but Stephen, being Stephen, manages to return her to her seat without anything being awkward—a feat that perhaps only Stephen Aston could pull off. With Pamela out of the way, the bride squeezes into the tiny space beside the groom, and the celebrant—a pigeon-shaped woman in a crisp white pantsuit—invites everyone to be seated.

The room is charged with aggressive goodwill—big unnatural smiles, wide eyes, comments about the bride's dress (which is exquisite). Miriam recently observed that the vast majority of brides resembled the Barbie on a child's birthday cake in their strapless gowns with skirts large enough to smuggle half a dozen leprechauns down the aisle. (*Leprechauns,* she'd whispered pointedly at the wedding of her niece last year. *At least a dozen.*) But not this bride. Heather looks positively elegant in her A-line gown.

As the celebrant starts her spiel, there's the usual rustling in seats as people shift to get comfortable. A baby cries and is removed by his or her father. A few guests fan themselves with the wedding booklets while simultaneously trying not to touch the person on either side of them (a challenge in the cramped space). Then, just as everyone seems to have settled, Pamela stands again. The energy of the room shifts from aggressive goodwill to scandalized breath-holding as she wanders onto the altar, observing her surroundings casually as if perusing produce at the supermarket. Stephen smiles, dispelling the panic in the room. "Carry on," he says to the celebrant.

"I now pronounce you husband and wife," she says uncertainly as Pamela charges past them. She appears to be interested in the stained-glass windows. They are quite beautiful. "You may kiss the bride."

The kiss is chaste and imbued with what appears to be genuine affection. When they separate, Stephen, impossibly pleased with himself, gives a little fist pump and the crowd erupts in applause, with a few whistles thrown in for good measure. The noise spooks Pamela, who looks around worriedly. She grabs an ornate brass candlestick, holding it up in front of her like a shield. Stephen beams at the crowd. He's a newlywed. An ex-wife with Alzheimer's isn't going to rain on his parade.

"Now, if you'll excuse us for a moment," the celebrant says, "I'm going to take the bride and groom into the sacristy to sign the register."

She leads Stephen and his new wife into a room to the side of the altar. The trio is followed by the two little boys, plus Rachel and Tully and Pamela, who is still clutching the candlestick. *Will someone take that poor woman home?* I think.

With the bridal party out of sight, the guests start chatting among themselves.

"Wasn't that lovely?"

"What a beautiful bride!"

"Isn't it wonderful that he found love again?"

"Couldn't have happened to a nicer man!"

It seems as good a time as any to take my leave. I stand, gathering my things, and that's when I hear it. A young woman's scream and then, a dense, meaty thud. I rise at the same time as every other guest. I look to the front of the room, but my view is obscured by large hats and bald heads. I am craning to see through the gaps between the guests when the celebrant reappears. Her face is ashen and her white pantsuit is covered in blood.

1

TULLY

The moment she laid eyes on Heather Wisher, Tully knew this woman was going to destroy their lives. Tully was sitting in the restaurant, fiddling with the salt and pepper shakers, when Heather walked in, half a pace behind Dad. She looked exactly like Tully had pictured her: doe-eyed, soft-featured, chock-full of cunning. She was Rebecca De Mornay in *The Hand That Rocks the Cradle*. A wolf in sheep's clothing. A viper poised to strike.

Game face on, Tully told herself as she rose to her feet. That's what Dad had always said to her. *Game face on, Tully-girl. Smile, be courteous, keep it together. Don't let them see any chinks in the ol' armor. Fall apart later, when you get home.* Tully was already looking forward to falling apart. She had it all planned. She was going to lock herself in the bathroom, where she would take a long, hot shower and cry until she slid down the wall, racked with those deep, guttural sobs that you saw in the movies. The catharsis of a shower cry could not be overstated for a woman in her thirties. Recently, Tully had taken to booking them into her schedule ahead of time—to get out in front of them, as it were. It was a form of self-care, really. Like personal training. And Botox.

"Natalie," Dad said, when he was close enough. He smelled the same as always: Omo laundry detergent and a hint of toothpaste. No aftershave, no fancy deodorants. Dad had always been old-school in this regard. At least the new woman hadn't changed *that* about him. Yet. "This," he said, glancing back over his shoulder, "is Heather."

Heather smiled carefully. Up until that moment, Tully hadn't known it was possible to smile *carefully*, but there it was: the perfect smile for someone in her position. It reminded Tully of the smile you flashed when you bumped into someone you hadn't seen for a while at a funeral. *Rob—it's fantastic to see you . . . and Beverly, I heard about your new business venture . . . but yes, very sad occasion. It was a lovely service.* Careful smile.

Heather looked like a New York fashion editor. She wore an un-creased white shirt with tailored black pants and flat gold sandals, and she carried a Burberry trench over one arm. Her dark hair was center-parted and tucked behind her ears, her lips were painted a tasteful nude-pink. The most striking thing about her was her youth, which Tully had been warned about, yet still found herself inadequately prepared for. *Thirty-four.* Three years younger than Tully. One year younger than Rachel. *Twenty-nine* years younger than Dad. The funny thing was, Mum was six years *older* than Dad. "I like older women," he'd said for most of Tully's life.

"Nice to meet you, Heather," Tully said, offering her a small, strange wave. There was always something a bit awkward about the lack of a handshake. Australia had fared exceptionally well during the COVID-19 pandemic—and since the strict lockdown had been lifted, life had continued more or less as normal, apart from a little more handwashing and people standing slightly farther apart than usual. Still, some people were nervous about the handshake, and Heather, with her perfectly white shirt, seemed like the classic germophobe who would wave away a handshake and then spray Glen 20 disinfectant on her palm "just to be sure." Like Tully did.

"It's lovely to meet you too, Natalie."

"Tully," she corrected. "Only my parents call me Natalie."

It sounded like a barb, Tully thought. Maybe it was.

"My apologies," Heather said sincerely. "Tully."

Tully had to hand it to her—she was bloody faultless. The question was, what was she doing with *Dad*?

Tully tried to see her father through Heather's eyes. He had sandy-gray hair—a full head of it, not bad for his age. He was tall and quite athletic. Actually, now she thought of it, he *had* stepped up the exercise recently. You heard about this kind of thing all the time: middle-aged men taking up marathon running to try to catch the eye of a younger woman. Often they ended up with a six-pack or some biceps before invariably having a heart attack and leaving their formerly penniless younger wives with a sizable inheritance and the freedom to marry a man their own age. Maybe that explained Heather's interest in Dad?

As for Dad's intentions with Heather, that remained unclear. Tully knew that some men liked to have young girlfriends—age-defying, midlife-crisis sort of men with something to prove—but Dad didn't have anything to prove. He was a heart surgeon at the top of his field. A scratch golfer. Chairman of the board of Australia Gives Life, a charity that flew patients to Australia from developing countries to have lifesaving surgery. More importantly, he was a self-confessed dork. A man who was perfectly comfortable running outside in his dressing gown with one last bag of rubbish as the garbage truck approached. A man who prided himself on being able to estimate the exact amount of milk to froth for Mum's cappuccino in the morning. A man who resisted mounting pressure to buy an iPad because he didn't understand what was wrong with a good old-fashioned desktop computer. He was . . . *Dad.*

"What a view!" Dad said, holding his arms out wide to take in Half Moon Bay. It was a beautiful day and the bifold windows were open, letting in a light breeze and offering sweeping views of the sea. There were only four window tables available, and as they were not able to be booked, Tully had arrived an hour and fifteen minutes early to secure one . . . all to impress a woman she already hated. Tully recognized the absurdity of this, but she also understood this was how it had to be. The Astons weren't the type of family to make a scene. They never spoke ill of each other outside the family circle. They never spoke ill of each other *inside* the family circle. The Astons did things nicely. Civilly. And a little bit absurdly.

"You did good, sweetie," Dad said, winking at Tully.

Tully knew she'd done good. She might not be running a successful business like Rachel, but she knew how to find a nice restaurant. Lunch would cost a small fortune, but one of the upsides of going out with her father was that he always paid. If Sonny was present, he and Dad would have a polite scuffle over the bill, but Dad always won. Tully wondered if, given what Sonny was calling their "new financial situation," those polite scuffles would soon be a thing of the past.

"Shall we sit?" Heather suggested.

Heather's voice, Tully noticed, was imbued with a solid upper-middle-class accent, prompting Tully to reassess her hypothesis that

Heather's interest in Dad was an attempt to improve her status in life. She could be a gold digger, but judging by Heather's Burberry trench, the woman wasn't hard up. Which left Tully a bit stumped. If not for money or social standing, why would an attractive woman of thirty-four be interested in Dad?

They all sat. Already Tully was exhausted. She'd spent the evening before on two-year-old Miles's bedroom floor, holding his hand as he got used to his new big-boy bed. She managed to sneak into her own bed around two A.M., before awaking again at daybreak for Pilates followed by packing lunch boxes, cleaning for the cleaner, and heading to preschool drop-off, where she was bailed up by Miles's teacher for half an hour to discuss his "issues." This, plus the extra half hour she spent crying in the car afterward, made her late for her blowout appointment—an unnecessary expense that, in light of their new financial situation, would almost certainly cause problems when Sonny saw it on the credit card statement. But it was going to be a tough day for Tully. A day that required her game face and a blow-out.

Heather reached for the wine menu. "What shall we drink?"

"Let's stick to water for now," Dad said, taking the wine list from Heather and setting it to the side in a gesture that Tully found curious. "At least until Rachel gets here."

Rachel! Tully had nearly forgotten Rachel was coming. At the sound of her sister's name, she felt a curious jolt of emotion. Relief, mostly. Things were always better when Rachel was here. Which was what sparked the other emotion Tully was feeling: irritation. Why did Rachel always have to be the one to make things better?

Tully glanced at her watch: 12:35. What kind of person would be late to meet their father's *new girlfriend*? Annoyingly, Dad wouldn't be bothered in the least. Rachel would stroll in fifteen minutes late and Dad's face would light up because of what Tully thought of as "the Rachel effect." The superpower that rendered all men, including her own father, putty in her hands. Not only was she funny and charming, she was also sickeningly beautiful—an attribute which was wasted romantically, as Rachel hadn't so much as *looked* at a man since she was sixteen. For years, Tully had been holding her breath for the announcement that she was gay, but it had never come. It seemed a travesty to Tully that no one, male or female, should get to enjoy her dark eyes, tumbling chestnut hair, and body that rivaled Kim Kardashian's. Man, how Tully envied that body. As an adolescent, Tully had assumed she was just a late developer—but her curves had never come, and Rachel's just kept coming. Lately, in fact, Rachel was looking downright . . .

"Fat," Rachel had said to her, when Tully had used the word "voluptuous" to describe her. "You don't have to whisper it or use some euphemism like 'generous' or 'plus-sized' or 'Botticelli-like.' 'Fat' doesn't mean disgusting, slothful, or lazy . . . that's just the meaning society attaches to it."

Tully had been mortified. She didn't think Rachel was disgusting or lazy or slothful. She thought Rachel was beautiful. She merely couldn't use the word "fat" at full volume. It felt wrong somehow. Like being asked to say "fuck" in church. That, she suspected, was Rachel's point though, and, she had to admit, it was a good one. Why *couldn't* she say the word?

"Stephen has shown me about a million photos of Miles and Locky," Heather was saying. "I know people say all kids are cute, but I have to say, they are *particularly* adorable."

"They are, aren't they?" Tully said, her ears pricking up at the sound of her sons' names. It was a smart move on Heather's part; only a serial killer could fail to warm to someone who called their children adorable. Tully found herself reaching for her phone and pulling up a photo she'd snapped of them that morning, eating Weet-Bix at the kitchen counter, a pair of beaming, blue-eyed angels. A second later Locky dumped his bowl of cereal over Miles's head, and Miles lost his mind because the texture made him feel like he had slugs in his hair, and slugs were on Miles's most recent list of phobias.

Heather took the phone and gushed appreciatively. "They're two and five?"

"Nearly three and five," Tully said. There was supposed to be a birthday party coming up, but given that parties had also appeared on Miles's list of phobias, it was anyone's guess whether that would happen.

"So, Heather, why don't you tell me about yourself?" Tully said, when conversation about the boys dried up. She pasted on a smile, which faded when Dad gave her an odd look. Sometimes, when she wasn't concentrating, Tully had been known to smile a bit too hard. Apparently everyone didn't have Heather's skill for smiling *just the right amount.*

"Well," Heather said, "I'm sure Stephen told you I'm an interior designer."

Stephen had. In fact, Heather had been the one responsible for the redesign of Mum and Dad's house. Tully didn't know all the details about how Heather had progressed from employee to girlfriend, but it wasn't difficult to piece together. Clearly Heather arrived at Mum and Dad's very nice, very expensive house, took one look at Mum, and saw an opening. Yes, Dad was old, but he was wealthy *and* a doctor. All you needed was a daddy issue or two and *Stephen* was a lamb to the slaughter.

"I'm also a keen gardener," Heather continued, reaching for her water glass.

Her teeth belonged in a movie star's mouth, Tully noticed. Almost certainly veneers. Tully glanced at Dad's teeth. Not movie-star teeth, but surprisingly white. It prompted a recollection of a tooth-whitening kit Tully had spotted in his bathroom last time she'd visited. She'd meant to ask him about it, but she'd been distracted when she noticed his grout desperately needed a clean. She'd ended up giving him a rundown of the best grout cleaners to use and then just cleaning it herself to make sure it was done properly. As a result, she'd forgotten all about the whitening kit. Until now.

"I also love yoga. I'm a bit of an addict, if I'm honest."

Yoga. Gardening. Interior design. It was as if she'd just plucked her profession and hobbies out of a how-to-be-dull catalog.

"Wow," Tully said, monotone. "Amazing."

"I've also taken an interest in cooking recently," Heather added, giving Dad a playful smile.

"Her specialty is charcoal chicken," Dad said, giving her an affectionate nudge.

Heather giggled. "I'm getting better!"

The strangeness of this flirtation sent a mild electric shock through Tully. It dawned on her almost anew that Dad was . . . *dating* this child. Probably having *sex* with her! As soon as the thought entered her head, Tully tried to quash it, but it was too late, it was spiraling. Dad. Heather. Sex. Tully closed her eyes, but that only made it worse. Her gag reflex triggered and she pushed back her chair and bent forward at the waist.

"Natalie!" Dad sounded alarmed. "Are you all right?"

Tully judged it to be a rhetorical question, since it must have been obvious to anyone that she was not all right. Her eyes were closed and her forehead rested on her knees. She inhaled deeply, trying to force oxygen in, and the images of Dad and Heather out. Unsuccessful on both counts. With her face between her knees, Tully opened her eyes. Heather's bag was under the table, unzipped and open. Her wallet sat right at the top.

"Tully?" Dad pleaded.

Tully's hands acted on autopilot, from muscle memory, from instinct—like a baby moving to music. One minute the wallet was on top of Heather's bag; the next, it was deep inside Tully's. By the time Tully sat up again, the air was already returning to her lungs. "Sorry," she said to Dad and Heather. "I'm fine."

2

RACHEL

As soon as Rachel hurried through the doorway of the restaurant, she saw that there were bigger problems at play than the fact that she was late. For one thing, Tully's head was between her knees (dramatic, but not altogether unusual for Tully, especially at a lunch of this magnitude). For another, there was not a morsel of food on the table yet, not even a bread roll! Rachel was entertaining the idea of skipping out of there and claiming car trouble when Tully sat up, and Dad noticed Rachel in the entrance.

"Oh, look," he cried, feverishly pleased to see her. "It's Rachel. *Rachel!* Over here!"

Rachel made her way to the table, ignored the barista, who winked at her. She hated it when people flirted with her.

"Sorry I'm late!" she said brightly.

"Rachel's not known for her punctuality," Dad said to the immaculate woman beside him, presumably Heather, as he rose to greet her. "Luckily she has other talents."

"Like what?" Rachel asked. She shot a quick glance at Tully, who appeared to have recovered from whatever spell had caused her to put her head between her knees, then held out her hand to Heather. She was, as expected, exceptionally young. Other diners would almost certainly assume Dad was taking his three daughters to lunch. The idea very nearly made Rachel laugh. Nearly.

"It's a pleasure to meet you, Heather," Rachel said as she shook Heather's delicate hand.

"Pleasure," admittedly, was a stretch. After all, "pleasure" was a good bottle of wine, a belly laugh, a perfectly iced chocolate éclair. Under different circumstances, Rachel might have felt pleasure at this meeting. For example, if her father had started dating someone *after* Mum died. A nice widow named Beryl, perhaps—someone he'd met down at the tennis club, who had adult children and plans for a huge blended-family Christmas with vicious games of Stealing Santa. After all, the idea of Dad not having to spend his golden years alone did indeed bring her pleasure. But the way things stood? Pleasure was a bit of a stretch.

Heather smiled as Rachel sat down. "It's good to meet you too, Rachel. I've heard a lot about you. Your dad says you make cakes."

"The best wedding cakes in Australia," Dad chimed in. Rachel didn't bother clarifying that she also made other baked goods for other occasions. She'd deduced a while back that her father only had the capacity to understand high-powered jobs. Banker. IT professional. Businessperson. She was fine with this. In her opinion, when you saved lives for a living, you didn't have to remember jobs.

Rachel tried to catch the attention of the waiter.

"Where have you been?" Tully asked curtly.

"Sorry," she said. "I dropped in to see Mum on the way here."

Rachel wasn't sure how that particular piece of information would be received. Mum had been moved to a high-security nursing home

with a specialist dementia wing a month ago. She had been diagnosed a couple of years back, after many more years of searching for
a diagnosis before that. First, her doctor thought it was a concussion
(she'd had a fall before the confusion started), then depression (Pam's
own mother had died around that time), and they'd even blamed a
urinary tract infection briefly. By the time they'd got the diagnosis
and a second opinion, Mum was already lost to them.

Upon admitting her to the nursing home last month, the doctors had advised that it would be good to give her time to settle in
before visiting. Rachel had agreed and then promptly showed up
daily, with cookies for the nurses. She felt sheepish about it, but
the idea of leaving Mum there alone, without anyone who cared
about her, was simply too much to bear. Her guilt was eased by the
knowledge that Tully was doing exactly the same thing.

"How was she?" Tully asked.

"A little agitated," Rachel admitted.

In fact, when Rachel arrived in her room, Mum had been irate.
She'd spun around and pointed at Rachel. "Did you take my bag
thingy?"

"No," Rachel had said.

Pamela narrowed her eyes. "It must have been your father. He
was just here, you know."

"Dad? No, I don't think he was here."

Her mother shook her head, tutting. "He's an awful man. I don't
know how I ever put up with him."

Rachel walked to the cupboard where the nurses always put her
bag. "Here it is, Mum."

"She wanted to go shopping," Rachel explained to Dad and Tully.
"And she was upset because she couldn't find her handbag."

"At least she was planning to take it with her this time," Dad said to Heather. "A few months back, she wandered away from me at Westfield and I got a call from security saying she'd tried to walk out of Kmart with a full trolley. Then, a few weeks ago, I found a bunch of stuff in the back of her closet. Random stuff. A Nintendo Switch, some candles, a screwdriver. A hot-water bottle. Most still with tags on. Which reminds me, I still haven't returned any of it. I've been driving around with stolen goods in the back of my car for months."

"I'll return it for you, Dad," Rachel said. "I'm at Westfield every other day. Now, have we ordered?" She waved madly at the waiter. "I'm happy to do the honors!"

"Happy" was an understatement. Rachel got terrible anxiety whenever she wasn't in control of the catering, and particularly when she was with Dad, who always wanted to start with a drink, then maybe some bread and dip or an appetizer. Rachel, on the other hand, couldn't relax until she knew her main course was in the oven. Rachel's family laughed about it, considered it a quirk of hers, a trademark of being a *foodie*. Usually Rachel considered it in the same light. Only occasionally did she hear a little voice at the back of her head that told her there was a bit more to it than that. That her foodie persona was nothing more than a glorified distraction from the one thing she didn't want to think about, dwell on, obsess about.

The waiter appeared—a handsome, charming Italian man full of compliments for Rachel, including a quite risqué one about wanting her in his bedroom (Rachel had excelled at Italian in high school). She ignored the compliments, got a quick rundown of the specials, and ordered for the table in a matter of minutes. Then, in consultation with the others, she ordered a bottle of pinot gris. She was relieved to see that Tully was drinking. Tully had been known to go on some strange diets or, heaven forbid, detoxes from time to time, which was always a bummer because, surprisingly, Tully and alcohol went together very nicely. It relaxed her, slowing her brain to a more normal pace. In fact, some of Rachel's favorite times with Tully had been when her sister was flat-out drunk.

"So, what did I miss?" Rachel asked.

"Heather was telling me a bit about herself," Tully said. "She enjoys gardening and yoga."

"Is that right?" Rachel said. She hoped her pleasant tone would compensate for Tully's sarcastic one. "Anything else? Have you told us about your family?"

Heather shook her head, pushing a strand of hair behind her ear. Her hand, Rachel noticed, was shaking slightly. "No family, really. I'm an only child, and my parents died in a car accident ten years ago."

"That's awful," Rachel said. "I'm so sorry."

"It's fine," Heather said. "It was a long time ago."

Tully sat forward, suddenly animated. "How did it happen? The car accident, I mean. Was it a head-on collision? Did they drive into a tree?"

"Tully!" Rachel said.

"It's fine," Heather said again. "Their car was hit by a drunk driver. I never got the details of whether it was head-on or not."

"Didn't you want to know?" Tully said. "I'd be desperate to know."

"So no other family?" Rachel said, over the top of Tully. "No cousins or aunts?"

"None that I'm in touch with. It's sad, really. When I was younger, I always envied people who had big families with lots of cousins and in-laws and grandparents. It felt like . . . insurance. If something happened to someone, there were spares."

"Must make you want to have a big family of your own," Tully said. "Lots of kids."

Rachel's instinct was to reprimand Tully again, or deflect her, but she let this one go, out of curiosity. Rachel half expected Dad to come to Heather's rescue, but he seemed to be more flustered than she was.

"I do love kids. I always thought that one day I would have as many kids as I could," Heather said. "But I've grown accustomed to a quiet life now. It suits me. So I wouldn't say kids are in the cards."

"It *is* a lot of work," Tully said.

Rachel had to hand it to her: Heather was doing a great job, coming up with the right answers. In fact, for the first time since Rachel arrived, Tully was looking almost relaxed, sitting back in her chair rather than perched on its edge in her customary rigid stance.

Then the waiter returned suddenly. "I forgot to mention," he said, "we also have freshly shucked Tasmanian oysters. Their aphrodisiac quality is at its height in spring, you know." He raised his eyebrows suggestively at Rachel, which was unsettling enough. Then Dad winked at Heather. "We'll take a dozen," he said.

"Excuse me," Tully said abruptly. "I need to use the bathroom."

"I'll join you," Rachel said.

By the time Rachel stood, Tully was already halfway across the room, pushing on the bathroom door. Rachel hurried after her.

Being Tully's sister required a very specific skill set. You had to be an animated conversationalist (Tully was easily bored) but also a calming influence. You had to be fully invested in whatever she was talking about, but be prepared for the fact that Tully would lose interest five minutes later. You had to love her with your whole heart but do so from arm's length. Getting close to her was like trying to get close to a helicopter—you always ended up windswept and breathless . . . and occasionally you lost your head.

Tully had always been a bundle of neuroses that equaled no particular diagnosis. A little OCD. A little mania. Some ritualistic behavior. As a child and teenager she'd had periods of being plagued by intrusive, obsessive thoughts. It had settled down to a generalized eccentricity as an adult, but since Mum's Alzheimer's diagnosis and subsequent move to the nursing home, Tully had regressed significantly, descending into odd bouts of hysteria at inopportune times. Sometimes Rachel envied Tully's propensity for wild reactions. It seemed healthier somehow to get all those feelings out. Sometimes she pictured her own insides, full of all the things she'd pushed down over the years rather than articulated. She imagined a series of ugly deposits, masses of secrets and regret, wedged around her lungs and stomach.

"Tul?" Rachel called, as she pushed open the heavy bathroom door. It was one of those trendy bathrooms with large hexagonal tiles and wood and pink marble. Tully's handbag sat on the counter. Only one stall was occupied, and Tully's nude flats were visible at the bottom. "It's me."

The toilet flushed and then the door to the cubicle swung open to reveal Tully's tearstained, frazzled face. "I'm not coping, Rachel."

"I can see that."

"The thoughts." Tully's eyes were closed tight and she was pressing her fingers to her temples as if she had a terrible migraine. "They're in my head. I can't get them out."

This wasn't good. "Thoughts?" Rachel said. "You mean like when you were a kid?"

"No! Thoughts about Dad and Heather . . . you know . . . *doing it*."

"Oh! Right."

"It's horrific. Sex is weird enough without imagining your dad doing it, right?"

Rachel was still trying to think of an appropriate response when Tully jumped in.

"Oh. Well, take my word for it."

"Anyway," Rachel said, "just take a deep breath and banish those thoughts from your head. I'll . . . do the same."

"Okay," Tully said, inhaling slowly. She looked relaxed for a quarter of a second before her expression became intense again. "So what do you think of her? Tell me everything, every single thought in your head."

"Well—"

"I just can't believe she's so young!" Tully cried. "I mean, we knew she was young. But I must have been in denial. I mean . . . why would he go for someone so young? She's not even very pretty. There's no way she's into Dad for the right reasons. She must want money or status or something. But even that I don't get. She's pretty enough. Why not find a rich *young* doctor?"

"Hang on, is she pretty or not?"

Tully started pacing. "Look, I get it—who *doesn't* want money? Her parents are dead, and presumably they left her with nothing. And life is hard on the breadline; believe me, I know."

Tully didn't know. She lived in one of the nicest neighborhoods of Melbourne in a mansion with a library and a cinema room. Sonny was a criminal barrister and Tully hadn't worked a day since Locky was born, if you didn't count charity dinners (and Rachel didn't). Rachel didn't begrudge her any of it, until she started talking about her deep understanding of the breadline.

"But setting your sights on an old man isn't right," Tully finished. "It's *immoral!*"

Rachel waited a full five seconds before attempting to respond. Still, the moment she opened her mouth, Tully started talking again. "I'm sorry. I don't know what I'm saying. I miss Mum. I miss her so much."

"Me too."

Tully sighed sadly. "It's just . . . the moments of lucidity are so rare these days . . . and so short. And I feel like we're betraying her by having lunch with Heather. What would she think if she knew we were sitting here, breaking bread with her replacement?"

"Heather isn't Mum's—"

"—replacement, I *know*." Tully ripped a useless square of toilet paper from the dispenser and attempted to wipe her face. "She's not Mum's replacement—for *us*. But she is for Dad. I guess I'm just . . . angry on Mum's behalf."

Tully made a reasonable point. Tully often did.

"I get it," Rachel said. "It's totally weird seeing Dad with Heather."

Tully grabbed Rachel's hand. "It *is* weird, isn't it?"

"Of course it is. She's younger than us!"

Tully smiled, as if Rachel's recognition of this was a delightful surprise. "She *is* younger than us!"

"It's true there's a lot of stuff to digest, Tul, but I'm trying not to worry about it. It's not like they're getting married or anything. He's still married to Mum, for God's sake! We're having lunch, that's it. Let's keep things in perspective."

Tully nodded, grabbing another square of toilet paper to blow her nose. "You're right. It's just lunch."

Rachel nodded, walking over to Tully's bag. "So, how about you reapply your lippy and we'll head back out there." Rachel unzipped her bag and rummaged around for the lipstick. "Why do you have two wallets in here? And . . . is this a saltshaker?"

"Doesn't everyone have two wallets?" Tully said, taking the bag from Rachel. "I don't need lipstick. Let's just go."

Tully led the way through the busy restaurant. As her father came into view, Rachel gave him the thumbs-up and he nodded in response, visibly relieved.

"All good?" he asked Tully, who smiled and nodded too many times. "Good. In that case, I think it's time to order champagne."

Rachel knew then what was about to happen. She got these feelings from time to time—premonitions of a sort. She had one the day Mum lost her keys for the third time in a week, even after Dad laughed it off as a normal sign of aging. She had one on a family skiing holiday when she begged Tully to go for hot chocolate instead of skiing another run (Tully refused and broke her leg on the next slope). And she had one when she was sixteen, a split second before that man jumped out of the bushes.

Her father cleared his throat. "Heather and I have an announcement to make . . ."

3

HEATHER

Stephen was standing in his driveway in sweatpants and a T-shirt the first time Heather laid eyes on him. It was a Saturday morning. He had a newspaper tucked under his arm and he was chatting to his neighbor over the fence. Heather had just pulled up in front of his house, ready for their first appointment, and when she got out of her car Stephen waved as if she were an old friend.

"You must be the interior decorator," he said.

In fact, she was the interior *designer*, and it was a source of great irritation to her that people often confused the two, since the difference had meant an extra four years at university for her. But on this occasion, she recalled, it hadn't bothered her.

"Just been for a jog," he explained, gesturing at the clothes.

"You don't need to explain yourself to me," she said, opening the passenger door and retrieving a box filled with samples and swatches.

Stephen laughed. "Force of habit. I have a wife and two daughters. I spend my life explaining myself to women. Oh God, that sounds terribly sexist, doesn't it? Don't tell Pam I said so."

Heather had already characterized him as an affable sexist, which was fine by her. She worked in an office full of affable sexists, and they weren't as bad as people made out. If anything, she felt most powerful around this kind of man. They tended to be largely confused by, and subservient to, women. Sure, they were surprised when women proved to be their intellectual or creative equal—often disconcertingly so—but by and large they didn't impede her existence in any way. So, affable sexist it was.

Stephen appeared beside her and took the box of samples out of her hands without asking. He was a big man, she noticed, with a ramrod-straight back and a broad chest. "Just so you know, I explain myself to men a lot too. To everyone really."

"Well . . . that's a nice quality. A lot of people I know never bother to explain themselves at all. I'm Heather Wisher, by the way."

"Stephen Aston."

They shook hands, as people did back then, and then walked side by side toward the grand front steps of the Astons' home, an upside-down house with the kitchen and living areas on the top floor so they had a view of Brighton Beach. At the bottom of the stairs, Stephen slowed a little. "Listen, before we go in, I need to fill you in about Pam. I probably should have called you earlier but—"

"You're here!" a woman called from the top of the stairs. "Are you early or am I late?"

"You're both right on time," Stephen said.

They started with a home tour, which was typical, but it was led by Stephen, which wasn't. Usually husbands made themselves scarce for these visits, apart from a brief speech on arrival about how the budget was not to be blown, and to insist that no space be taken from the garage. But that day, Stephen did all the talking. As they made their way around the house, he kept his hand on Pam's shoulder, guiding her through the house as if she didn't know the way. It was curious. Pam didn't say much, and whenever Heather asked her opinion, she shrugged and asked if anyone wanted a cup of tea. After the fifth or sixth time of this, Stephen put an arm around her shoulders and said, "All right, we'll take the hint. It's tea time." He grinned at Heather. "Pam makes a mean cup of tea. She has just about every flavor you could think of."

They'd sat in the living room, which was cluttered and a little chaotic. As an interior designer, Heather was one of the minority who actually liked clutter. Stark, vast spaces, with clean lines and sharp surfaces, always seemed so unlivable to her. Naturally, she would do whatever a client asked of her, but when it came to her own personal style, she favored warm wood, rugs, eclectic artwork, texture. Love. So different from her own childhood home, with its mismatched op shop couches that perennially smelled of dog even though Heather's family had never owned one. There was always a terra-cotta pot in the middle of the coffee table, filled with cigarette butts, and a giant TV on the wall, one of the few things her dad could always seem to find money for.

"What is it you want from the renovation, Pamela?" Heather asked, as they finished their tea and Stephen carried the mugs back to the kitchen. "What is your style?"

"I like cozy," she said. "Cozy and comfy, that's my style. Stephen prefers modern."

"I prefer what Pam likes," Stephen countered cheerfully as he returned to the room. "Happy wife, happy life."

They both chuckled. Heather did too. But after a few seconds, the smile faded from Pam's face. "How rude of me. I haven't even offered you a cup of tea! Will you have a cup?"

When Heather looked at Stephen, he held her gaze for just a second longer than would be considered normal. And then she understood.

"Oh, thank you," she said to Pam. "But I'm fine for now."

"What is the announcement?" Tully said, looking from Stephen to Heather and back again. "Come on. Out with it!"

"Just hold on a minute," Stephen said. "We need champagne!" He glanced around for a waiter; Tully shot Heather a wary look.

"The girls are going to love you," Stephen had said last week, when he suggested the meeting. She asked him to tell her as much as possible about each of them, and Stephen, to his credit, had done a reasonable job. He told her about Tully's neuroses. About the fact that Rachel, to his knowledge, had never had a serious—or even casual—relationship. But there were things Stephen left out of his summaries. Like the fact that Rachel was not just "pretty" but breathtaking—as divine a creature as Heather had ever seen. And the fact that Tully's entire being came alive when she talked about her little boys. And the fact that both girls looked at Stephen with an adoration that was palpable, but also something else, something she couldn't quite put her finger on.

"Dad!" Tully tried again, but the waiter was already approaching the table.

Stephen glanced at the wine list for a second or two before sighing helplessly. "A bottle of your best champagne, please. And four glasses."

"Three," Heather corrected. "None for me."

Stephen frowned at her. "Really? You're sure?"

Heather wasn't sure. Heather was rarely sure of anything. It was an unappealing trait, she'd always thought. *Get a spine,* she told herself constantly. *Be more decisive.* She'd decided yesterday that she wasn't going to drink today. Or at the very least, she'd only have one. It had felt like a prudent decision at the time.

Heather never trusted herself after a couple of drinks; she relaxed a little *too* much. All the bad decisions she'd made in her life, all the ones she regretted, had happened after a couple of drinks. Today she wanted to be on her best behavior. After all, she knew how she must look to Stephen's daughters. A new, younger girlfriend. They'd assume she was a gold digger or someone with daddy issues. She'd suggested they wait another six months or more before she met the girls, but Stephen had insisted. She envied his certainty that they would love her. It was yet another thing that she wasn't sure of.

Three sets of eyes were staring at her. She had, she realized, made a faux pas. Heather had spent enough time in the middle-class world to know the rules, even if she didn't understand them. Champagne was a team sport. When it was suggested, regardless of the time, date, or occasion, the correct response was to squeal and clap. If someone didn't want to partake, the wind was taken out of everyone's sails.

"Just one glass," Stephen cajoled. "It's a special occasion."

"All right," she said. "You've twisted my arm."

"So," Tully said, the second their glasses were full, "what's this announcement?"

"Tully has always been like this," Stephen told Heather. "When she was little, she was the one up at dawn, desperate to open her Christmas presents, while Rachel was still fast asleep."

"Dad!" Tully said.

"Fine." Stephen smiled, reaching for Heather's hand. "I'm very excited to tell you that Heather and I have decided to get married!"

Heather hardly dared to look at Rachel or Tully. Unlike Stephen, who seemed utterly certain that his daughters would be delighted for them, Heather knew how this was going to land. No matter how polite this family was, no matter how hard they slapped on the strained smiles, this was not good news for them.

"Well," Rachel said. "Well, that's . . . Wow, that's really . . ."

Tully didn't even attempt to hide her horror. "You can't get married. You're already married to Mum!"

Stephen's smile dimmed only the slightest bit. "Straight into the logistics, that's my Tully-girl." He laughed. "I'll admit, there are some things that need to be worked out. And I'll include you both every step of the way. But the main thing is . . . Heather and I have decided we want to spend our lives together."

"Include us every step of the way with *what*?" Tully demanded.

Heather picked up her drink and took a large sip. She felt a whisper of irritation at Stephen. Why had he been so determined to announce it now? They should have taken it slower. Met the girls a few times first, then announced the engagement down the track. She hadn't even worn her engagement ring. She was delighted about the engagement—ecstatic, even!—but sometimes even the most charming of men were hopeless when it came to reading a room.

"You'll wait until . . . until after Mum passes away, I assume," Rachel said. "It's not like this is going to happen soon." It was ostensibly a statement, but Rachel looked at her father for confirmation.

Heather took another sip of her drink.

"Well," Stephen said, "obviously Mum is very healthy—physically, at least. And"—Heather felt his gaze on her, but she studiously avoided eye contact—"we can't keep our plans on hold forever."

The girls fell silent. At a table nearby someone started singing "Happy Birthday" and a waiter appeared with a cake.

"So . . . what *are* your plans?" Rachel asked finally.

Stephen sighed. "I've met with Bill Thompson, and he said we can be granted a divorce, under these circumstances."

"You're going to *divorce* Mum?" Tully cried.

"It's just a formality, Tully-girl. Mum doesn't even know we're married most of the time. And of course I'd continue to look after her—and you. Mum would get sixty percent of our assets, which would be handed down to you two after she passes."

Tully and Rachel appeared so bewildered, Heather didn't know where to look.

Eventually Rachel was the one to speak. "This is a lot. I don't know quite what to say!"

"Why don't we drink to it then?" Stephen suggested, lifting his glass.

Hesitantly, the rest of them followed suit. But after they clinked their glasses together, Heather was the only one who took a sip.

4

TULLY

The day after the lunch, Tully sat in the car park of Westfield and looked in the rearview mirror. Items were strewn all over the back seat of her Range Rover, spilling into the footwell—a silk camisole, a pair of Lululemon running leggings, a leather wallet. There was also a fine gold necklace, a pair of toddler scissors, and a packet of Post-its. A random assortment of items, but it didn't matter what it was. That's what most people didn't get about her habit. It wasn't about the getting. It was about the *taking*. She'd determined, a while back, that she was an addict. When the urge to put something into her handbag or stuff it under her sweater overcame her, she was powerless to stop herself. Most of the stuff she stole was later stored in the garage, stuffed under beds, or dropped off at charity shops. Heather's wallet, for example, she'd handed in to the police station yesterday with all cash and cards accounted for.

Like any addict, she knew that soon she'd feel the guilt and self-loathing and remorse. But since this was a given, she decided she might as well enjoy the high.

And enjoying it she was. It was exactly what she needed after all the "meeting Heather" malarkey yesterday. Tully had been unaware of the stress she'd been carrying around in the lead-up to that meeting. Heather hadn't been a welcome relief, nor had she put any of Tully's fears to rest. Heather had been exactly as she'd feared . . . though perhaps slightly less trashy, with slightly smaller boobs. And now she was going to become Tully's stepmother! The idea was too horrific to contemplate.

She'd spent the last twenty-four hours analyzing and unpacking every moment of the lunch, sorting out what she did and didn't have to worry about. There was a lot to work through. Every flickering eyebrow, every moment of discomfort, every slightly-longer-than-normal pause, required analysis and conclusions to be drawn. Little wonder she didn't have time for a job. She had no idea how all those type A lawyerly types did it. For Tully, managing her anxiety was a full-time occupation.

If there had been one highlight of the lunch (and "highlight" was pushing it), it was the declaration that Heather didn't want children. If she was honest, Tully had never understood those women who didn't want to have children. She nodded along and loudly championed their rights on social media, and she'd have been aghast if anyone expressed her views out loud at a dinner party and would immediately take the side of the childless woman who argued her case. But she thought it was strange.

Admittedly, when you looked at it practically, making the decision *to* have children was much stranger. If her own children were any sort of representation, children were difficult, anxiety-inducing little parasites. *Cute*, difficult, anxiety-inducing little parasites. Parasites with an aptitude for kindness, poignant observation, and the most adorable pad of fat on the backs of their hands that Tully liked to press. "Mummy loves my squishy hands," Miles said whenever she did it.

In any case, when Heather had refused the champagne, Tully had worried for a moment. She'd been relieved when she finally drank the champagne. Even if that didn't necessarily prove she wasn't pregnant. After all, Tully herself had had the odd drink during her pregnancy. She'd had four champagnes at Anna and Jake Silverstone's wedding! (She'd always wondered if that was the reason for Locky's slightly odd gait.) But still, reassuring. Unless Heather was an alcoholic? This was the problem with your father getting a girlfriend. There was so much you didn't know. So much to worry about.

Tully put the car into reverse and backed out of her parking space. This morning she'd had a phone call from an old friend, Bec Saunders, asking how the lunch went. Tully had confided in Bec, which, in hindsight, hadn't been the smartest move. Bec was a sympathetic ear who could be strikingly wise at times, but she was also, at her core, an insatiable gossip. She actually lit up when she heard an interesting tidbit, glowing as if she'd just had a facial at an expensive salon. When Tully had said, "I have to tell you something," she'd practically levitated! It was an annoying trait, as it made Tully want to share information with her, even though she knew she shouldn't.

Anyway, Bec had been full of sympathy and platitudes. "Well, do you know what Amber said when I told her? She said it was just not right that your dad is doing this, not while Pam is alive. Viv said the same. We're all shocked by Stephen's behavior. It's just so unlike him." And she laughed, a short, perfunctory laugh. Everyone would be laughing, Tully realized. Heather had made their family a laughingstock.

No wonder she had turned to her old habit of stealing things for stress release.

Tully was eleven the first time she shoplifted. Mum was convalescing at home, having broken her wrist playing squash, and she and Rachel were delighting in playing nursemaid. So, when they realized they'd run out of bread, Tully had practically fallen over herself to be the one to run to the store to get more. It wasn't a long walk to the shops, less than five minutes each way, but she did have to cross a main road. She was about halfway there when she realized she hadn't made this particular trip without Rachel before. Tully had been no stranger to anxiety, even then, and she felt it creeping from somewhere deep within, but she continued on. She just had to get the bread and return home; it wasn't that hard.

The bell dinged as she entered the shop and the man behind the counter looked up from a little television set and then immediately looked back down.

Tully was feeling sick to her stomach by then. She made her way to the bread and selected a loaf, intending to get out of there as quickly as she could. Then a packet of Nerds, on the shelf beside the bread, caught her eye. She didn't remember ever making the choice to take the Nerds. Probably because, for her, there was no choice to make. It felt like swimming to the surface for air after being held under water. Her body was doing what it needed to do. She was as powerless to stop it as the body that needed oxygen.

The stupid thing was, she had enough money to buy them. Mum wouldn't have minded, especially if she shared them with Rachel. But she didn't want to pay for them. She didn't even want the Nerds. She wanted *escape*.

On the way home, Tully shoved the Nerds into her neighbor's

letter box, too horrified to eat them and wanting to get rid of the evidence. She knew what she'd done was wrong. And yet, the peacefulness remained. She felt cushioned from herself. Buoyed. She'd found a way to escape from herself. But the sense of calm didn't last long. By that evening she was lying in bed in the throes of a panic attack, waiting for the police to appear on the doorstep. But by the next morning, she knew she'd do it again. She had to. She had no choice.

At the boom gate, Tully glanced into the back seat again for a glimpse of the things she'd taken. There were too many to fit into her handbag; she was going to need to get creative. This was the problem with flexible working arrangements. COVID-19 had a lot to answer for, in Tully's opinion. In the old days, Tully was free to bring home her goods during the day, knowing they could be safely hidden or disposed of by the time Sonny got home at 6:00 P.M. Now, if he wasn't in court, Sonny was often at home, which was highly inconvenient for someone with a habit like hers. She thought about the picnic blanket in the boot of the car. That would have to do. She'd pull over before she got home and cover everything up with it.

She just had to hope Sonny wasn't in one of his helpful moods. Lately, it felt like every time she nosed her car into the driveway he appeared, ready to help her with the bags. She suspected he was keeping tabs on her, making sure she wasn't spending any money they didn't have. How she would *love* to tell him that he needn't worry about that! But how could she? Sonny was the ultimate law-abiding citizen. He drove the speed limit, he refused to park in no-standing zones, he waited his turn in line and told people off for pushing in. One of the biggest fights of their marriage had been when Tully had lied on her travel insurance forms, saying she'd lost her sunglasses in Italy when she'd actually misplaced them months before, back home in Australia. Her responses of "everyone does it" and "we can't afford to replace them" only seemed to infuriate him more. "Not everyone does it," he replied. "And we *can* afford to replace them."

Except now they couldn't, because their money was gone. Or, if not all of it, a sizable chunk. The most shocking part about it was that Sonny had always been so good with money. Not only had he always made a stack of it, he also did wonderful-sounding things with it, like investing it to offset their tax burden, self-managing their superannuation, and setting them up as "companies" and "individual entities" and other important things that she didn't understand. So when he announced two weeks ago that there was a problem with one of their investments, she hadn't understood that either.

"Remember last year when I met with that financial adviser about reducing our tax burden?" he said.

Tully didn't. "Yes," she said.

"Yeah, well, he told me about an investment—a solid, long-term investment that would deliver good returns and significantly reduce our tax liability . . ." He trailed off.

"And?" Tully prompted.

"And we lost our money."

Tully started to get nervous. "What do you mean, 'lost our money'? How much money are you talking about?"

He paused, which made Tully more nervous. "Two million."

"Two million *dollars*?" She gaped at him. "Do we even *have* two million dollars?"

Sonny's cheeks were pink. "I borrowed it. And the loan was secured against our house."

"You mean we'll lose the house? We'll be homeless?"

An image of the four of them in their car flashed into her mind. It was dark and they were in a deserted car park. She was tucking Miles and Locky into the back seat with blankets and pillows and singing them a lullaby while Sonny sat in the front, illuminated by the light of his laptop, typing furiously, trying to find a way to get them out of this mess. As horrific as the scene was, something about it felt vaguely romantic to her.

"We won't be homeless," Sonny said. "We'll just have to rent for a while until we get back on our feet. And tighten our belts—no more spending."

Tully thought of the bill from lunch yesterday. After Dad announced his engagement to Heather, she'd slipped into an odd sort of mania and insisted on paying the bill. She'd expected her father to fight her, and he did a little, but she was adamant. Sonny would choke on his own saliva when he saw the credit card statement, but in her defense, she was still getting used to her new life as a pauper. And, in her very recent old life, if she wanted to do something, she did it. She didn't have to save up or shop around for a bargain. How privileged she'd been. She pictured herself in a sumptuous silk gown, dripping with jewels, her hair adorned with feathers and pearls. *Let them eat cake!* she cried in the fantasy.

She was going mad. Maybe she'd always been a bit mad?

She stopped at the traffic lights. The high from her retail therapy was starting to wear off. She felt so jittery that when her phone started ringing she screamed.

"Oh," she said, when she realized where the sound was coming from. The phone. She accepted the call. "Tully Harris."

"Tully, it's Rachel."

That was a surprise. Rachel never called her. Rachel preferred text messages—short perfunctory statements with clear action items. Dad's birthday. Might get wine from Laura's vineyard on Saturday. Want to chip in? Or, Visited Mum today. Dad says she needs more underwear. Bonds cottontails, size 12, 4 pairs. Can you drop them off tomorrow? Why was she calling?

"Hi, Rach," she said. "I'm just leaving Westfield."

"Bought anything good?"

Tully glanced at the back seat again. "Some running leggings. I thought I might start running. Hey, maybe we could go together sometime?"

Rachel used to love running. As a teen, she used to disappear for hours, running along the beach path, and would come back sweaty and resplendent. She used to say there was nothing that made her feel as good as running. But when she was about sixteen, she stopped abruptly and never ran again.

"I'm not sure I could run to the end of the street right now, Tul," Rachel said. "But thanks. Anyway, how are you?"

How are you? How long had it been since someone asked her that? Tully would have been touched if she weren't simultaneously worried that the question was directly related to an *R U OK?* day or something. Rachel was always so tapped into those sorts of days. So "woke." And there was nothing wrong with being woke, obviously. But in this particular instance, the question would have meant more if not the result of wokeness.

"I'm fine," Tully said cautiously. "Why do you ask?"

"A girl can ask her sister how she is, can't she?"

"A girl can," Tully said. "But a girl usually doesn't."

"Anyway, I just wanted to check in. There's been a lot going on. Mum moving into the nursing home. Dad starting up with Heather. The engagement. The *divorce.*"

"Did Dad ask you to check on me?" Tully asked.

"No."

"Right," she said. "Well, you'll be pleased to know that I'm fine. Or I will be when I can get Miles sleeping in his own bed! I haven't had a full night's sleep in weeks.

"Lately I've been wondering if I should pull him out of pre-school. He's been so funny about going. He cries when I drop him off and cries when I pick him up. When I ask him why he says it's because they make him 'have fun.'"

"Why don't you pull him out?" Rachel said. "Have another year with him at home. It'd save you some money. Not that you have to worry about that, I suppose."

Tully hadn't told Rachel about the money they'd lost yet. She'd started to, once or twice. She fantasized about Rachel putting the kettle on, producing something freshly baked, and telling her about something much worse that had happened to someone she knew, which would make Tully feel much better about it. Tully *knew* that's what Rachel would do, and yet she hadn't told her. If she were to admit that Sonny had lost their money, they would think he was irresponsible or stupid. Smart, responsible people didn't lose their money—that was the act of a cowboy, a salesman, a get-rich-quick kid, and perfect Tully didn't marry men like that.

"Yesterday was a weird day, wasn't it?" Rachel said, as Tully turned onto her street. It was a beautiful street. Sunny and tree-lined, it was often visited by camera crews in spring to get footage of the blossoms for their "Spring Has Sprung" news segments. Tully supposed she should feel grateful that she'd been able to live here for a little while. Instead, she felt like crying.

"Heather seemed more like one of our friends than one of Dad's," Rachel said.

"She didn't seem like one of *my* friends," Tully said immediately. But, again, it wasn't true. In different circumstances, Tully would have been utterly enamored of Heather, with her trench coat, pretty hair, and understated style. She probably would have invited her over for tea already.

"I meant age-wise," Rachel clarified.

"Oh," Tully said, pressing the button to open the gate. "Age-wise, yes."

The garage door was open, and the sight of Sonny's car reminded Tully that she'd forgotten to cover up the stuff in the back seat. She saw him notice her through the window of the front room and rise from his chair. Tully put the car into park.

"Anyway," Rachel was saying, "I guess I felt a little weird after yesterday, so I thought you might too. The idea of Dad divorcing Mum? It's . . . a lot."

There was something different about Rachel's voice. It was softer. More . . . vulnerable. It occurred to Tully that maybe Rachel was the one who needed to be asked if she was okay. Tully was about to, but before she could get the words out, Sonny opened the front door.

Tully felt her heart rate rise. She needed to get the stuff out of her car before Sonny saw it. The heady feeling she'd had at the shopping center was long gone, and she just felt breathless, strung out, and a little sweaty. That was the thing about addiction. The high got shorter and shorter.

"Rach, do you mind if I call you back? I've just got home."

Sonny trotted down the front steps.

"Oh, you don't need to," Rachel said. "I was just checking in."

"I'd like to, though. It would be nice to—"

Sonny yanked open the passenger door. His face was like thunder. And he hadn't even seen what was in the back seat. This was going to be bad.

"Why is there a six-hundred-dollar charge on the credit card, Tully?"

5

RACHEL

Rachel stood in the kitchen in front of three enormous chocolate mud cakes. They were for a wedding cake for Peter and Emily, a couple who were so particular about their cake that they came for three tastings last month, along with the entire bridal party and both sets of parents. Rachel wasn't prone to stress, but she'd had the odd anxiety dream about this cake. She'd started making the sugar flowers five days before. They were made petal by petal and took hours. Last night, she'd dreamed that she'd accidentally lain in a bed of sugar flowers and ground each one into dust. Bizarrely, Heather and Dad had also been in that dream. And why not? They'd been in her every *waking* thought ever since their lunch.

She threw a couple of chocolate buttons into her mouth, and then realized the packet was finished—the second packet she'd finished this morning. This morning when she got dressed, her underwear had felt tight. Her underwear! Rachel was not the sort who weighed herself, or worried about weight gain, but she'd noticed her weight creeping up lately. Her thighs, her breasts . . . even her face was rounder. She attributed the stress-eating to everything that had been going on in the family. Everyone had their coping mechanisms. This was hers. Better than drugs, she told herself! Or was it? She had to admit, in a lot of ways, it was exactly the same as drugs. A way to obliterate. A way to hide.

When she'd called Tully yesterday, she'd really wanted to unpack the lunch with Heather. It had been a gamble, obviously. Tully was rarely a good person to unpack things with, at least metaphorically speaking. Literally, she was a fantastic person to unpack with. She had helped Rachel move last year and the entire house had been unpacked in twelve hours, efficiently, with a clear system. But when it came to mentally unpacking things, it was trickier. Tully tended to become caught up in emotion and Rachel preferred to remain clearheaded and practical. Still, Rachel had to try. After all, no one in the world understood what she was going through as well as Tully did.

But as soon as Tully answered the phone, Rachel regretted calling. For one thing, Tully was in the car and she was always mildly hysterical in the car. Sure enough, she'd immediately started rattling on about the boys and running and then, just as Rachel thought they were getting to the heart of things, she hung up. So that, she supposed, was that.

What else could she do other than bake her feelings?

Once upon a time, Rachel had run her feelings, but baking had taken over when she was sixteen and she'd never looked back. It was amazing how she could suddenly breathe when surrounded by butter, sugar, and eggs. The methodical nature of baking provided an equilibrium of sorts, an opportunity to process her feelings. And lately, she'd had a lot of feelings. About Mum, who'd already slipped away. About her nutty sister. About Dad, who was starting a new life in his sixties. About Heather, who was a frustrating blend of perfectly nice and ordinary; nothing about her to hate, nothing to love. The most difficult type of person to withstand, really.

On the table, already cooled and iced and boxed, was a gender-reveal cake, ready to go off to a baby shower. Her new delivery girl—Darcy—was supposed to be here five minutes ago to collect it. *Not a good start to a new job, Darcy,* Rachel warned her mentally. She'd hired the girl from a long-term unemployed list at an agency, thinking she was doing a good deed, but now she worried that had been a mistake. Maybe there was a reason Darcy had been unemployed for so long?

While she waited, Rachel perused the pile of bizarre goods on the dining table—souvenirs from Mum's shoplifting period that Rachel had told Dad she would return. Mum's *shoplifting period.* How ridiculous that sounded. Mum, who'd once driven forty-five minutes back to a service station when they were on a road trip and she realized they'd driven off without paying for their soft drinks. Now she was a *shoplifter?* Dad had been so grateful when Rachel offered to take care of it, and Rachel had to admit she enjoyed the gratitude. It reminded her of a time when she was twelve or thirteen and she'd accompanied him to David Jones to help him choose a birthday present for Mum. He'd looked so panicked as the sales assistant showed him fragrances and hand creams that Rachel had stepped in. To this day, she basked in his gratitude.

Among the pile of pilfered goods she found a hot-water bottle. It was the only item from the pile that Rachel could actually imagine her mother using. Mum loved hot-water bottles. Nana, Mum's mother, had made her one every night when she was a little girl, and Mum was always nostalgic about that. When Rachel and Tully were little, she'd often put a hot-water bottle into their beds "to warm their bones." This hot-water bottle was pink, and inside its own cream knitted cozy. Rachel decided she might use it to warm her bones now. It would be nice to make sugar flowers with toasty feet. She flicked on the kettle at the same time as the doorbell rang.

About time, Darcy.

She abandoned the hot-water bottle, grabbing the gender-reveal cake instead. Darcy was ten minutes late. She'd make a comment, she decided. Just something small to let her know that tardiness wasn't appreciated. She was a friendly, forgiving boss but it was important to set expectations and boundaries from the beginning.

But when Rachel opened the door, instead of Darcy she found a man standing on her doorstep.

"Hi," he said.

"Oh." Rachel closed the door slightly, placing herself in the crack, blocking the way. "Sorry, I was expecting someone else."

The man looked surprised. "Who?"

Rachel blinked. "I beg your pardon?"

It had to be said, the man on the doorstep was gorgeous. He was tall and lean, with a sweep of dark brown hair across his forehead. His eyes were green with a hint of mischief about them. "Who were you expecting?"

"Why don't you tell me who you are, and we'll go from there," Rachel said coolly.

"I'm Darcy."

"*You're* Darcy?"

He frowned. "You're Rachel, right? You *were* expecting me?"

She definitely wasn't expecting *him*. "You're my new delivery person?"

He lifted his hands demonstrably. "It's crumby work . . . but I need the dough."

Rachel stared at him.

"Sorry," he said. "Couldn't think of a batter joke."

"Well," Rachel said. "Let's hope you are as good at delivering cakes as making jokes about them."

Rachel felt entirely discombobulated. She cursed herself for assuming Darcy was a girl. After all, now that she thought of it, Darcy was a gender-neutral name. But the fact was, if she'd known he was a man—well, she wouldn't have hired him. She was sexist, she realized. Who knew?

"All right then," Rachel said finally; since he was here, he might as well deliver this cake. She let go of the door and held out the cake. "It's for a gender reveal. The address is on the side of the box."

Darcy took the box and opened it. "Wow. This is amazing!"

Rachel looked at it. She'd been limited in her decoration options due to it being a gender reveal, and as a result it looked plainer than she would have liked. "I feel like it needs something," she said. Then, noticing the wattle growing in her front garden, she grabbed her secateurs from the hall table, snipped a couple of yellow flowers, and quickly arranged them on top. "There," she said. "Now it's perfect."

"It really is," Darcy said. Then he looked up at her. "So what is it? Boy or a girl?"

"I can't tell you that."

"Why not?"

"Because it's a secret. Even the parents don't know!"

"Come on!" Darcy pleaded. "Who am I going to tell?"

"I will not break my baking code of ethics for you or anyone."

Darcy grinned. "Principled. I like it."

He really was extraordinarily cute. It was disconcerting. Rachel started wishing he'd just take the cake and go.

Instead, he looked down at the cake, closed his eyes, and whispered "I love you" into the box.

Rachel stared at him, aghast.

"Sorry," he explained. "It's just that last time I forgot to tell a cake I loved it, it burst into tiers."

Darcy didn't give her time to respond, just turned on his heel. Rachel stared after him. It had been a mistake, hiring Darcy, she could see that already. Not because of his tardiness, not even because of his terrible jokes. The problem was, had she not sworn off romance, Darcy would have been exactly her type.

When Rachel returned to the kitchen, she debated if she even needed her hot-water bottle. She felt hot under the collar, unsettled by Darcy's easy, jokey—*late!*—demeanor. Still, for sentiment's sake, she unscrewed the lid and was about to pour the hot water into the bottle when something caught her eye. It looked like cash, sticking out of the top.

She put down the kettle and plucked it out. A hundred bucks. *Cheers, Mum,* Rachel thought. Then she decided to take a quick look inside. After all, she didn't want to leave any more money in there.

She lifted the bottle to her eye—then, seeing what was inside, nearly dropped it again.

"Jesus, Mum," she whispered. "What the hell did you do?"

6

HEATHER

Heather had only intended to step out of the kitchen for two minutes. She'd left Stephen in the steam shower a few minutes earlier, promising that dinner would be ready soon. It had sounded funny, even to her own ears. As if she were the kind of person who could *make dinner*.

She'd given it a shot, at least. She'd got as far as putting the steaks in a pan before she'd had to consult Google for the next step. (Google had informed her that the steak should have been room temperature. Who knew? Heather's mother had always taken meat straight from the fridge—though, admittedly, it was usually burgers and sausages rather than Wagyu beef.)

With the chilled steaks cooking, Heather refilled her wine and went in search of a mirror to reapply her lipstick. There was no mirror in the kitchen/dining room—a failing for which she could only blame herself—and so she'd headed into the front hallway, which boasted a specially ordered mirror, one that had required four men to hang it, one that bounced the light all around the entryway.

As she touched up her lips, she thought about Tully and Rachel. Any idiot (apart from Stephen, apparently) could see that the lunch hadn't been a resounding success. They'd both looked horrified when Stephen announced the engagement. Heather got it. For one thing, their mother was still married to Stephen. For another, there was the age difference. There was also the fact that, though Heather didn't want to admit it, she was just a little bit different. She might have tried to act the part, and she'd even managed to convince Stephen of it, but women were another story. Women could *feel* differences. Which meant Heather just had to work harder to hide them.

Heather had spent her life working hard to look better than she was. Admittedly, you had to when you worked in interior design. No one wanted an ordinary person to fit out their home. When she'd graduated and got her first job in interior design, she'd used her first paycheck to buy a pair of secondhand Christian Louboutins on eBay. She wore them with cheap black dresses (all she could afford back then) because black, she'd read, was the most forgiving if you were going to go cheap. A couple of paychecks later, she bought a second pair, and alternated them. In the years that followed she'd bought Jimmy Choos, Manolo Blahniks, and most recently Golden Goose trainers, always on sale or secondhand. She followed all the Buy, Borrow, Swap pages to find used designer clothes, and she had an A-grade fake Louis Vuitton bag that was so good she doubted even Louis himself could tell the difference. It had taken some time, but now she had enough high-quality pieces that she could wear them on rotation and look like the kind of person who lived in the kind of homes she designed. In fact, in two weeks' time, she would live in one.

Growing up, Heather had lived in a single-story orange-brick home on a housing estate that had cows and sheep on one side and an electrical substation on the other. Her clothes came from op shops or Best & Less or from the daughter of Mum's friend who was a couple of years older and favored dark, ripped clothing or skintight miniskirts. Her friends lived in similar homes and had similar clothes. While other kids were learning to ride bikes, Heather was learning to bring her father a beer. While other kids were learning phone manners, Heather was learning to answer the phone and the door with the words "Daddy is at work." While other kids were having their first alcoholic drink, Heather was already switching from wine and beer to something stronger.

Heather always knew she would leave. It was a feeling she had even before she knew anywhere else existed. And leave she did: When she turned eighteen, she moved to the center of Melbourne and rented an apartment with her friend Chantel. They both got jobs at fancy restaurants at Southbank—restaurants attended by men who left her large tips but didn't try to feel her up and women who asked her where the bathroom was with a motherly hand on her forearm. Chantel wasn't as enchanted by it as Heather had been, and she returned home after a few months. Heather stayed and enrolled in an interior decorating course and that was where she met Lily.

Lily had the kind of family that Heather thought only existed in movies. Her father was some kind of businessman, her mother was a stay-at-home mum. She had two older sisters, Lucinda and Annaliese, who were impossibly beautiful and sophisticated, even while lying around the house reading magazines. Lily was always insisting that Heather come for dinner, and even if they showed up unannounced, there was always food in the fridge and faces that were delighted to see them. Lily's parents offered them wine at dinner, and they sat at the vast table—it could seat twelve easily—with matching dinner plates and a water jug and a salad. Afterward, everyone except Lily's dad rose in unison and argued over who would clear the plates.

After a few months, Lily's mother said she would like to meet Heather's parents. "We should have them for dinner," she announced brightly.

Heather tried to imagine it. As she did, she felt a twinge of shame.

"My parents are dead," she said for the first time.

That Christmas, Heather was invited to spend the holidays with Lily's family at their beach house. Her own parents, who celebrated Christmas by buying some slightly more expensive beer, were unbothered by her absence. Christmas at Lily's was like nothing she'd ever experienced. The house, perched on a cliff top, was straight out of a travel brochure: sandstone with shutters, rolling lawns, and its very own jetty on the beach below. On Christmas Day, Heather awoke to gifts for her under the tree—beautiful gifts. A pair of silk pajamas. A bottle of perfume. A thick plush beach towel. As she opened them, Heather began to cry. Everyone mistook her tears as a sign she was missing her parents, and Heather allowed Lily's mother to hold her as she cried.

After a year, both she and Lily transferred into the interior design degree course. Lily's father owned a luxury apartment in South Yarra, where Lily and Heather lived together and paid minimal rent. Heather started to associate with different kinds of people. Slowly, she *became* a different kind of people.

Heather was so lost in her memories as she applied her lipstick in the beautiful mirror in the foyer that she forgot entirely about the steaks. By the time she returned to Stephen's chef's kitchen, the air was thick with smoke. Panic shot through her. She wrenched open the sliding door. As the smoke billowed outside, the shame set in. Pamela, she knew, had been adept at cooking extravagant three-course meals. Canapés and charcuterie boards and seafood paellas. Together, she and Stephen were "famous" for entertaining. It was a reminder to Heather, another little nudge that told her: *You'll never fit in.*

Her stomach fluttered as she heard Stephen's footsteps on the stairs—an illogical feeling, as she knew she was entirely safe with Stephen, and yet old habits died hard. She remembered hearing her father's footsteps as a child, the way her mother would glance around to make sure everything was in order. She never understood the point of it. If he wanted to punch her in the face, it didn't matter how cold his beer was or how clean the kitchen. She would have been better off just bracing for it.

Heather mentally braced herself now, as Stephen appeared at the bottom of the stairs, fresh and clean from the shower, in jeans, a gray woolen sweater, and bare feet. She reached for her wine and drained the glass, but misjudged the closeness of the bench as she brought it down a little too hard, smashing it into tiny pieces. At the very same moment, the smoke alarm sounded.

"Uh-oh," Stephen said, waving his hand around to clear the smoke. He came into the kitchen, hitting the switch on the fan on his way in. Then he grabbed the broomstick and batted it against the smoke alarm on the ceiling until it went silent. "What's going on here?"

"Clumsiness," Heather said. "And poor cooking."

She reached under the sink for the brush and dustpan as Stephen glanced at the steaks.

"Anything salvageable?" he asked.

Heather shook her head sadly. "I don't know what happened. It said to put the steaks on high heat."

He lowered the broom. "*It* said?"

Heather finished sweeping up the glass, then hesitated. "Google."

"You *googled* how to cook a steak?"

He stared at her, and she wondered for the hundredth time if this was going to be it—the moment that he would see her for who she really was.

"Wow," he said finally. "How did I not know you could google that sort of thing? Google can probably tell you how to perform heart surgery these days! Soon I'm going to be out of a job."

His phone beeped and he pulled it out of his back pocket.

"Who is it?" Heather asked.

"Good question." He rolled his eyes. "Tully's set up a family chat via some app. What's Up, maybe? But I can never find the message when it beeps. I wish she'd just text me."

"WhatsApp?"

"That's the one."

Heather took the phone from him, opened WhatsApp, and handed it back.

"That simple, eh?" he said ruefully. Then, after a moment, his eyes lit up. "Hey—we should add you to the group, since you're going to be part of the family. Then you could read all the messages and pass along any pertinent information to me."

"I'm not sure how Tully and Rachel would feel about that."

He looked up from his phone and considered her a moment. "Why? You all got along at lunch, right?"

"Yes," she said. "But I think it might be too soon. We've only just announced the engagement; let's give them some time to—"

"Nonsense," Stephen said. "You just need more time to bond. You should have lunch!"

"We just *had* lunch."

"No, I mean the three of you—you, Rachel, and Tully—without me hanging around, cramping your style." Stephen nodded, clearly warming to the idea. "You can do your girl talk, have some drinks . . . Rachel is mad about her baking. Get her going about that and she won't shut up. And Tully, she's mad about her little boys. Actually, she's just plain mad. Gets it from me. The point is, you're all going to have to get along, because none of you are going anywhere."

Heather smiled. "Fine," she said. "We'll have another lunch."

She got out a fresh glass and filled it with wine. As she did, she noticed Stephen watching her.

"Sorry," she said. "Would you like a glass?"

Stephen lifted his gaze, his brow ever so slightly furrowed. After a second, he shook his head. "No," he said. "I'm fine."

THE WEDDING

"Is there a doctor in the house?" someone shouts, which tells me Stephen is the one who is hurt. If not, he would be assisting, surely?

Of course, this being Stephen's wedding, there are dozens of doctors present. A woman in the row in front of me passes her husband her handbag before pushing her way through the crowd, and a gentleman a few seats down from me stands too. I dutifully move out of the way, make myself smaller than I already am.

I should leave now, I realize. I wouldn't want Stephen to know I was here. But given the dramatic turn of events, I find myself compelled to stay. I feel what must be a jolt of adrenaline—not common for me these days. I want to know what is happening. Did Pamela hit Stephen with the candlestick? Did she hit someone else? What happened?

There is the low hum of anxious conversation in the chapel. No one is quite sure what to do. The sacristy is out of eyeshot from where I sit and to venture closer would seem voyeuristic. After all, it's not as if I could assist in any way. In the distance, I hear the sound of sirens. Someone must have called an ambulance.

A woman at the end of our row with a sensible bob and a flouncy floral dress suggests that perhaps we should head outside to give the doctors some space. It is, after all, very tight in here. People stand and start shuffling out of the chapel, spilling out the doors and into the courtyard, where the ambulance has just pulled up.

It isn't long before the theories start. The consensus is that Heather was injured. A few speculate that one of the daughters went for her. It's a fair assumption, as it's no secret they weren't happy about the wedding. But a man in a bowler hat is adamant that Pamela attacked Heather. Someone else is sure that Stephen had a heart attack. My money is on the thin daughter being involved. Very neurotic girl, apparently. Mental problems, I think.

Two paramedics unload a stretcher from the back of the van. A police car arrives. Everyone moves out of the way to make space.

7

TULLY

Heather Wisher has been added to the group.

Tully was searching her family WhatsApp for a photo of one of Rachel's wedding cakes when she saw it. Heather had been added to the family WhatsApp chat.

So many questions went through her head. First, who had done this? Dad didn't know how to add people to the family chat—he could barely reply to a message via the family chat. When he did manage to respond to one of Tully's pictures of the boys, or one of Rachel's pictures of a wedding cake, it was usually with one word, all lowercase—"wow" or "cool" or even just a thumbs-up emoji (oddly, Dad loved emojis; often his one-word messages were accompanied by no less than four of them). But emojis notwithstanding, Dad's technological capabilities were pitiful. There was no way he was adding someone to the family chat on his own.

High on the list of reasons this was inappropriate was the fact that *Mum* was still in the group. She didn't interact in it, obviously; they had taken her phone from her before she'd gone to live in the nursing home, and even if she did have the phone she would not have understood how to use it, but that wasn't the point. They'd left Mum in the group as a matter of principle. The same principle that said Heather Wisher had no business in their family chat.

"I couldn't find the cake," she said, tossing her phone back on the table and tried to ignore it. She and Sonny were sitting at the back of her garden, in the paved area that butted up against the outdoor kitchen. They were being civil to each other—even pleasant—but it was for the benefit of their lunch guests, Rob and Michelle. It was almost as if they hadn't spent the last twenty-four hours ignoring each other entirely.

"You paid for *lunch*?" Sonny had cried when she'd explained the charge on the credit card. "Why on earth would you do that?"

The truth was, she had no idea why she'd insisted on paying. It was a spontaneous gesture, a burst of desire for her father's approval, maybe. A mistake—she could acknowledge that now—but a well-meaning one. "I . . . don't know."

"You don't know? Tully, we don't have any spare money at the moment, do you understand that? None. We have to sell our house, our cars—I'm not sure how I'm going to make the mortgage payment. As it stands, we're well short."

Tully was flooded with shame, both at what she'd done and at the idea of the bank noticing something was up. She'd always felt so proud, so secure in the fact that they paid off their credit card debt in full each month and that all their payments were made ahead of time. The mortification of people having to follow up, wondering where their money was . . . it was simply unthinkable.

Sonny had also seen the items on the back seat of the car, which only served to make the argument worse. Tully assured him that she would return each and every one—and she had indeed dropped them all off at the nearest charity shop—but he'd still given her the silent treatment. In fact, the only time they'd spoken in the last twenty-four hours was when Tully asked him not to tell Rob and Michelle that they'd lost all their money.

Sonny had looked baffled. "They're going to find out sometime."

"I know that," Tully said tersely. "I just don't want them to find out today."

Sonny had agreed and now here they were, sitting in the sun. It was the classic setup. Sonny and Rob commandeered the barbecue, while she and Michelle sipped white wine spritzers and yelled at the children not to be too rough on the trampoline.

"So, we've been dying to know," Michelle said. "What was the new girlfriend like?" She laughed a little. It wasn't a mean sort of laugh; it was the polite, slightly scandalized sort. A testing laugh—a laugh that was aware of the sensitivity of the issue but hopeful for a bit of salacious gossip. Tully didn't blame Michelle. How many times had she enjoyed a scandalized laugh of this nature over a friend's child who'd been caught sexting or a politician who'd been caught with his pants down? How superficial she'd been. This was not content for titillation—this was someone's life! She vowed to change from now on. Everything would be different.

"She was . . . as expected," Tully said. "Young, pretty. Did I mention young?"

Rob and Michelle nodded expectantly. They were waiting for more, of course. And Tully had more. She could tell them that they were getting married. That Dad was planning to divorce Mum. She could have given them what they wanted. But for some reason, her throat started to close up and she couldn't seem to project the words.

"Are you having chicken, Michelle?" Sonny said, in a clear attempt to change the subject. "Or I have a nice steak here?"

He met Tully's eye and, for the first time in ages, she smiled at him gratefully.

Sonny had always been a skilled host. She loved the ease with which he chatted to people, the way he kept everyone's glass full, the effort he always made to talk to even the most boring person and make them feel special. He was equally competent with the kids—their own and other people's—doling out icy poles or putting on a movie when the other parents were too drunk or tired to deal with them. After everyone left, he always helped her clean up, and while his standard of cleaning was well below hers, she appreciated that he didn't slope off to bed like other husbands. Often, because of this dedication, he got lucky at the end of the night. It was unlikely this would happen today. Today, they were playing a part. The part of a happy couple.

She and Sonny had met at a university trivia night. Tully had arrived with two friends, but because they didn't have enough people to make up a table, they'd been put on a table with a bunch of know-it-all law students. Tully hadn't bothered to argue when they insisted they knew the correct answer to several questions (they hadn't), but when it came to the final question (How many children did Madonna and Guy Ritchie have together?) she had to speak up.

"It's two," she said.

"No," one loudmouth, drunken law student had exclaimed. "It's one. The little boy. Rocco."

"They also adopted a little boy from Malawi," Tully said. "David. That's two children."

Tully remembered the way she'd leveled her gaze at Sonny, the scribe, and gestured for him to write it down. She'd acted more confident than she felt. She didn't have numbers on her side, after all. The law students all knew each other. If they sided with the drunken loudmouth, she wouldn't stand a chance.

"I think she's right," Sonny said. "I'm going with two." And he wrote it down, without waiting for any input from the table. When it turned out that Tully had been right, Sonny had nodded at her, a faint look of approval in his eyes. That was the moment, he told her later, that he fell in love with her.

The relationship went full speed from that night, which was fine with Tully. She always preferred traveling at high speed. For a while, she even thought Sonny had cured her of her unspeakable addiction. Or at least got her hooked on a different drug. When he looked at her, and when she looked at him, she got so high she didn't need to think about stealing. Sonny was her drug, and she could have as much of him as she wanted.

But like all drugs, Sonny eventually lost his potency. And when he didn't provide the hit that he once had, Tully needed to go looking for that rush of adrenaline in the place she'd always found it.

"Boys!" Michelle called. "Not so rough!"

Tully looked over, thrilled to see that Miles was playing on the grass with Rob and Michelle's boys. He was often timid when other children came over, and usually spent the whole time sitting on Tully's lap. Perhaps he was sick of Tully, given that they spent every night together? Three weeks in, he still hadn't slept in his big-boy bed and Tully was starting to think he never would. One day, his wife would kiss him good night, tuck him into his crib, and then head into her own bedroom. If this was his reaction to a new bed, Tully wondered, what would be his reaction to a new house?

"Is that a new top, Tully?" Michelle asked her. "It's gorgeous."

This caught Sonny's attention. The word "new" had a way of

sending an electric shock through him lately. "I don't think I've seen it before either," he said.

Tully avoided his gaze. "This one? Sure you have."

"Michelle has a lot of clothes that aren't new but which I haven't seen before," Rob said, sipping the froth off the premium beer that Sonny must have bought without receiving the third degree from her about its cost. "The next thing I know, there's an eye-watering charge on the credit card from Zimmerman or Scanlan Theodore."

"And Rob has so many golf clubs that aren't new but which *I* haven't seen before," Michelle replied. "If I looked at the credit card statement, I'm sure I'd find some eye-watering charges from House of Golf."

They both laughed with the airiness of people without money problems. This was how it happened, Tully realized, opening a new bottle of sauvignon blanc. You married a kind, generous progressive man, and within a decade he became George Banks from *Mary Poppins*. (The boys had been watching *Mary Poppins* lately and Tully had been shocked by what poor Winifred had had to put up with. No wonder she joined the suffragette movement.)

"You won't find any eye-watering amounts on the credit card from me," Tully said, holding up her hand to imply scout's honor. "You have my word."

She wasn't sure if it was the scout's honor or giving her word that did it, but Sonny seemed to relax then. It had the effect of relaxing Tully too. Until her phone started ringing and she saw Heather's name on the screen.

"It's Heather," she said, her eyes widening.

"Answer it," Michelle demanded.

"Should I?" Tully said. The group nodded unanimously so she raised the phone to her ear. "Heather?"

There was a longer than normal pause.

"Tully, hi . . . I hope I'm not catching you at a bad time."

"It's not a great time," Tully said. "I have some friends here at the moment."

She looked up. Rob, Michelle, and Sonny were all watching her eagerly.

"In that case, I won't keep you. But I was just talking to your dad, and he suggested it might be fun for us to get together again. Another lunch, just the girls this time. I wondered if you would be interested?"

Tully had a vision of herself sitting at a table with Rachel and Heather, no Dad. It made her stomach lurch. It was one thing meeting up with Heather and Dad at his request, but . . . socializing with her? It felt like the ultimate betrayal of Mum.

"It might sound a little too much," Heather continued, "but I just thought it would be nice if we got to know each other better as women . . . without your dad around."

Rob and Michelle were sitting forward in their chairs, absolutely thrilled, mouthing things to each other and beaming. The new girlfriend. Calling!

"I'm sorry, Heather—like I said, this isn't a great time. I have guests here."

"Oh." A pause. "Of course. So sorry."

Tully knew she should say, *I'll be in touch about lunch,* or, *I'll call you later and we can make a plan.* But her brain seemed to have temporarily cut off access to such social graces, so instead she said: "Bye," and hung up the phone.

As she returned her phone to the table she noted Rob's and Michelle's delighted, scandalized faces and knew she was expected to provide juicy details. She herself would have appreciated the juicy details in a similar situation. And why not? Not only would it please her audience, there was a good chance it would be therapeutic to share all the sordid, peculiar details. The problem was, she wanted to save those details for the one person who would understand exactly how she felt. The one who'd reached out to her just a few days ago. The one who, no matter how hard she tried, she just couldn't seem to connect with.

Rachel.

8

RACHEL

Ninety-seven thousand three hundred and seventy-two dollars.
Rachel sat on her bedroom floor, surrounded by crumpled bills. She had pulled the money out of the hot-water bottle bill by bill, first with her fingers, then with tweezers, and finally, when the cash kept coming, she'd taken a pair of scissors and cut through the bottle. The hot water bottle cover was also full of bills.

Ninety-seven thousand three hundred and seventy-two dollars. Where did Mum get that kind of money?

Was it even hers?

Logically, it couldn't have been. Even before Mum started showing signs of dementia, she and Dad had been old-school when it came to money. Back in the day, Dad gave Mum "housekeeping" money; more recently, if Mum needed something, Dad just bought it for her, or Rachel or Tully did. Mum simply didn't have access to this sort of money. Which meant it had to be stolen—but from where? And how?

It was true that Mum had done some strange things these past few years. On top of the shoplifting, she'd signed up with virtually every energy company that rang up to offer special rates. She'd taken the dog for a walk using an old scarf because she couldn't find the leash (only to realize later that they didn't have a dog; it belonged to the neighbor). She'd repeatedly tried to enter the house via the window rather than the door. But unlike the shoplifting or the dog-stealing or window-entering, stashing away this amount of money required some premeditation and planning. After all, even if she was to swipe an entire grocery store till (which Rachel couldn't imagine), it still wouldn't contain $97,000.

It made no sense.

"Where, Mum?" Rachel said out loud. "Where did you get all this money?"

She looked at it, laid out on the floor. The only thing she'd found inside the hot-water bottle besides the cash was a folded piece of paper, torn from a spiral notebook. On it were two names: *Tully* and *Fiona Arthur.*

Rachel had never heard the name Fiona Arthur, so she focused instead on Tully. Why had Mum written Tully's name? Did it mean the money was meant for Tully? Admittedly, Mum was always worried about her oldest daughter. *A mother is only as happy as her unhappiest child,* she used to say. And while Tully wasn't unhappy, exactly, she was never exactly happy either. True, she'd settled a bit since meeting Sonny and having the boys, but she was still . . . Tully. Maybe this money was supposed to help with that . . . somehow.

Rachel jumped as her phone began to ring. It was Heather. She was intrigued, but not enough to answer. She had enough to deal with right now without adding her father's fiancée to the equation. She stabbed at the screen to silence it, but unfortunately, in her haste, she accidentally accepted the call. Worse still, it was a WhatsApp call—with video. After a second, Heather's face appeared on the screen.

"Rachel?"

"Heather!" Rachel scrambled to grab the phone and then turned away to ensure the money wasn't visible. "Hello. Sorry, I . . . um . . . dropped the phone."

"No, *I'm* sorry . . . I didn't mean to do a video call. Your dad added me to the family WhatsApp and it's not my strong suit."

"It's fine," Rachel said. "What can I do for you?"

"I won't keep you. I just wanted to see if you and Tully might be free to have lunch. You know, just us girls?"

Rachel heard a knock at the door.

"I thought it might be nice to get to know each other better."

"It would," Rachel said, getting to her feet. "Definitely. But there's actually someone at the door right now. Do you mind if I call you back?"

There was a short pause followed by a quick: "Sure. Of course." Then Heather hung up the phone, leaving Rachel to wrestle with her guilt.

There was another knock at the door. All right, all right. Rachel shoved the cash under the bed and headed for the door. Before she could get there, there was a third knock. Seriously? Did people not know that she had just uncovered tens of thousands of dollars that her mother had potentially stolen and stashed in a hot-water bottle and she was trying to figure out what to do, while also trying to get off the phone from her soon-to-be stepmother, who was one year her junior? Rachel threw open the door, ready to tell whoever it was to take a hike. But it was Dad.

Of course it was.

When Mum got sick, he'd started coming around all the time.

Three times a week he'd stop in, on his way to or from work, ostensibly to give her an update on Mum but more likely to have a conversation with someone who didn't merely repeat the same question over and over again. Rachel enjoyed the visits, but she could never seem to instill in him the importance of calling ahead.

"I run a business, Dad," she'd tell him, and he'd apologize then come in anyway. She knew that her cake business confused him, even if he made an effort to seem proud. Whenever he saw her he'd say, "So . . . er . . . how are things in the kitchen?" She knew he meant well, so she resisted the urge to roll her eyes.

"What are you doing here?" she asked him now.

"Do I need a reason to visit my equal favorite daughter?" He kissed her forehead on the way inside, as sure as a child that his company would be a welcome delight.

"No," she said. "But you might want to try calling first."

"Why, I'm not interrupting anything, am I?" He paused, glancing around as if expecting to find a lover hiding somewhere. Rachel wondered what he would do if he *had* interrupted something. Keel over and have a coronary, possibly.

Dad had never commented on her lack of a partner—not when she was younger and not now—but she knew he must wonder. Who wouldn't? At fourteen she was dating a new guy every week, to the point that Dad refused to answer the landline because he couldn't stand to listen to another stammering adolescent boy asking for Rachel. Then, at sixteen, she hung up her dating boots. It must have surprised him. She was certain he'd made some kind of pact with himself never to ask. Back when Mum was lucid, she used to ask often. "Why don't you have anyone? Surely you could have your pick of the men!" But Dad never said a word. She'd always been grateful for it, but suddenly she wondered why.

"You interrupted me watching TV, actually," she said, closing the front door. "Cup of tea?"

"What a good idea!" he said, as if that hadn't been his intention all along.

Rachel led the way to the kitchen, where Dad immediately settled himself at the round table and waited for her to produce a cup of tea. She should have found it insulting, the way he expected to be waited on, but he always seemed so happy when she handed over the tea that it was almost a delight to make it for him. This was why men ruled the world.

"Lemon cake?"

Dad grinned. "With cream, if you have it."

Naturally, she did. She even had lemon-infused cream, made specially. She flicked on the kettle and cut them each a generous slice of cake, which she doused with cream. She placed a plate in front of Dad.

"It was nice meeting Heather the other day," she said carefully. "She seemed . . . great."

"She can't cook," he replied, spearing a piece of lemon cake. He was trying to be brave, but Rachel could see he found this a little distressing.

"Well," Rachel said, "lucky you already have a cook in the family."

"Indeed." His cheeks were bulging with cake. "I don't suppose you offer cookery classes?"

"For you, or for Heather?"

"Both," he said diplomatically.

Dad wasn't always diplomatic. The old Dad would have said, "Cooking? Me? I don't think so," and Mum would roll her eyes and say, "Your father would struggle to make toast without me." Now he was considering cookery classes?

"Speaking of Heather," Rachel said, "she called a few minutes ago."

Dad looked up from his cake. He had a bit of cream on his chin. "Oh?"

"I was in the middle of something and I had to end the call prematurely."

"Ah," Dad said. "She was hoping to arrange lunch with you and Tully. That's why I stopped by. I want to make sure you and Tully are making an effort."

Rachel thought about the way she'd hurried Heather off the phone and felt another stab of guilt.

"Listen," he said. "I know these last few years have been a trial. And I know that strange doesn't even begin to describe what it must feel like to have your father find himself a younger girlfriend while still married to your terribly ill mother. I know this, and I'm sorry. But, Rach, all of this is because of me. *I* made a decision to pursue a relationship with Heather at this time. Meeting Heather brought me the most joy I've had in years, and perhaps because of this I wasn't as sensitive to what that would be like for you as I should have been. But that's on me. And I'd hate for you to blame Heather for decisions that really have nothing to do with her."

"I don't blame her, Dad."

"You don't?"

"No. And of course I'll have lunch with her. I'll do it here. I'll make coq au vin. I'll call Heather later to tell her."

Dad looked relieved. "That sounds great. Do you think you can rope Tully in?"

"I can try."

He smiled. "Thanks, sweetie."

"No problem," she said. "And actually . . . since you're here, there's something I want to talk to you about," she continued.

"Oh?"

"You know that stuff you gave me at lunch? The stuff that Mum had stolen?"

"Yes."

"There was a hot-water bottle in there."

"Oh yeah?"

"And it had money inside. Quite a lot of money."

He looked up, cocked an eyebrow. "Well," he said, after a moment, "maybe she was saving up for something. Or stashing it away for a rainy day. How much?" He speared another piece of cake and put it in his mouth.

"Almost a hundred thousand."

Dad choked on his cake. After a moment, he swallowed. "A hundred thousand *dollars*?"

Rachel nodded. "I was about to fill it up with boiling water when I saw a fifty-dollar note sticking out the top. Where would Mum have got that kind of money from?"

He was silent for several seconds. "Honestly, I have no idea. She would have had to be putting away her housekeeping for her whole life to save that much."

"I thought the same thing."

Dad drifted off into thought for almost a minute. When he finally looked at her, his expression was still just as bewildered.

"What should I do with the money?" she asked finally.

Dad picked up his tea. "Well, you know the expression: finders keepers."

"Oh no. I couldn't."

"Nonsense," he said. "Why couldn't you?"

Part of his eagerness for her to take it made Rachel wonder if he was the one behind it. It wouldn't be unlike Dad to try to give her something without having to receive thanks for it. In fact, nothing made him more uncomfortable than being acknowledged for a kindness or good work. At the same time, she always knew when Dad was lying. It was a tic he had—his eyes flickered. Her mum had pointed it out once, and she was absolutely right. And there was no tic now.

"Dad, really it's too much. Besides, what about Tully? Her name was—"

He held up his hand like a stop sign and Rachel fell silent. Such was the effect a father had on you, even when you were in your thirties. "Keep it, Rachel. Tully has plenty of money. If anyone deserves it, it's you." He drained the last of his tea and then stood up. "Now, I have to run. You'll arrange the lunch with Heather?"

"I said I would, didn't I?"

He smiled, and made his way to the door.

"Oh, Dad, one more thing?" she said, as he stepped over the threshold. "There was a note with the money that had Tully's name on it, and also the name Fiona Arthur. I thought you might know who that was."

He frowned for a minute, then shrugged. "I'm sorry, sweetie, I don't."

She shook her head and waved him off before returning inside. It was only after he was gone that she allowed herself to think about the fact that, when he said he didn't know Fiona Arthur, Dad's eyes had flickered.

9

TULLY

Tully stood in the doorway of her mother's room at the nursing home. She was already exhausted, and she hadn't even gone inside yet. In the days since their barbecue with Rob and Michelle, Tully could recognize she'd been spiraling. Commitments not to steal had been broken almost as soon as they'd been made—first at the supermarket, then the petrol station, then the department store. The self-loathing had been quick to set in each time and she'd ended up stopping at the charity shop on the way home and leaving the items in a pile on the doorstep. At least that way she didn't have to worry about Sonny finding them. Unfortunately, she couldn't leave the guilt and shame on the doorstep with the stolen goods, along with her habit, which was slowly taking over her life.

"Hi, Mum," Tully said.

Mum was sitting in the corner chair with a bowl of soup pushed up to her, staring out of the window, while the television played quietly. Upon hearing Tully's voice, she looked over, suspicious. "Are you talking to me?"

"Yes," Tully said, walking into the room. "It's me, Tully."

Tully had introduced herself on arrival the last few times she'd visited. She reasoned that even if Mum *did* recognize her that day, saving her from searching her mind for her daughter's name would free up brain space for other things. She'd deteriorated even in the last couple of weeks, since Tully and Rachel and Dad had come into the nursing home to have Christmas lunch with her. That day, Mum seemed to know who they were, but today, even after Tully called her "Mum," there was no recognition in her mother's eyes.

If she doesn't know who you are, don't push it, Rachel always said. *Just pretend you're a stranger, there for a visit. It upsets her if she thinks she's supposed to know who you are and she doesn't.* Tully suspected Rachel was right, but she had never been able to do it. This was her mother. She couldn't pretend she was a random visitor. She wanted to grab her by the shoulders and shout, "Look, Mum, it's me. Tully. Your daughter. You gave birth to me!"

"Are you here to clean the room?" Mum said after a moment. She pointed to a feather duster lying on a side table. "Someone left this thingy here. Is it yours?"

Mum had a fresh bruise on her temple, Tully noticed, which wasn't a huge surprise. Mum always had one bruise or another, even before the dementia. She was terribly clumsy, always tripping or stumbling on something, and the worse her dementia got, so too did the falls. Still, Tully made a mental note to ask the nurses about it. She'd watched a documentary about elder abuse and it was worth letting them know that she had noticed.

"Is it yours?" Mum repeated.

"Oh . . . yes. Yes, it is."

Tully picked up the feather duster and Mum turned back to her soup. She looked interested in it, even leaning down to smell it, but she didn't reach for her spoon.

"What's for lunch?" Tully asked.

"Red watery stuff," Mum said. "Smells all right."

Tully nodded doubtfully. "What does it taste like?"

A pause. "I'm not sure."

"Why don't you try it and see?"

"All right," Mum said.

Tully only realized what she was doing a second before it happened. Mum leaned down as if to smell the soup, but instead of sniffing, her mother—the woman who used to sit at the end of the table even when she wasn't eating, simply to ensure that she and Rachel were using their table manners—lowered her face into the bowl.

"Oh, Mum, no," Tully said, dropping the feather duster.

Mum looked up, startled. She had soup on her chin and her nose. "What's wrong?"

"Nothing," Tully said. "It's just . . . may I help you?"

Tully pulled up a chair opposite her mother. She filled the spoon and lifted it to her mum's mouth, which her mother dutifully opened wide. As strange as it was, there was something lovely about caring for her like this. For so long Tully had felt useless when it came to helping her mother. Now, finally, there was something she could do.

Tully was concentrating so hard on feeding her that she almost missed the fact that Mum was looking at her intently. When Tully finally met her gaze, Mum's face softened. "I know you . . . don't I?"

Tully nodded, tears welling in her eyes. "Yes, Mum," she said. "You do."

It was, Tully realized later, the perfect storm. She left the nursing home and went straight to the main street of Armadale, the part with all the shops. She could feel it coming, like the change in the air before a storm. She was like a balloon filling with air. The pressure would grow until it managed to find a release.

When she saw the homewares store, she knew it was the place. It had a double shopfront, which was unusual for this strip of shops, and it was jumbled and chaotic enough to allow Tully to disappear deep into the store, where she wouldn't be seen. She wouldn't be watched; Tully never was. She was well presented, upper middle class, and looked like she had money to spend.

"Good morning!" the nicely dressed woman behind the desk said, looking up from the item she was gift-wrapping then immediately down again.

"Good morning," Tully replied brightly.

"I'm Sophie. If there's anything I can help you with, just sing out."

"Just browsing for now," Tully said, plunging into the cozy, cluttered space.

It was still quite shocking to Tully, how easily she played the game. Even as her whole body trembled, she morphed into the role of snobby affluent mother without so much as a thought. She did it on autopilot, the same way she shoved small items into her purse. It was as if she were temporarily inhabited by an alien.

At the back of the room, in a large wicker basket, she spotted a pile of eccentric doorknobs. Tiny little things that would be perfect for a shabby chic bedside table. She fingered one carefully, already feeling her anxiety abate. She never, at any point, decided to take it, no more than she ever decided to breathe. Rather, it was like getting swept up in a hurricane. Her purse was already unzipped when the saleswoman, Sophie, suddenly appeared be-side her.

"I love those doorknobs," she said. "Did you have a piece of fur-niture in mind for them?"

Tully dropped the doorknob and it went clattering to the ground.

"Sorry," Tully said. "I'm a bit jittery today."

"I noticed." The saleswoman bobbed down to grab it, then con-tinued to hold it in her own hand. Her expression was a little warier now. "You live around here, don't you? I think I've seen you with your little boys on the way to the park."

Tully tried to force herself to smile, to raise her eyebrows with interest, to be the breezy Armadale mother she'd been a few min-utes ago. But the skill had deserted her.

"I noticed because I also have two little boys," Sophie said. "I bring them in here sometimes, during the school holidays. They stand behind the desk and play shop." She laughed. "They tell all the customers proudly that it's their mummy's shop. It's so import-ant that our boys are proud of us, don't you think? I feel like I'm doing my bit for feminism when I make them proud."

Tully nodded and muttered, "Yes, very good."

"Sorry, I didn't catch your name," Sophie said.

Tully didn't want to give the woman her name. She wanted to end this conversation. Leave this shop. She had a bad feeling. But what else could she do? "It's . . . Tully."

"Tully," Sophie said. "That's pretty. Well, Tully . . . I would hate for your little boys to feel anything other than proud of you. That's why I'm going to pretend I didn't know what you were about to do with that doorknob."

Tully smiled in what she hoped was a polite, indignant fashion. "Ex*cuse* me?"

"And I'll pretend I didn't see you take a candle the last time you were in here. Because I don't think that would make your boys proud of you."

Tully's smile faded.

"But as I said, I want my boys to be proud of me too, and for that reason, I'm going to have to ask you not to return to my shop. I hope you understand."

"Yes," Tully said. "Yes, I understand."

And then, because there was nothing else to say, Tully barreled toward the front door, practically bowling over another customer in her haste to get away.

10

HEATHER

Heather sat on Stephen's bathroom floor nursing a glass of whiskey. She'd got home from work an hour ago, poured herself a drink, and immediately took it to the giant en suite. She'd always found it soothing, drinking in the bathroom. Beyond the privacy the bathroom offered, she liked the way her thoughts felt in there—the coolness of them, the space they had to bounce against the tiled walls.

In a way, it was a tribute to her mother, who used to drink in the bathroom. The first time she saw her do it, Heather was just eleven years old. The night before, Heather had woken to the sound of her mother crying and her dad shouting. They'd been at a party and Heather had expected them to be gone most of the night, but they'd got home early. It wasn't even midnight.

"If you ever embarrass me like that again," Dad was saying to her mum, "I'm going to kill you. Do you understand? I promise you that's what I'll do."

Heather had got out of bed and followed the noise as far as the lounge. By then her mum was crying loudly, saying "please" and "stop" in halting bursts. Heather peered around the corner. Mum's back was against the fridge and Dad was holding her by the throat.

"It would be so easy. I could just press my thumbs a little harder. Like this . . ."

Her mum made a gagging sound. *He's killing her,* Heather thought. *My dad is killing my mum.* The worst part was that Heather didn't do anything. She didn't run to help her. She just stood there, frozen.

After what felt like an eternity, he let go and Mum fell to the ground, gasping for air. Heather heard the sound of her scrabbling away from him on the kitchen floor.

"*So* easy," her dad repeated.

Heather ran back to her room, but she didn't fall asleep for hours. In the morning, when she came out of her room, Mum was in the bathroom. The shower was running, but when Heather opened the door she found her mum sitting on the floor drinking wine straight from the bottle. Her eyes were glassy and tired.

"Why is the shower running?" Heather asked.

"Because when the shower's running," Mum said, not looking at her, "he doesn't come in."

"I wanted to check you were all right," Heather said, closing the door and sitting beside her. "You know . . . after last night."

Her mum frowned for a second, as if trying to remember what had happened last night. Then her hand rose to the pinkish mark on her neck. "Oh." She took another sip of wine. "I'm fine."

"I thought he was going to kill you," Heather said.

"Nah." Another sip. "He just likes the drama."

"But he was strangling you. He said he would kill you."

Mum held out the bottle out to Heather. She took it.

"Don't worry," she said, after Heather took a sip. "He's too fuck-ing chicken."

But, as it turned out, Mum was wrong about that.

Since that day, drinking in the bathroom had helped Heather to deal with many things. For example, the baby thing.

She and Stephen had had the discussion the first morning she woke up in Stephen's bed.

"I have a tricky subject I'd like to bring up and I think it would be pertinent to bring it up sooner rather than later," he'd said.

It was one of the things she loved about him: his forthrightness, his refusal to shy away from difficult discussions. Also, his casual use of words like "pertinent."

"The fact is, I'm at quite a different life stage from you. As such, I feel it would be irresponsible of me to proceed with you any further—and, to be clear, I very much want to proceed further—without making you aware that I am not interested in having any more children."

It wasn't a surprise. Heather understood there weren't many men in their sixties with adult children who wanted more kids. Some might be willing to go there for the sake of the relationship—but no one *wanted* it. And it was fine with Heather. Or if not *fine,* at least it didn't injure her the way it might have injured a different, more maternal sort of woman. For Heather, it was primarily something she felt intellectually rather than physically or biologically.

"What do *you* want?" he asked.

It was such a middle-class question. People her age spent so much time musing on it. What do I want? *What do I want?* Heather didn't bother. After all, it didn't matter what she wanted. Life hap-pened; you didn't get to choose it. And sure enough, it had just happened to her again. "I want to be with you."

Stephen accepted that at face value. He didn't press her on whether she had ever wanted children, or whether this would be a sacrifice. He didn't want to know and she didn't want to tell him. She just needed to reframe, that was all. People reframed all the time. People who realized they weren't going to live a long life. People who lost a loved one, suffered an accident, lost use of a limb. They reframed. And Heather would too. No babies for her. They wouldn't be part of her journey.

She heard the rumbling of the garage door opening. Stephen was already home from work. She downed the rest of her whiskey, left the glass on the counter, and turned on the shower. She'd just stepped out of her clothes and into the stream of water when there was a knock at the door. "May I come in?"

Stephen was always wonderfully respectful like that. They hadn't reached that point in the relationship where they barged into the bathroom when the other was in there demanding to know where the car keys had been left. Heather felt an unexpected pang of yearning to reach that point with Stephen.

"Of course," she replied.

The door cracked open. "I like coming home to find you in my shower."

"I like that you like it." She heard him drop his keys on the vanity. "How was your day?"

Through the glass she saw him prop himself up on the bathroom counter. "Well," he said, "I started divorce proceedings with Pam, so good and bad."

Heather turned off the shower and wrapped a plush towel around herself. "Oh."

"It's fine. Nothing for you to worry about."

"Are you sure?"

"Totally sure. How was your day? Did you arrange that lunch with Rachel and Tully?"

"Oh," Heather said. "Not yet."

"My guess is that you'll be hearing from Rachel very soon." He said it at the very same moment that Heather's phone began to ring. She glanced at the screen. It was Rachel.

She held it up to show Stephen, amazed. "Told you," he said. "I know things." He gestured for her to answer it.

"Rachel," Heather said. "Hi."

"Heather! I hope this isn't a bad time? I just wanted to follow up about lunch. I was thinking I could host at my place, if that works for you."

She lifted her gaze to gape at Stephen. "That would be lovely," she said. "And . . . Tully will be there too?"

"Of course," Rachel said, after a slight pause. "Tully wouldn't miss it."

When Heather hung up the phone, Stephen looked positively triumphant.

She shook her head. "How did you know?"

He tapped his temple, still smiling, but with a slightly different look in his eyes now. Then he opened the cupboard under the sink and pulled out the whiskey bottle.

Heather's heart sank.

"Told you," he said. "I know things."

11

TULLY

As Tully sat on one of Rachel's counter stools with a glass of wine in hand, she felt herself relax for the first time in weeks. Part of it was the wine. The other part of it was Rachel. As silly as it sounded, she was *touched* that Rachel had invited her to lunch. It was out of the ordinary. Generally, they caught up as a family—or they had before Mum went into the nursing home—for birthdays and Christmas, or to shop for a gift for Mother's Day or Father's Day. And there were the other odd things—like their cousin Caitlin's hens' party or the time they got tickets to see *Frozen*, the musical. But intimate one-on-one meetups at Rachel's house weren't something they'd ever done before, and Tully was excited.

Rachel lived in an unappealing blond-brick unit on the hip north side of Melbourne. It should have been ugly as sin, and yet somehow she'd managed to make it charming, the kind of place people wanted to hang out. Even her tiny courtyard was lovely, decorated with fairy lights and hanging plant pots. She also had a gift for entertaining—being able to produce a good bottle of wine, spectacular lasagna, and a salad with absolutely no notice, and without any apparent effort. Any time you went to Rachel's, your glass was full, your plate was warm, and conversation flowed all night. It was a vibe Tully had been unable to re-create, even when paying caterers.

Today, as Tully sipped her wine, Rachel stood on the other side of the counter, piping intricate flowers onto a wedding cake that she'd been making for days.

"That one isn't straight," Tully said helpfully. At least, she hoped it was helpful. If it was *her* cake, she would definitely want to know. And Rachel, to her credit, didn't seem bothered; she merely examined the crooked flower, said, "You're right," and straightened it.

Rachel had called the day before to invite her to lunch. Tully had been in the middle of hiding a pile of recently acquired goods in the garage and she'd been about to ignore the phone when she got a case of the what-ifs.

What if it was Dad? He was their only living functioning parent—what if he'd had a heart attack? What if he was lying on a table in an emergency room somewhere, taking his last breaths thinking, *I'd love to see my daughter Tully one more time before I go,* and she didn't answer the call? What if it was Mum? Before she'd moved into the nursing home they'd received several worrying phone calls about her. The one from the supermarket cashier who'd found her wandering around the car park when she couldn't remember which car was hers. The one from the cleaning lady when Mum had gone ballistic at her for "breaking into her home." They'd had fewer worrying phone calls since Mum moved into the nursing home, but Tully knew enough about Alzheimer's to know that more worrying phone calls would be coming. What if it was bad news about Rachel herself?

Why were there always so many bloody what-ifs?

As it turned out, it wasn't bad news at all. Quite the opposite.

"Can you strain the potatoes for me?" Rachel asked, placing a sugar flower just so on the side of the cake.

Tully leaped to her feet. It was a rare moment when she was able to help to Rachel and she wasn't going to miss the opportunity. The funny thing was, if a guest of Tully's ever tried to strain the potatoes, she would have been mortified. If Tully was having guests over, even if it was just Rachel, the potatoes would have been strained hours ago, the pots would have been washed and put away, and the place would be devoid of all evidence of life, allowing her to devote her entire attention to her guests for the duration of their visit. It was good manners, she thought. But now, straining potatoes for Rachel while her sister decorated her cake, Tully had to admit that Rachel's lack of attention on her wasn't harming her experience in the least. On the contrary, Tully felt charmed at being authorized to assist in the lunch-making while watching Rachel do something as special as icing a wedding cake. She felt more special, more privileged, than if she'd been given Rachel's undivided attention.

She placed the strainer in the sink and tipped the potatoes in.

"Hey, Tul," Rachel said, still focused on the cake, "did Mum ever say anything to you about money?"

The steam from the potatoes rose from the sink. "What do you mean?" Tully said. "What about money?"

"I don't know. I just wondered if she might have put any aside for"—Rachel shrugged—"emergencies or something."

"Why?" Tully looked at her. "Do you need money?"

"No, no."

"Because if you do, all you need to do is ask, and Sonny and I will . . . It wouldn't even have to be a loan."

The offer rolled off her tongue so fast she couldn't stop it. This was, after all, how they'd been raised. *Don't be mean with money. Always pay more than your share. Money isn't something to hoard; it is to be shared and enjoyed.* If someone you loved needed it, you gave it, no questions asked. Tully had always thought of herself as generous for that reason. Now she saw it for what it was. A privilege. Giving money was an easy way to support someone. A lot of people didn't have that ability. Now, neither did Tully. Funnily enough, the ability to be generous was one of the things she would miss the most.

"Thanks, but I don't need money," Rachel said. "I was just thinking about how Mum always told us we should be more independent than she was financially, and I wondered if she had ever put anything away for us."

Tully tipped the potatoes into the serving bowl that Rachel had left out. "Like in a trust or something?"

"Yes," Rachel said. "Or something."

Tully felt a surge of hope. If Mum had put money in a trust for them, she and Sonny could be saved! They wouldn't have to sell the house. They wouldn't have to endure any humiliation at all. Depending on the amount, she supposed. But every little bit helped. "Well, Dad would know if she'd put any away for us," she said eagerly. "Why don't we ask him?"

"Oh," Rachel said. "No, I'm sure he would have told us."

Tully deflated. "Yes," she said. "Yes, he probably would." She took a long sip of wine.

"But you don't need money, right?" Rachel said after a moment. "You and Sonny, you're . . . pretty comfortable?" She paused in her icing and looked at her sister.

This was, Tully knew, the opportunity she'd been waiting for. She could tell Rachel about Sonny losing their money. About them selling the house. Maybe she could even tell her about her . . . habit?

The shame of it would be immense, but there would be relief in it too. And Rachel wouldn't judge her. She might not be able to help her, but at least she'd send her home with a frozen meal and an offer to babysit the boys. (Tully would take her up on that offer too, as Rachel was one of the few people Miles was happy to be left with.) Yes, she decided. She was going to tell Rachel.

But just as she opened her mouth to begin, the doorbell rang.

"Oh," Tully said, irritated. "Who is *that*?"

She expected to see her confusion reflected in her sister's face. Instead, Rachel looked wary. "I invited someone else," she said, putting down her piping bag. "To lunch."

"Who?" Tully asked. But her body was already tense. This happened to Tully when something caught her off guard: her body reacted. Tully liked to think that she would have been excellent in the caveman days, when your fight-or-flight response was critical to your survival.

"Heather," Rachel said. Her face was scrunched up as if expecting a punch.

Admittedly, Tully did think about it.

"Heather? *Heather* Heather? Dad's Heather?"

Now her flight instinct was in full swing. She was already reaching for her handbag and looking at the door in panic.

The doorbell rang again.

"I know I should've told you but . . ." Rachel started but her words disappeared into the ether because, all at once, the fight instinct had caught up. Tully had been so delighted when Rachel invited her to lunch. She'd been *touched*! She'd thought Rachel wanted to spend some quality time with her. Instead, it turned out she'd been *lured* here.

"Why on *earth* would you invite Heather here?"

"Dad thought lunch would be nice opportunity to bond."

"Which is why we had the last lunch with her!"

"Listen," Rachel said, "I should have told you sooner, and I'm sorry. But I promised Dad that I would get you to come and I wasn't sure you if you would if I told you the truth."

"I'm insulted," Tully said, even though she was certain that Rachel was right.

"Let's just be nice," Rachel said as she left the kitchen to answer the door.

"I'm always nice," Tully muttered, following her. "Nicer, in fact, to people I don't like."

Rachel opened the door. Heather was dressed in a black flowing dress, sandals, and large tortoiseshell sunglasses. She carried a bottle of wine and a small posy of pink peonies. She really was the picture of understated elegance. It was *magnificently* irritating.

"Heather, hello!" Tully cried from behind Rachel. Her voice sounded high-pitched and strange. For goodness' sake—what was the matter with her?

"Hi, Heather," Rachel said, in a normal-sounding voice. "Come on in. Shall I put this on ice? We already have a bottle of chardonnay open."

Heather handed over her bottle and the three of them headed for the kitchen. Almost immediately the doorbell rang again.

"Invited someone else?" Tully said to Rachel.

She gave Tully a beseeching look. "It's my delivery person," she said, picking up a white cardboard box. She disappeared, leaving Tully and Heather alone in the tiny kitchen. Tully pretended to busy herself moving the potatoes around in the bowl, but the silence was thick. It made it easy to hear the conversation happening at the door.

"So," a deep voice said, "what have you got for me today?"

Tully's and Heather's eyes met. There was something . . . sexy . . . about the voice.

"Cream buns," Rachel said. "For an office farewell."

"I like cream buns and I cannot lie." There was a short pause. The owner of the sexy voice must have opened the box to take a look, because a moment later she heard a deep inhalation. "I swear, this is what Heaven smells like."

Tully pictured her sister. She would be struggling with this scenario. On the one hand, she'd want to be giving the man with the sexy voice the cold shoulder, which was what she always did to men. On the other hand, he'd just complimented her baking, which was Rachel's actual kryptonite.

The pause dragged on for a couple of seconds before Tully heard a sigh. "Hold on."

Tully resumed moving the potatoes around in the bowl as Rachel reentered the kitchen. But her attempts to act natural were wasted, as Rachel didn't even make eye contact with her. Instead, she grabbed a bun from the cooling rack, piped cream into the center, and popped it into a foil cupcake case. She dusted it faintly with icing sugar and slipped it into a cellophane bag. Then she hurried from the kitchen.

Tully resumed her eavesdropping position.

"For *me?*"

The voice sounded genuinely thrilled. The cellophane bag rustled and then . . . a distinct, masculine moan of pleasure. Tully couldn't help it; she had to get a look at him. She figured she'd think of an excuse by the time she got there, but unfortunately, the moment she laid eyes on him, all excuses—and words—deserted her. He was even better-looking than his voice had suggested. Dark hair and piercing green eyes and a nose to rival Elvis Presley.

"This is my sister," Rachel said.

The man waved, swallowing the last of the bun. "Hello, sister."

"This is Darcy," Rachel said to Tully.

Tully continued to stare at him unselfconsciously, as Darcy's attention was fixed solely on Rachel. Over the years, Tully had seen a lot of men look at Rachel like this, as if she were a rare and precious treasure. The difference this time was that Rachel was staring back.

"What do you call a stereo made of cake?" he asked.

Rachel rolled her eyes. "Just take the—"

"A gâteau blaster!"

He laughed heartily at his own joke, which was oddly endearing. Tully supposed you could do things like that if you looked like Darcy did. Tully snuck a look at Rachel, and saw she was fighting a smile.

Tully started to feel like she was intruding.

"Right then," Rachel said. "Better get those buns moving."

Darcy grinned delightedly. "Good one!"

As Rachel closed the door, the tiny smile crept back onto her face. When she turned around, Tully was right there.

"What?" Rachel said.

"Better get those buns moving?"

Rachel scoffed, pushing past her and walking into the kitchen. "It was a silly joke."

Tully followed her. "You were flirting with him!"

"I wasn't! I was just . . . making conversation. Sorry about that, Heather."

"No problem," Heather said.

"That's not how *I* make conversation with delivery people," Tully muttered.

Rachel opened the fridge and retrieved the open wine bottle. She filled her glass nice and high. "Heather, help me out, would you? Was I making conversation or was I flirting?"

Tully and Rachel looked at her. Heather looked like the prover-bial deer in the headlights.

"I'd say," Heather ventured bravely, "that you were making con-versation. Slightly flirtatious conversation."

Tully looked at Rachel triumphantly. Maybe Heather wasn't so bad after all.

12

RACHEL

Rachel stood with her back to Heather and Tully and her head in the pantry, pretending to survey the spices. There were two French madeleines in there that she'd made yesterday, and she picked up one and shoved it in her mouth. She'd worn her black wraparound dress, so she could loosen it, if need be. The way things were going with this lunch, she suspected she'd need to.

"He was definitely flirting," Tully was saying, from where she sat in the dining area. She was utterly delighted, stretched out and looking more relaxed than Rachel had seen her in months. Probably because she was already on her second glass of chardonnay. Heather was on her third. Meanwhile, Rachel hadn't even managed to have a sip of her first. Her mouth was full, so she turned around, rolled her eyes, and turned back again.

"Where on earth did you find him?"

Rachel swallowed. "Long-term unemployed list. It was a government program."

"Wow," Tully said, mystified. "Who wouldn't want to employ *him*?"

"Maybe he's unreliable," Rachel said. "Or forgetful. Or lazy. He was late the first time he showed up for a delivery."

"Who cares?" Tully cried. "Do I need to remind you what he looks like? Sometimes I wonder if you actually have red blood running through your veins, Rachel, I really do."

Rachel picked up the other madeleine and stuffed it in her mouth, saving herself from having to answer. The truth was, Darcy's visit *had* rattled her a little. It was hard to put her finger on what it was about him. Probably it was the dumb jokes or the fact he complimented her food. She enjoyed dumb jokes and people complimenting her food. But she was wary of him too. He'd been unemployed for over a year before working for her, which was a long time for an able-bodied, charismatic young man like Darcy. There had to be a story there.

"Rachel doesn't date men," Tully explained to Heather, as if they were suddenly best friends. "Or women. When we were younger, she did. She was the rebel child, always wanting to go out at night, always hanging out with boys in places she shouldn't. Every boy at school was in love with Rachel. It was her hair. She had this long, shiny hair. . . . A boyfriend of mine once told me he had a dream about Rachel's hair and I had to break up with him. Do you remember that, Rach?"

"Aaron Henderson," Rachel said without looking up. "He was a giant tosser."

"A *colossal* tosser," Tully agreed, before turning back to Heather. "Anyway, one day when she was sixteen or seventeen, she shaved it all off. I'll never forget coming home from school, and there was Rachel, sitting up at the kitchen counter, bald."

"I wasn't *bald*," Rachel corrected. "It was a *pixie cut*."

"Mum made her grow it back, but she never wears her hair out anymore. You really should, Rach. You have the best hair. It's your crowning glory."

"Shall I put the dressing on, or would you prefer it on the side?" Rachel asked.

"Pour it on," Heather said at the same time as Tully said, "On the side."

Rachel poured it into a jug. She wished she'd made canapés so she could shove one into Tully's mouth. It was always feast or famine with Tully. She either didn't mention the fact that Rachel didn't date—tiptoeing around the subject as if it were a shameful secret one didn't discuss—or she just went all out, airing Rachel's dirty linen for all to see. Or, in this case, for Heather to see.

"You need to date this man, Rachel," Tully said. "Seriously. Doesn't she, Heather?"

"Well," Heather said uncertainly. "I don't know. If she doesn't date . . . maybe not?"

It wasn't as if Rachel had *never* dated. She'd kissed eight boys in her life, though admittedly only two of them were boyfriends— Cameron Fidler and Jason Swift. She'd lost her virginity to Cameron when she was fifteen, and then had sex with him two more times because she'd been told it got better, but it hadn't, so she'd ended things.

She was sixteen when she started dating Jason, and she'd been hopeful it would be different with him. Certainly, the chemistry between them was different. When they lay around after school, doing homework and reading magazines, the urge to kiss and touch him had been almost overwhelming. And when they stood on his doorstep, or hers, to say goodbye, the pain of having to separate felt almost physical. So when he'd told her his parents were going away for the weekend, she'd acted cool, but inside she was bursting. She started preparations immediately. She had a bikini wax. She bought a new matching bra and underwear set from Bras N Things—black and lacy. She applied fake tan, nail polish, and eyelash tint to the appropriate parts of her body. But then, instead of having sex with Jason when his parents went away, she broke up with him.

"Rachel used to be an amazing cross-country runner," Tully was saying now. "We used to have guys calling the house all the time, asking if she wanted to"—Tully drew inverted commas in the air with her fingers—"go for a run." She laughed. "Is that why you quit running, Rach?" Tully didn't wait for an answer. "Anyway, what was my point? Ah! Darcy. The *flirting*!"

"Please, no more about the flirting!" Rachel opened the drawer and pulled out her good salad servers. TO RACHEL, LOVE MUM was engraved onto each handle. Mum had given them to her for her twenty-first birthday. *Georg Jensen*, her mother had said proudly. *Acorn pattern. Antique.* Rachel had no idea what that meant at the time, but she couldn't help but catch on to her mum's enthusiasm and they had remained her favorite salad servers ever since. "I'll talk about *anything* else. Heather, help me out! What's news with you?"

"Actually," Heather said, "I visited Pam this morning."

There was a beat of silence. That was not what Rachel expected. Tully went oddly, unnaturally still.

Heather seemed to realize her error and responded by stammering. "It's just . . . the nursing home was on my way here so I . . ."

"You and Dad went?" Tully asked after a moment. Her voice sounded funny.

"Er, no—just me."

Heather looked very unsure of herself now. Rachel wanted to jump in and say something to ease the tension but she found herself, once again, at a loss. Heather had gone to see Mum? Why would she do that? Why would *anyone* go and see a person with advanced dementia if they weren't a loved one?

"It probably sounds odd to you," Heather said. "But I've spent quite a bit of time with Pam over the past year and we became—not friends, exactly, but . . . I don't know." Heather's hands trembled as she continued. "Obviously her condition deteriorated a lot over that time, and our conversations became more limited, but when she wasn't agitated, I found her to be good company. We had some . . . some great chats."

"Wow," Rachel said. "I hadn't thought about the fact that you actually met Mum. It makes sense that you developed some sort of . . . relationship with her."

Rachel glanced at Tully, who was deathly still.

"What did you and Mum chat about?" Rachel asked.

"Cooking, mostly," Heather said. "I'm a terrible cook. Pam was always asking me what I was having for dinner, and when I said I didn't know, she'd give me a recipe. Then she'd give it to me again. And again. I can recite her recipe for chicken, lemon, and feta pie verbatim."

"The chicken, lemon, and feta pie?" Rachel exclaimed. "That recipe is meant to be a family secret!"

"If it helps," Heather said, "I struggle to fry an egg."

"Sorry," Tully said, "I'm still confused as to why you would want to go to see our mum—your boyfriend's current wife. It's a bit weird, don't you think?"

"Tully—" Rachel started.

Tully put down her glass—which was nearly empty—and shrugged. "I'm just saying, I don't know why you'd *want* to." She looked at Heather.

"I guess because I don't have any family of my own . . ."

"You want *us* to be your family?" Tully finished.

"Actually, yes," Heather said. She looked from Tully to Rachel and sighed. "I know how strange it must be, having your dad dating someone while your mum is still alive—not to mention someone so much younger. And I'm so sorry about it, honestly I am. But the fact is, I'm in love with your father. So, yes, I want to be part of his family. And, odd as it sounds, that includes your mum."

There was something about the simplicity of it, the straightforwardness, that Rachel found compelling, if a little jarring. Even Tully was stunned silent by it. But despite the certainty with which Heather spoke, the hand holding the glass of wine was still shaking.

"Well," Rachel said finally, "we want what Dad wants. And if Dad wants you—and he's made it very clear that he does—that means you're family. Right, Tully?"

Tully shifted uncomfortably in her seat. Her head tilted forward ever so slightly and Rachel decided to take that as a nod.

"Good," Rachel said. "Well, then, shall we eat in the courtyard?"

Rachel didn't wait for a response; she just picked up the potato salad and carried it outside. The other two grabbed a dish each and followed her.

"Whoops," Rachel said as she set down the salad. "Forgot the salad servers."

She returned to the house for the servers, but though she scanned the bench, the table, even the dishwasher, they seemed to have disappeared.

13

HEATHER

You're not following the rules, Heather, a little voice told her. Stephen had instructed her to talk to Tully about her little boys and to Rachel about baking, and so far she'd done neither. The wine was to blame. She hadn't intended to drink today. Stephen had been so strange after finding the bottle of whiskey under the sink, she'd been determined to prove he had nothing to worry about.

"What I don't understand," he'd said, "is why you would hide it?"

Habit was the answer. Growing up, if anyone left alcohol lying around, it was as good as gone in a matter of minutes. But she couldn't say that to Stephen. After all, she understood how it must look. But it didn't mean she had a drinking problem, which was what Stephen was suggesting.

"I'm fine," she'd said to him. "In fact, I'm going to go off alcohol for a while."

She'd brought a bottle of wine today as an offering, but she didn't intend on drinking any. She amended this to "just one glass," to be polite. Since then Rachel had determinedly kept her glass full, or Tully had. What was she supposed to do?

"More potatoes?" Rachel offered, holding up the bowl.

"No, thank you," Heather said. "But they were lovely. All of this is lovely. I'm having a lovely time."

Perfect. She'd just said "lovely" three times. She often said words like "lovely" and "delightful" and "gorgeous" when she was around people like Tully and Rachel. The stupid thing was that Heather wasn't sure if she was having a lovely time or not. On the one hand, she was sitting in a charming courtyard, sipping good wine and eating delicious food. On the other hand, she had a feeling she was on very tenuous ground with these women.

Rachel was easier to like, obviously. Though she was the younger of the sisters, she gave the impression of being older, wiser, calmer. Perhaps it was the fact that she kept her distance, watching from afar, remaining carefully neutral. It had been interesting to hear that she'd cut off all her hair as a teen. What had been more interesting was the flippant way that Tully mentioned it—much like the way Stephen mentioned the fact that Rachel hadn't ever had a proper relationship. As though they were normal, if quirky, decisions that any person might make, rather than clear signposts of adolescent sexual assault. Growing up, Heather knew a handful of people who'd been sexually assaulted. Radical changes in appearance were commonplace, as were weight gain or loss, retreating from threatening environments, and drug abuse. Heather supposed things like this didn't happen very often to nice middle-class people, so they didn't know the signs, but even so . . . it seemed a fairly large thing to miss.

"Have we finished the bottle?" Tully asked, after trying and failing to fill her glass.

"I'll get another one," Rachel said. A more perfect hostess Heather had never known.

As Rachel disappeared into the kitchen, her phone, which was on the table, beeped. Tully glanced down at it and her eyes widened.

"It's from him!" she whispered. "Darcy!"

Heather felt a jolt of excitement. "What does it say?"

Tully snatched up the phone. "It says: *What did the cake say to the fork?*" She looked at Heather, her nose screwed up in confusion. "What on earth . . . ?"

"It's a joke!" Heather whispered, glancing back toward the house. She could see Rachel squatting down in front of a low cupboard. By the time she looked back, Tully was thumbing a reply. "What are you doing? You can't answer him!"

"I can," Tully said, thumbs moving at an astonishing rate. "I told you, Rachel doesn't go out with men. What we saw earlier was the closest she's come to flirting since she was sixteen. We need to help her make a move." She pressed send, then held up the phone.

Heather blinked. *Eat me?*

"I panicked!" Tully cried. "I'm not good under pressure."

"Give me the phone," Heather demanded. She thought for a minute, then typed: Do you want a piece of me? She showed it to Tully, who nodded enthusiastically. Heather pressed send.

Almost immediately three dots appeared. Both women let out a hushed squeal.

"Are you girls okay with rosé?" Rachel called from inside. "I haven't got any more chardonnay."

"Fine!" they called in unison, as a message appeared on the screen.

Even though I love your cakes . . . it said, I would never dessert you.

Heather and Tully chuckled.

"What's so funny?" Rachel asked, coming outside with the bottle of rosé. "Sorry, I can't find—Why have you got my phone?"

Heather dropped it, just as it beeped again. She couldn't help it; she looked at the screen.

If you're enjoying my sweet jokes, you're going to love my savory ones. I can tell you all about them over dinner... maybe tomorrow night?

It was followed by a winking emoji.

Rachel grabbed the phone and paled. "What did you do?" Frantically she scrolled back through the texts. After a second, she looked up. "'Eat me'?"

"Sorry," Tully said. "I wrote that."

Rachel sat down heavily in her wrought-iron chair and filled her glass to the top. "I can't believe you did this."

Tully looked suitably sheepish. "*Are* you free tomorrow?"

"No," Rachel said. "As it happens, I'm not."

"What are you doing?"

"None of your business."

"She's not doing anything," Tully said to Heather.

"I am!"

"Are not."

Heather watched the back-and-forth interestedly. It was funny. During the last lunch, it had seemed to her that the sisters were not particularly close. Today, perhaps because of the wine, or maybe because talking about Darcy felt vaguely adolescent, she saw an intimacy that she hadn't seen before. And despite Rachel's protestations, she got the feeling that she might be losing some of her reluctance.

"Look," Rachel said, "we don't even know him. He's probably a serial killer or something."

"Who *cares*?" Tully cried.

Rachel rolled her eyes, but there was a hint of a smile on her face. Heather took another sip of her drink as the phone lit up again. All three women screamed.

I could do the next night? he wrote. Or the night after that.

"See?" Rachel said. "He doesn't have plans for the next three nights! He's definitely a serial killer."

"You could meet in a public place, if you're worried about the serial killer thing," Tully suggested. "I could even come to the restaurant in dark glasses and hide behind a menu so I can make sure everything is aboveboard."

Rachel appeared to be wavering. Whether it was because of Tully's suggestions or not, it was hard to tell. "It's not a good idea," she said. "Yes, he's good-looking, but he's got to have issues. Why else would he have been unemployed for so long? Besides, we work together."

"Actually," Tully corrected, "he works *for* you. If things don't work out you can sack him. It's not as if you can't find another person to deliver your cream buns!"

"Pretty sure that's illegal."

"Again," Tully said, exasperated, "who *cares*?" She grabbed the phone out of Rachel's hand, thumbed, tomorrow night works, and handed it back. "There. Now let's move on to the next stage of the day, which is drinking to calm your nerves." Tully refilled their glasses all the way to the top. "Look at that," she said. "We've gone through another bottle."

"There's plenty more inside," Rachel said, and Tully and Heather cheered.

Maybe Stephen's daughters were her kind of people after all?

. . .

Heather was drunk. The most marvelous part about it was that Rachel and Tully were too. The comfort of being around drunk people when you were also drunk was not to be underestimated. Heather was sinking into the pleasure of it, really enjoying it, when the air was pierced by a very annoying noise. "What is that?" Heather said.

The three women looked around, at first in that dopey, half-interested way, but when it continued, with more desperation.

"It's my phone," Tully said when she realized. "Where is the damn thing?"

Heather was already out of her seat. She followed the ringtone into a Gucci handbag. She dug past some salad servers, a single patent-leather shoe, and an expensive-looking candle, still in its box, before clasping her hand around the phone. It was funny; she'd imagined Tully's bag would be just so, but it was an unholy mess.

"Here it is!" she cried, and Tully claimed the phone and accepted the FaceTime.

"Hi, babe," she said as a face appeared on the screen.

"Uh-oh. 'Babe'? Does this mean you're drunk?"

Heather glanced at the screen and recognized Tully's husband Sonny from a photo she'd seen at Stephen's house. He looked faintly amused.

"That's right, babe," she said, laughing. It was hard to match up this Tully with the uptight Tully from the other day. Even from a few hours ago. Her whole body was loose and relaxed.

"I take it this means I am your Uber driver this evening?"

Evening? Heather looked around. Sure enough, the sky was starting to darken. It felt like only a few minutes ago that Rachel had cleared the dishes away and produced the most delicious sponge cake Heather had ever tasted. Now, even the sponge remains had been cleared away and the picked-over remains of a magnificent cheese platter lay on the table before them.

"Only if you give me a five-star rating," Tully said.

"Promise not to vomit in my car and we have a deal."

Due to her proximity to Tully, Heather had no choice but to eavesdrop. But she felt like she was witnessing something very personal. Tully was drunk. Sonny thought it was funny. He was offering to give her a ride home. No one was yelling or getting into a fight. It was like something out of a TV show.

"Can I get you anything else, Heather?" Rachel asked, as Tully continued chatting to Sonny. "Tea? Coffee?"

"There's nothing else I could possibly want," Heather replied. "Honestly, I've never known a host to be as considerate as you are."

Rachel waved the compliment away, but she looked pleased. "I love to make people feel comfortable and welcome. And to feed them, obviously. It's a bit of an obsession of mine."

Heather picked up her wineglass and took a long sip before returning it to the table. "I went to high school with a girl who had an obsession with feeding people. She used to bring homemade cakes and slices to school nearly every day."

Rachel was looking at her intently.

"After high school, I heard through a friend that the girl had been sexually assaulted by her uncle during high school. Apparently baking was her escape—almost like therapy. If she was stressed or angry or upset, the only thing that could calm her down was cooking. And it didn't hurt that the weight she gained made her a little less attractive to her uncle."

Rachel was still looking at her, but her face had become a little gray. It was all the confirmation Heather needed that what she had suspected about Rachel was true. It made her wonder about the Aston family, ostensibly so close, and yet completely blind to something Heather had been able to extract in a couple of minutes, using a made-up example about a girl from school.

"All right, Uber driver," Tully was saying. "You can pick me up. But don't be late or your rating is ruined!" She laughed and hung up the phone. "My ride's on its way."

"What about you?" Rachel asked Heather. "Should I call Dad? You won't be able to drive home now, will you?"

Heather was definitely too drunk to drive. But thankfully she wasn't so drunk she thought calling Stephen was a good idea. "Actually," she said, "I thought maybe we could hang out for a bit longer. Maybe open another bottle?"

"Of course," Rachel said, ever the amenable host.

It seemed like such a good idea at the time. But, as it turned out, it definitely wasn't.

14

TULLY

Tully woke at 3:00 A.M. with a dry mouth, a thumping headache, and *all* of the anxiety in the world. This was what happened when you got drunk in your thirties. She had memories—distant memories—of being drunk in her twenties, nights when she'd collapse happily into bed at the end of the night (often with a nice-looking boy), and when she finally got to sleep she'd drift into a slumber so deep she wouldn't wake until noon the next day.

Today, when she woke for the second time, it was 6:21 A.M. and Locky was sitting astride her stomach. "Daddy says you're feeling sick," he said unworriedly.

"I'm sure you sitting on her stomach doesn't help, mate," Sonny said, lifting Locky off her.

Tully rubbed her eyes and glanced around. "Where's Miles?"

"Asleep," Sonny said. "In his bed."

"His *big-boy* bed?"

"Yep. Been in it since seven last night."

Tully couldn't believe it. "Tell me the truth: Did you drug him? Lace his bottle with alcohol?"

"You were the only one laced with alcohol last night," Sonny said, smiling. It was strange, seeing him smile at her. Tully started to wonder if she was still drunk and imagining it. Then he said, "It was nice to see you so relaxed last night. I haven't seen you like that in ages."

"Are you saying you *like* me drinking?"

"I like you letting your hair down," he corrected, then he took Locky's hand. "Come on. Let's let Mummy sleep."

"Wait, I can go back to sleep?" She gazed at him with an intensity that made her headache a little worse. "But . . . I'm a drunken disgrace. You should be reporting me to the police. Taking my children away from me and putting them with a very nice elderly foster family who still have one of those old-fashioned cookie jars filled with homemade biscuits!"

"I'll let you off with an official warning this time," Sonny said, and disappeared out the door.

Tully sank back into the pillows. She had almost forgotten how great Sonny was. People always reminded her, of course. *Sonny's so great! So good with the children! Such a caring husband! Just an all-around good guy!* Lately, when people said it, Tully felt resentful. *What about me?* she wanted to cry. *I'm great! Why is everyone always talking about Sonny?* But they were right. Sonny *was* great. It was just that, when you'd been married awhile, you tended to forget these things.

With that thought in her mind, Tully stretched out and fell asleep in a matter of minutes. The next time she woke it was 10:00 A.M. Not noon, but a very nice sleep-in for an old goat like her. Her mouth still didn't taste right, but her headache was gone and she felt more human than she had four hours earlier. Best of all, there was no small child bouncing on her midsection. She closed her eyes again, planning to doze for a bit longer, when suddenly she remembered her bag, and lurched upright.

It was a rookie error. Last night her bag had been jam-packed with things—a candle, a silk scarf, a single shoe that she'd swiped from a boutique around the corner. And Rachel's salad servers. She felt particularly bad about taking those. She was going to return them—today, if she could find her bag. But where the heck was it?

She found it half wedged under Sonny's side of the bed—bulging, but still zipped. Thank God. Usually, Tully stored any goodies she'd acquired in the garage as soon as was reasonably possible. It was, after all, not unusual for Sonny to rifle through her bag—for keys, a ringing phone, a breath mint. How horrible it would have been for that to happen this morning of all times, when Sonny was being so lovely. How would she have explained it? After all, she was far too hungover and pathetic this morning to come up with a lie.

She bundled all the items into her bedside table, making a mental note to move them to the garage when Sonny left the house. In the meantime, she thought a shower might be a good move. She padded across the carpet into their en suite bathroom, and got the water going nice and hot.

When she emerged again, Sonny was sitting on the edge of the bathtub.

"If you're hoping for shower sex, you're going to be sorely disappointed," Tully said. "I could barely stand up in there." She reached for a white fluffy towel and wrapped it around herself. "Why is it so quiet? Did someone die?"

"I gave the boys a Kit Kat and an iPad each. I even put Miles in a nappy so he wouldn't need us to take him to the toilet."

"Bloody hell. You're much better at this parenting thing than I ever give you credit for."

He gave her what started as a smile but turned into a grimace halfway through.

Tully's brain was working so slowly it took her a minute to compute that this wasn't normal. "What's wrong?"

"I just got off the phone from the real estate agent." He exhaled, looking at his hands. "The house is officially on the market. They're sending photographers this week. And those people who . . . you know . . . stage the house."

Tully sat down on the edge of the tub beside him. It wasn't unexpected; Sonny had already said the house would need to be sold. Still, there was something about this next step that felt like a sharp kick to the kidney.

"Okay," she said. "Well, that's that, then."

"God, I'm just so sorry, Tul," he said. "I know this is your dream house. And the boys . . ."

"It's not my dream house," she said, scooting up beside him. "At least, it's not my only dream house. My dream house is wherever you and the boys are. As for the boys, do you think they give two hoots what kind of house they live in?"

Sonny looked unconvinced. Admittedly, Locky did have a taste for the finer things. When they went to Fiji last year, he'd located a button by their beach loungers that summoned the waiter. When the waiter arrived he ordered hot dogs and waffle fries and vanilla milkshakes. On the flight home, they'd asked him what was his favorite part of the holiday was and he'd replied, "The button." But now was not the time to focus on that.

"I'm sorry, Tul," Sonny said again. "I'm just so sorry." He was hunched over. After a moment, he dropped his head into his hands. "I have a headache," he said.

"It's going to be all right," she said, putting an arm around his shoulders. "It's really not that bad."

"Daaaaad!" Locky called. "Miles has taken another Kit Kat, even though I told him you said we could only have one."

Tully stood up. "I'll go. You take some Panadol and get yourself together. It's all okay, Sonny. Really."

Tully pulled on her dressing gown and gave him a quick kiss on the head. On her way out the door, she felt a stab of optimism. If things were good between her and Sonny, she could handle this. This wasn't just going to be fine; it was going to be better than fine. They would live simply for a while, that was all. If they did ever get back to a similar financial position, Tully would find charities to donate to. Perhaps she'd start volunteering her time at the local charity shop? There was so much more to life than shopping and going out for lunch. She'd end up so much more fulfilled. She actually couldn't wait. Most importantly, she was going to stop stealing. This was just the shot in the arm she needed to make a change. This whole thing had been a blessing in disguise.

"Tul," Sonny called after her, "there's no Panadol in the medicine cabinet."

"Try my bedside table drawer," she called back.

She was almost in the living room when she realized her mistake. She turned on her heel and ran back immediately, but she was too late. Sonny was holding the shoe, the candle and the scarf in his hands. They still had the price tags on. The scarf still had the security tag. He spun around when he heard her come in.

"What's all this?" he said.

Tully stared at him. Her mouth started to bend around some lies, something that would explain it. But no words came out.

15

RACHEL

'm going on a date."

Rachel stood in her kitchen and said the words out loud. They sounded ridiculous, almost comical—at least when spoken in relation to her. When she'd agreed to the date, she'd been 100 percent sure that she would cancel—after all, a woman who hadn't dated since she was sixteen years old didn't just start dating because her sister decided to commandeer her phone one day at lunch. And yet today she was only 99 percent sure that she would cancel. She even put on a dusky-rose sundress, the one that always made her feel especially pretty. Then, to put the whole thing out of her mind, she made the finishing touches to Peter and Emily's wedding cake.

The cake, she could admit, was just as magical as she'd promised. Three-tiered, every inch covered in fondant, buttercream, or sugar flowers. It was, without question, the most beautiful cake she'd ever made. It was also the most labor-intensive cake she'd ever made, which made it all the more satisfying. She'd decided to deliver it herself, in fact, just so she could see the couple's reaction with her own eyes. When it was finally complete, she reached for her phone to snap a photo of the cake, and that's when she saw she the text message.

Hey, you.

Her phone slipped from her hand and clattered to the floor.

Hey, you.

A chill ran the length of Rachel's spine.

For goodness' sake, she chided herself. *Don't be so bloody dramatic.* And yet, just like that, her body pulsed with adrenaline. It was infuriating. *Hey, you,* after all, was such a common, benign turn of phrase. A common, benign phrase that cleaved her life neatly in two—"before" and "after."

She was sixteen when it happened, shockingly, in broad daylight. She was out jogging. It was around 10:00 A.M., that strange time of day when the early-morning joggers and cyclists had all headed off to work and the school run was done, and hardly anyone was around. She was at that part of the path where the scrub blocked the beach from the road. The stretch was only a hundred meters or so, but very secluded. She followed the dirt track as it snaked through the scrub. At the point where the scrub was the thickest, she stopped at a lookout to admire the view down over the water. What if she hadn't done that? she'd asked herself a thousand times since. What if she'd kept on running, like she usually did? Tully often talked about the endless "what-ifs" in her head. For Rachel they weren't endless. For Rachel, there was just that one.

She *felt* him a moment before she heard him. She'd heard people say things like that before, but she'd never understood it. It was a proper, tangible feeling, like an alarm going off in her body. Danger. It was possible, she knew, that the alarm in her body was overreacting. Girls her age were, after all, primed for the worst in these sorts of situations. Then she heard his voice—*Hey, you*—and she knew her instinct had been right.

She turned to face him. His mouth was hard. His eyes were mean. By his side was a large German shepherd.

Come here.

She tried to run, but she only made it a few paces before he caught a fistful of her hair. (The fact that her own hair had been accomplice to her attack was one of the things she fixated on, later.) Within moments she was on her stomach, her lips pressed against the dirt and sand. The dog stalked around, unperturbed by her position and her fear. Rachel had heard of people becoming superhuman in dangerous situations, able to lift cars or chew off their own arm in order to save themselves, but this didn't happen to her. Instead, her body went rigid. Frozen. All she could do was lie there and listen to the swish of the cars on the nearby road, as the tears streamed silently down her cheeks.

Now, Rachel squatted down to retrieve her phone from the floor with a shaking hand. The message was from Darcy, who couldn't possibly have known the effect the words would have on her. Indeed, he'd written a second message immediately after the first.

Pick you up at 6 p.m.?

How ridiculous she'd been, thinking she could go. How totally and utterly ridiculous.

She replied to Darcy saying she wasn't feeling well, then put her phone on silent and placed it upside down on the table. She needed to busy herself, she realized. Take her mind off things. Obliterate. The hunger had already started rumbling from deep within; she knew what she had to do. She sat at the table directly in front of the wedding cake, which was ready for delivery. She had two hours until it was due at the reception center. Two hours with that memory fresh in her mind.

Two hours.

She grabbed a fistful of wedding cake and began to eat.

16

HEATHER

Heather opened her eyes. She was fully dressed in the clothes she'd been wearing the day before—including her shoes. Mascara and lipstick were smeared on Stephen's crisp white pillowcase. Her mouth was dry, predictably, and tasted a little of vomit. This was bad, Heather realized. This was very, very bad.

She glanced at Stephen's side of the bed, sensing already that it was empty. He'd probably been up for hours. Meanwhile she was in bed, sleeping it off. What must he be thinking of her? She needed to find him, explain it was a one-off. That they'd had a lovely time and just let loose a little too much. She'd be sheepish and contrite. And, she hoped, he would forgive her.

She tried sitting up, but the room spun so fast she had to sink back into the bed. Her right elbow throbbed—what on earth had she done to it? There was no blood or graze, but she couldn't even manage to straighten it. What had she done? Why couldn't she remember?

She'd been at Rachel's house yesterday, she knew that much.

They'd had a lovely long lunch that had stretched on past dinner-time. She had a faint memory of someone arriving at Rachel's on a scooter, which was folded and put neatly in the back of Heather's Mini Cooper. The driver must have brought her here in his car, taken out his scooter and ridden away again. Heather recalled asking the driver to take her home, but she must have changed her mind en route. The details of this were a little fuzzy.

Heather stripped out of her clothes and stepped into a pair of Stephen's tracksuit pants, which were comically too big. She then pulled one of his T-shirts over her head. They were as comforting as she'd hoped. She wiped off her makeup, cleaned her teeth, and then tottered along the hallway and down the stairs, holding the walls for support. As she descended the stairs another memory eased into her consciousness, this one of arriving on Stephen's doorstep unannounced. He'd been in bed when she rang the doorbell (after searching and failing to find her key), and when he answered the door he was a little cranky. Her heart constricted at the memory. She had to physically force herself into the living room to face him, when everything was telling her to run away and hide.

Stephen was in the armchair in his running gear with one ankle balanced on the opposite knee. He'd made himself a short black, which sat on the coffee table beside him, and the newspaper was in his lap.

"Hi," she said weakly.

"Hi." He didn't appear to look unhappy. Heather was used to doing this quick analysis of people's moods. When she was little and she came out of her bedroom to find her parents awake, she had to assess them carefully. It could be a very good thing that they were up early, meaning they'd had an early night and were sober and calm. It also could be a very bad thing, meaning they'd just got in and were irritable and drunk.

"I like your tracksuit," he said.

"Sorry," she said. "I . . . I couldn't face putting actual clothes on."

"It looks good on you."

"Thanks." She sat on the coffee table in front of him. "I disgraced myself last night, didn't I?"

He hesitated a second. "I wouldn't say that."

"What would you say?"

He folded the newspaper and put it on the coffee table next to his cup. His eyes were kind. (Another thing Heather had learned growing up was to assess people's eyes. Kind. Mean. Lecherous. They could change quickly, so you always had to keep an eye on the eyes.) "I'd say you had a bit too much to drink is all."

"And I did something to my elbow?"

Now he looked surprised. "You fell on the stairs. Surely you remember that?"

With that prompt, a vague memory started to come. She had—dear God—been trying to waltz around the lounge with him. He'd been less enthusiastic than she'd anticipated, refusing to turn on the music and insisting that she "shush." Eventually she'd taken the hint and headed up the stairs. About halfway up she tumbled forward, landing hard on her elbow. Stephen had had to pick her up and put her to bed.

"I'm so embarrassed."

He scooted forward now and took her elbow between his hands. He manipulated it gently, perhaps feeling for injuries. "No need to be embarrassed."

"What happened?" she asked.

"You tell me. It must have been some lunch!"

"Actually, the lunch was wonderful. But I meant . . . why did I fall?"

Stephen shook his head. "I have no idea. One minute you were walking up the stairs, the next you were on the ground. You must have lost your footing somewhere."

"Oh."

"In any case, it doesn't feel like anything's broken, so no harm done. It's likely just bruised, but I can take you in for an X-ray . . ."

"No," she said quickly. The horror of having to get an X-ray for being drunk and falling down the stairs! "I'm sure it will be fine. As you say, just a bruise."

"I'll put it in a sling for today. That'll stop you putting pressure on it." He let go of her elbow and sat back in his chair. After a few contemplative seconds he said, "Heather, may I ask you a personal question?"

"Of course," she said, thinking, *No, you may not.*

"How is your relationship with alcohol?"

He's starting to see me, she realized. *He's starting to see me.*

"I know that sounds loaded, but it's a genuine question," he said. "I, for example, enjoy a drink with lunch or dinner. I consider myself a wine snob. I drink regularly but rarely more than one glass. As for you, a lot of the time you don't drink. Some days you don't intend to drink but then you change your mind. Last night, you were quite drunk. So . . . tell me."

She heard the subtext of what he was saying. Stephen's method was the right way. Drink good wine, and not much of it. Drinking too much, making commitments not to drink and then breaking them, flip-flopping from teetotal to drunk, was not the right way. She should have known this. She *did* know this. But it wasn't in her blood. It wasn't the real Heather.

"Were your parents big drinkers?" he asked. His expression was curious, concerned.

Heather's ability to craft a coherent lie was subverted, she suspected, by the amount of alcohol still in her system.

"I'm just trying to understand you better," he explained when she didn't answer. "We're engaged—don't you want to know more about me?"

No, she thought. *I know everything about you that I need to know.*

"My dad," she heard herself say, "was a bit of a drinker."

Stephen nodded. He didn't look surprised by this, nor did it appear to bother him.

"He was probably an alcoholic, though no one ever used that word. He drank every day, and not just one." And it wasn't just wine, she wanted to add. He drank beer, cider, spirits. He'd have drunk methylated spirits if he knew it was alcoholic.

"That must have been hard," Stephen said. "Thank you for telling me."

There was something about his acceptance. It undid something in her.

"You know, I think my drinking *has* got a little much lately. I might take a break from it for a while."

"Don't do it on my account," Stephen said. "But if that's what you want to do, I'll support you on one condition."

"What is it?"

"You don't stop wearing my tracksuit."

She smiled. "You're mad if you think you're getting these back."

"Glad to hear it. Panadol and coffee?"

"Please," she said.

Stephen leaned forward to kiss her forehead, then stood up and headed for the kitchen. As Heather watched him go, another memory burst forth from her foggy brain. Specifically, a tightening around her ankle when she was halfway up the stairs, followed by a tug. And a sense that she didn't lose her footing—she was pulled.

THE WEDDING

It's clear the wedding festivities aren't going ahead. The mood is solemn. Someone has been seriously injured or killed. I should head home now—yet I find myself unable to leave.

Another police car pulls up. Another ambulance. More people spill out from the chapel as if from a strange, somber concert. A few people start to walk toward their cars, but as they do they are stopped by a couple of young-looking police officers with notepads. The officers appear to be taking names. Witnesses? It makes me nervous.

I make my way determinedly in the other direction. But as I emerge at the other side of the crowd, I see another fresh-faced police officer standing there, notepad in hand.

"Were you a guest of this wedding?" he asks.

It's clear that I was. "No" is not going to be an acceptable answer. I nod.

"We're advising guests that there will be no wedding reception today, so everyone can head home. We do need to take down everyone's name and contact details before they leave, however."

"Why?" I say, as both a delaying tactic and an attempt to get information. I know I have to leave, but it will drive me crazy wondering what happened. "Did someone die?"

"All I know is that a crime has been committed here today. Everyone present is considered to be a witness and we may need to contact you in the future."

"Well, I didn't see anything. I was right at the back. Behind a tall man," I add.

"I understand. Still, I'm required to get everyone's details." His pen is poised above the page. "Name?"

I feel a pinch in my heart. Stephen will know I was here. The idea makes me so nauseated I'm afraid to open my mouth to answer him.

"Name?" he repeats when I don't respond.

"My name is Fiona," I say. "Fiona Arthur."

17

TULLY

stole them."

A few months back, Tully had been watching an old episode of *Dr. Phil* about infidelity. The guest, a woman in her forties who'd been having an affair for eight years, was discussing the moment she decided to tell her husband. She talked about how she thought it would be a crescendo moment—something that would come out after much deliberation and planning, or perhaps in the heat of a fight. As it turned out, she just walked into her living room one day while her husband was watching the footy, sat down beside him, and confessed. She didn't know why that was the moment when she felt she couldn't contain it anymore. And Tully didn't know why this was the moment she told Sonny her secret. It might have been the hangover. It might have been that she was feeling so warmly toward Sonny. It might have been because, after all these years, she'd finally reached her limit of lies.

"What do you mean you stole them?"

It seemed fairly self-explanatory to Tully. She wasn't sure how she could make it any clearer. "I stole them. Shoplifted. Took them without paying."

Sonny's face contorted as if he was going to laugh, but it stopped somewhere around a grimace. Then he looked back at the scarf at his hand, which still had the security tag attached. "But . . ."

"It's true," she said.

A few meters away, in the kitchen, the boys were semi-quiet because they'd been granted more screen time and an extra Kit Kat. In her peripheral vision, Tully could see Miles eating his Kit Kat directly off the kitchen table—a new eating technique that Sonny put under the "kids are weird" umbrella, but Tully knew was more.

"But . . ." He held up a battery-operated torch he'd found in the pile. "A torch? We have half a dozen of these. Much better quality, too."

"I know," Tully said. "I wasn't going to keep it."

Sonny looked like he was trying very hard to understand, and failing. "You weren't going to keep it, but you stole it . . ."

"Yes."

"Why?"

"It's like a release," she explained. "Imagine my anxiety is like air in a balloon. It builds up and up until I feel like I might burst. But when I steal something, it's like pricking the balloon with a pin. The anxiety rushes out of me and I feel kind of . . . breathless and elated. Does that make sense?"

Sonny's face said it didn't.

"Afterward I feel so ashamed," she continued. "I hide all the stuff in the garage or a drawer or under the bed. Periodically I get rid of everything—take it to a charity shop or the tip—but within a few days I take more stuff. I tell myself every day, *You won't do this again, Tully*. But by the end of the day, I'm shoving a chocolate bar or a packet of Tim Tams into my pocket at the supermarket. I can't control it, Sonny."

Sonny closed his eyes and massaged his temples with the thumb and middle finger of each hand.

"I know it's hard to understand."

"It . . . is hard to understand," he said slowly. "How long has this been going on?"

"Since I was eleven."

"Since you were eleven? How did I not know this?"

"I guess . . . it's not the kind of thing that you confess to the new guy you're dating: 'Hey, I've been shoplifting since I was eleven and I still do it.' By the time we got married it just felt too shameful. Besides, I always thought I would stop."

"But you didn't."

"No," she said. "I didn't."

Sonny started to pace. In the living room, Miles was using his chin to nudge the Kit Kat closer to the edge of the coffee table.

"You went to a counselor a few years back, right?" Sonny said. "Did you talk to her about it?"

Tully had indeed gone to a counselor a few years back, a serious young woman with thick black hair and a perpetually confused look on her face. The sessions had been pleasant, but not especially helpful, as Tully had found herself unable to admit the problem. Anxiety, she said, when she was asked what she was doing there. And strange compulsions. It wasn't as if she could just come out and say, "I steal things. Meaningless things that I don't even want and that I can afford to pay for."

"What kind of strange compulsions?" the serious woman had asked, looking confused.

It was little wonder she looked confused. It was, after all, a high-end practice in a very nice area. The serious woman likely spent her days talking to women who thought they had problems because their husbands couldn't send them first class to Europe for the second time this year. Or trying to put their marriages back together after their husbands strayed. The serious woman's clients wouldn't steal! Tully couldn't bear to admit to the woman that she did.

"Like . . . eating dirt," Tully said finally. It was the best she could come up with on the spur of the moment. She remembered hearing during her pregnancies about a pregnant woman who started craving things like dirt, metal, and rocks. It was a legitimate condition, apparently, though Tully herself had only ever craved carbohydrates during pregnancy. In any case, as the direction of counseling began to steer toward what she should do the next time she started to crave dirt, it didn't seem pertinent to continue the counseling, and Tully dropped out a few weeks later.

"I tried," Tully said to Sonny. "But I could never manage to say the words out loud."

He sighed. "Tully, what you're describing doesn't sound like regular shoplifting to me. It sounds like kleptomania."

Tully had heard the word. She didn't like it. It sounded so . . . awful. Like "necrophilia." Or "hemophilia." Or worse, "pedophilia." Nothing Tully wanted to be associated with. She preferred to think of it as her "little problem."

"Matt defended a kleptomaniac a few years ago. It was a very similar story. A young mother who had more than enough money and yet she kept stealing. They were things she didn't even want. Apparently, she was desperate to stop, but she couldn't. It was like an addiction."

"Yes!" Tully nodded desperately. "An addiction. That's exactly what it is."

Sonny sighed and began massaging his temples again. As much as Tully wanted to plead with him to understand, she knew he needed a minute to process this.

After a couple of minutes of silence, she asked, "What are you thinking?"

He looked at her. "I'm thinking that I haven't got the faintest idea who you are."

"Sonny," she started, and then the Kit Kat fell onto the floor and Miles began to scream like he was being attacked by wolves.

18

RACHEL

Someone was knocking at Rachel's door. She had no intention of answering, obviously. How could she? Peter and Emily's wedding cake had been destroyed, that much was clear. Rachel had eaten the top two layers. She was utterly stuffed, with cake, self-loathing, and shame. There was no way she could repair or remake the cake in time, which meant she was not only an unspeakable glutton, but also that her business was ruined. She could just see the reviews. It might even make the news.

Another knock.

"Go away!" she shouted. She sounded like a madwoman.

"Rachel?"

She swore internally. It was Darcy. Of course it was Darcy. Only someone who looked like he did could have the confidence to show up at your house after you'd canceled a date with a pathetic excuse.

"I know you have a wedding cake to deliver and I thought I'd deliver it for you since you aren't feeling well," he called through the door. "You can just put it out on the doorstep and I'll take it. I don't need to see you without your . . . beauty products or anything. Not that you need beauty products. But I have sisters and I know they don't even like the postman to see them before they've put their faces on. I can even close my eyes," he offered.

Rachel opened the door. She felt like the ugliest, most revolting woman alive.

"Hey, you don't look sick. You look great!" He looked at her searchingly. "What is it? Headache? Stomachache?"

"All of the above."

"You need to get to bed," he said, and to his credit there didn't seem to be any double entendre. "Off you go. I'll grab the cake. Where is it?"

She pointed toward the kitchen. Darcy got as far as the doorway before he stopped short. "Uh . . ."

"Please don't say anything obvious," Rachel said from the other room. "And if you make a baking joke, so help me."

To his credit, he didn't. He took another moment, then asked, "And . . . the cake is due at the reception when?"

"An hour and a half."

Darcy closed his eyes, his hands steepled over his mouth. After what felt like an eternity, he nodded.

"I have an idea," he said.

19

HEATHER

For most of the time that Heather worked for Stephen and Pam, things between her and Stephen were strictly platonic. She did her job creating the cozy space that was Pamela's style, and Stephen paid her invoices on time. It was a mutually acceptable arrangement. Or, it would have been, had Heather not been in love with Stephen.

The irony was that one of the reasons Heather fell for Stephen was the way he loved Pam. When they met to talk about plans for the house, he always insisted that she be part of the conversation, making sure she was on board with the plan, even if it took two or three tries to get her to understand. If she got up and went for a wander, he followed her with his eyes and was on his feet in seconds if she put herself in harm's way—like trying to boil the kettle or walk up the stairs. His patience, it seemed, was endless.

But Pam's condition deteriorated quickly. Each time Heather came to the house for a meeting, Pam's eyes were a little duller. She was more confused. Slower to understand. Stephen and Pam had planned to stay in the house during the renovation, but the more Pam started wandering, the more they realized how dangerous this could be. After a few months, Stephen and Pam decided to find a rental property a few streets away, and Heather started seeing Stephen at the house alone for meetings. It was during one of these meetings that Heather arrived at the house to find Stephen balancing on the wooden frame of what would soon be the new oak floorboards of their kitchen. His face was wet with tears.

"I'm sorry," she said. "Do you want me to come back?"

"No," he said. "Come in. I'm sorry."

"Are you sure?"

He nodded, and she crossed the floor from beam to beam, coming to a stop at the beam beside his. "Are you okay?"

He smiled. "When my patients ask, 'Am I going to be okay?,' I never know what to say. In the odd case I can say, 'Yes, after the surgery you will be as good as new.' But in most cases I can't say that. I have to give them a long answer, like, 'We hope that your heart will work as it should for some time to come, but we don't know how long that will be. And the life that you have known up until now will likely never be the same. There will be daily medication, treatment, lifestyle amendments.' As for whether *I'm* okay, that's a complicated answer too. I'm already feeling better after having a good cry. But Pam is going to get consistently worse and then she'll die. We don't know when that will be, or how it will happen. We'll never have her the way we used to have her." His face tensed with the effort, it seemed, of holding back tears. "We made the decision today to move Pam to a nursing home sooner rather than later. Which means she won't even get to enjoy this bloody renovation, which was all for her."

Now he *did* cry, in earnest. His face became mangled, and the tears began to flow. It was a powerful thing, Heather thought, watching a man cry while discussing his feelings so eloquently. Unfortunately, she didn't share his eloquence. Finding herself without words, she did something totally out of character. She stepped across to his plank of wood, and put her arms around him. As Stephen leaned into her, they overbalanced, landing heavily on the beam below them.

"Oh God," Stephen exclaimed. "Are you hurt?"

"No! I'm fine. I mean . . . I think I'm fine."

"Did you hit your head?"

"No." She had banged her side quite badly, and she would later find a bruise, but she definitely had not hit her head.

"Are you certain you didn't hit your head?" Stephen repeated, surveying her with a doctorly gaze.

"I'm certain. But . . . oh no! You're bleeding."

She lifted his arm. The elbow of his white business shirt was soaked through with blood. "Just a graze," he said. "But if you are hurt, please tell me and I'll take you to the hospital."

"I'm fine. Really. But I have Band-Aids in my car. Come and let me fix up your elbow."

They finished their meeting in Heather's car that day. And, after that interaction, things were a bit different between them. At each meeting Heather asked how Pam was, and Stephen would answer honestly, if sadly. When Heather gently probed as to whether Stephen would like to take another look at the plans—as Pam was unlikely to spend much time in the house, it was still possible to change the style to something more to his personal taste—he agreed this wasn't a bad idea.

"You know, you're right. No point mourning my wife in a house that I hate."

A not-unpleasant side effect of this was that the late changes required several more meetings. Some of these meetings happened in the hospital cafeteria. A couple of times they met at funny little shops that sold specialist taps or hardware. On one such occasion, a salesperson confused Heather and Stephen for husband and wife. As Heather hurriedly opened her mouth to correct them, Stephen chimed in, "Yes, you're right. Happy wife, happy life." And he threw her a wink.

Slowly, a closeness grew between them. It was never romantic—at least, not from Stephen's point of view, as far as Heather could tell. But he had a charming way of letting his guard down around her. Usually it was when he was talking about Pam, and the latest challenge. He was always respectful, never revealing anything that could be seen as humiliating her. That, combined with stories about lives he'd saved (always prized from him, he was very humble) meant Heather was soon ruined for all other men.

They had been supposed to meet the afternoon after Pamela moved into the nursing home. Stephen had moved into the house by then, but there were a few little i's to dot and t's to cross. Heather had suggested they change the time of the meeting, but he'd insisted they go ahead, saying he'd need something to take his mind off things.

She arrived just after 3:00 P.M., as agreed, to find Stephen in his sweatpants, drinking a glass of wine.

"Sorry. Didn't we . . . did we have a meeting?"

"Yes. Excuse the informality." He gestured to his clothes. "I took the day off today. Will you have a glass of wine? I just opened a bottle."

"Sure," she said. "Why not?"

They didn't even pretend to talk about interior design that afternoon. When Heather left, a couple of hours and a bottle of wine later, they hugged on the doorstep. And in the morning, when she stepped out of her front door, she found a bunch of flowers. *Thank you*, said the accompanying card. *I needed that.*

Three months later, after clinking their glasses in celebration of the new, minimalist house, he kissed her, right in the modern streamlined living room that she'd designed. The living room that was about to become hers.

Heather was moving in with Stephen. Moving into a mansion on the beach in the nicest neighborhood around. She wondered what her parents would say if they knew. "Let's pop the bubbly," probably. Heather would've liked to. She'd gone back and forth for hours, wondering whether to suggest it to Stephen. It was a special occasion, after all. It would make it more special to celebrate with bubbles. Then again, after her behavior the other night, she was fairly sure the suggestion wouldn't be well received.

"Another box?" Stephen moaned, gesturing to the one in front of her.

The question was tongue-in-cheek. He was in a wonderful mood. There was no need for him to be helping the men they'd hired to do the move. Heather had hardly brought enough stuff to justify hiring them, in any case. There were her clothes (several boxes of those). Some crockery. Some photographs and memorabilia. And two pieces of furniture—a mid-century modern sideboard that she'd been gifted by a client, and a marble coffee table gifted by another client. The rest of her furniture—her bed, sofa, and dining table—was old and didn't match the house, so she'd donated it to a charity for women in need.

She and Stephen probably could have transported everything in the back of his Porsche in a couple of trips, but that wasn't how the upper middle class did things. Upper middle class hired people to help them pack, take away the things they didn't need, and unpack again at the other end. In addition to paying them handsomely, Stephen had given the movers a slab of premium beer and instructed her to order pizzas for them. That had been particularly eye-opening. Heather had assumed—from movies and the like—that the more money people had, the worse they treated the staff, but she understood now that wasn't generally the case. She also understood why. When you were comfortable, you could afford to be magnanimous. Poorer people didn't help the movers unpack because they were tired from working two jobs. If the movers broke something, poorer people were mad, because they couldn't afford to replace it. They didn't order pizza or premium beer for the movers, because when was the last time someone did that for them? It was strange, seeing the world from both sides. Strange, and eye-opening. So few people got to see things from her vantage point. It seemed, to Heather, an awful shame.

"Will we have pizza too, or shall I order us something else?" Stephen asked.

"I'm not sure I feel like pizza," she said.

"Sashimi?" he suggested.

"Perfect."

As Stephen wandered off to order their dinner, Heather leaned back in her chair and admired her things in Stephen's house. Her elbow had healed now. Apart from a slight yellowish tinge, you wouldn't even know that the bruise had been there, and Heather's suspicion that Stephen had been responsible had faded along with it. It had been a trick of the mind, she realized. Seeing women getting roughed up by men was part of Heather's DNA; of course she'd carry that expectation into her life with Stephen. But she had found a new way of living now. Her old way of thinking was just another thing she'd need to unlearn.

"Sashimi is on its way," Stephen announced. "Shall I open some sparkling water?"

Again, she entertained the idea of suggesting a bottle of bubbly. It hovered on the tip of her tongue. Stephen watched her intently for a moment, as if he knew what she was thinking. It scared her sometimes, when he did that. More old thinking, she suspected.

"You know what?" he said finally. "It's a special occasion. Why don't I open a bottle of champagne?"

Suddenly Heather wasn't scared anymore. Just the opposite. "What a good idea," she said.

20

RACHEL

As she drove to visit her mum, Rachel was thinking about Darcy. This was nothing new; she'd lain awake half the night thinking about him and she'd probably spend most of the day thinking about him. Yesterday had been a long day. Darcy had clearly been surprised by the fact that she'd destroyed the wedding cake, but he wasn't noticeably disgusted. In fact, after he'd seen the state of the cake, his mind had seemed completely focused on damage control.

"I have an idea," he said.

Rachel stared at him. "Aren't you going to ask me what I did?"

"I can *see* what you did."

She must have made a face at this, because Darcy held up his hands. "Hey, I'm not judging. I have three sisters, I know the deal. When you have your period you can't be held responsible for what you do. Once, my older sister Suzanne legit bowled me over when I stood in between her and a tub of Ben and Jerry's. See this scar on my eyebrow? That's from when Lucy was on the rampage and I was eating some Oreos—"

"Okay, okay." Rachel was happy enough to let him assume it was period-eating for now. She sure as hell didn't have a better explanation—at least, not one she wanted to reveal to Darcy. "So . . . you have an idea?"

She tried to keep the hope out of her voice. She didn't have high expectations for his plan, but currently it was all she had. And who knew? Maybe Darcy, as well as being preposterously good-looking, was the MacGyver of getting out of work-related troubles.

"Yes," he said, grabbing her arm and leading her out of the house. With no other option, Rachel allowed herself to be led. "We're going to the supermarket."

"The supermarket?" She stopped dead. "That cake took me a week to make, Darcy. I don't have time to bake another one. Besides, I have ingredients here."

"We're not getting ingredients," he said, ushering toward his car. "We're getting cakes."

"Cakes? They paid four grand for this cake! You think the bride isn't going to notice that it's a supermarket cake?"

"Of course she won't. She probably won't even eat the damn thing."

He opened the passenger door and waited patiently until she got inside. It was, admittedly, a fair point. So many brides who'd been incredibly finicky about their wedding cake later admitted that they hadn't even eaten a slice of it. Still.

Darcy shut her door, then walked around to the driver's side and got in. "And the guests aren't exactly going to say, 'Hey, your wedding cake tasted exactly like Woolies's chocolate mud,' are they?"

"Even if that's true . . . it's the fondant that takes the time," Rachel said. "And I spent days on the sugar flowers."

Darcy pointed to the clock on the dash. "Sorry, no time for fondant. We're going to have to get Betty Crocker's buttercream frosting."

She gaped at him. "Darcy! I cannot give Emily and Peter a Woolies mud cake with Betty Crocker icing."

He waved his hand, unbothered. "You'll be able to fancy it up. Add some sprinkles?"

"Sprinkles!" she cried. "And what do I say when they ask 'Where is the cake we ordered'?"

"*I'll* say, 'This one has your name on it. Do you want me to take it away? Rachel's away for the weekend, though, so I won't be able to get you anything else today.' They'll have no choice but to take it. The next day they'll send you an angry email, you'll explain that the dim-witted delivery man got the cakes mixed up and offer them a fifty percent discount, and everyone will be happy."

It wasn't a brilliant solution. But it *was* a solution.

And if she said so herself, she did a pretty good job with the mud cakes and Betty Crocker icing. She'd got the icing the exact shade of the fondant, and decorated it with extra sugar flowers purchased from the specialist cake store. She added fresh flowers as well, and by the time she was finished, the cake didn't look half bad. Not exactly like the one Emily and Peter had ordered, but pretty close.

And, as luck would have it, the *groom* had accepted delivery of the cake, without noticing anything was amiss (despite having been present for three tastings), and when Rachel had emailed the bride the next morning to apologize for the mix-up, Emily had said the cake was delicious and there was no need for a discount. She also had had many requests from guests who wanted the same cake for their own wedding.

All in all, it was a spectacular save. And not only had Darcy come up with the idea and driven her to the supermarket, he had also stayed with her while she assembled, iced, and decorated the cakes, making no mention of the fact that she didn't seem unwell.

When she told him he was welcome to go, he'd merely smiled and said, "Nowhere else to be." At one point, as she was adding the final layer of icing, she looked up and saw him watching her intently.

"What?" she said.

"I've never seen an artist at work before," he said. "It's pretty awesome."

She waited for him to turn it into a joke. He didn't. She wasn't sure she believed him, and yet there was something about him standing there that made her feel a little taller.

When she was done, he took the cake to the wedding. He returned afterward to let her know it had been successfully delivered.

"I'm not sure how I can thank you," she said.

"Go on a date with me," he replied, without missing a beat.

"Unfortunately," she said, "I don't date."

"You don't date?" His confused expression nearly made her laugh out loud. "You mean . . . not at all?"

"Not at all."

"Are you religious?"

"No."

It was as if she'd told him she didn't eat food, but feasted on the spines of lizards instead. "Then . . . why?"

"I just . . . don't."

Darcy stared off into space for a minute, as if trying to get his head around this unexpected piece of information. It seemed to take him a while. And then, just when Rachel thought he was going to move on, he straightened. "If you don't date, then why did you agree to the last date?"

Rachel felt a pulse of shame. "Actually," she said, "my sister agreed to the last date. She took my phone."

A beat of silence. "Your *sister*? So you didn't want to go out with me?"

He looked so stricken, Rachel had to look away. She wondered if it was possible to die of shame.

"Listen," she heard herself say, "as I said, I don't date. But after what you've done for me today, I think I can make an exception to my rule."

They'd agreed to have dinner. Just a casual dinner, in a public venue. She avoided asking herself what was the worst that could happen, because, well, she didn't want to go there.

Rather than agonize over it advance, Rachel decided to focus on her mother.

It always took her a little time to get into the headspace to see her mother. It was just so hard to anticipate what would happen. She had to prepare for the possibility that her mum would be having a bad day. That Mum might not want to see her . . . or would be delighted to see her because she thought Rachel had come to take her home. Once, when Rachel visited, Mum had screamed at her to "get the fuck out of my room." Each day was a fresh, new, heartbreaking challenge. And today, as well as dealing with that new challenge, she was hoping to get some information out of her mother.

She found Mum in the communal area of the home, flanked by two older ladies who appeared much more on the ball than Pam. One of the ladies held her mother's hand. The sheer volume of emotion Rachel felt at witnessing this was overwhelming. Gratitude to the lady for her kindness. Sadness for Mum, who had never been particularly tactile, and generally didn't like anyone to touch her other than her husband and daughters. But Rachel's new mum didn't seem to mind the hand-holding. This too made Rachel sad.

Rachel kneeled in front of her mother's chair. "Hello," she said, holding back the word "Mum." If it was a bad day, a day when she didn't remember Rachel, that would just confuse her. But today she perked up a little.

"Hello there," she said.

Rachel scanned her eyes. She definitely saw some lucidity.

"Would you like to take a walk?" Rachel asked.

"Why not?" Mum said, letting go of the older woman's hand. Rachel smiled at the woman as she helped her mother to her feet.

"Where to?" Mum asked.

"How about the garden?"

"Sounds beaut," Mum said. "Lead the way."

Rachel felt her heart lift. "Beaut" was one of Mum's words. At her fiftieth, two of her friends, Elsa and Mary, had made up a song called "Beaut" and performed it for the crowd while Mary's husband accompanied them on the guitar. It had been a while since Rachel had heard her say it.

Rachel led Mum to the sensory garden, a lovely space where residents could explore all five senses, including eating the snow peas that grew there. She and Mum sat in the wrought-iron chairs at one end.

"So," Mum said, "what's news?"

This was Mum's go-to conversation starter of late. Rachel assumed it helped to kick things off without her having to remember her shared history with visitors.

"I've been going through some of your stuff, actually," Rachel said. "Stuff that you left at home. Dad . . . Stephen gave it to me."

"Stephen?"

"Yes. He found a bunch of things in your wardrobe."

Rachel trailed off, watching her mother's face and preparing for disappointment. More than half the time, Mum didn't even know who *Rachel* was, so the chances of her remembering shoving a stack of cash into a hot-water bottle were slim to none. Still, there was a tiny part of her that hoped.

"One of them was a pink hot-water bottle," Rachel continued. "Pale pink in a knitted cozy."

Mum looked her in the eye now. "Stephen is a *sadistic bastard.*"

Rachel sighed. Mum had been saying this sort of thing a lot lately. The nurse who supposedly stole her stuff was a "witch." The person in the room beside her was "loud as fuck." Last time Tully visited, Mum apparently called her "an irritating little troll." Rachel had coughed to hide her giggle. Before Mum got sick, Rachel had never heard her use a single swear word.

"I found money inside the hot-water bottle," Rachel continued. "A lot of money. Almost a hundred thousand dollars."

Mum glanced away, not interested in the slightest. It was just so frustrating. Mum *had* to have had a plan for this money. Otherwise how did she get it? Why did she hide it? Rachel had so many questions. Maybe she should have brought the remains of the hot-water bottle to jog her mother's memory?

"Actually, I'm looking for someone called Fiona Arthur," Rachel said, changing tack. "You don't happen to know her, by any chance?"

Mum's reaction to this question, unlike the last, was palpable. It was as if the name sent an electric current through her.

"Who is she, Mum?" Rachel asked. "Who is Fiona Arthur?"

Mum's eyes filled with tears. She dropped her face into her hands. "That poor, poor woman," she said.

"Why do you say that?" Rachel asked. "Why is she a poor woman?"

Mum raised her head and looked Rachel right in the eye.

"Stephen hurt her," she said. "Stephen hurt that poor woman terribly."

21

TULLY

We're getting McDonald's for dinner!" Tully announced cheerfully. The boys, who were in their car seats in the back of her Range Rover, blinked at her in confusion.

"What's McDougal's?" Locky asked.

Tully understood their bemusement. She had never fed the boys McDonald's before. They were, after all, upper-middle-class preschoolers. They ate bliss balls and drank organic green smoothies and sugar-free cocoa. The one time Locky had been invited to a birthday party at McDonald's, Tully had fed him before he left and told the birthday boy's mother that Locky was a celiac so he couldn't eat the food. She'd told Locky that the food was really yucky and if he didn't eat any he could have an extra bliss ball when he got home. What was wrong with her? she wondered now. Too much time? Too much money? Too much choice? Now that all three of those things had been taken away from her, McDonald's sounded rather good. She could have just about murdered a Big Mac right now, just quietly. She hadn't eaten one since university!

She and the boys had headed out to give the real estate agent and photographer space at the house. They wanted to get photos in the early-evening light, so they could turn on the interior lights and let the "buttery yellow spill out into the garden" (the photographer's words). Admittedly, the house did look magical. It took her back to the day when she was seven months pregnant with Locky and they'd inspected the house for the first time.

"This will be the baby's room," Sonny said. "And this could be another baby's room. This could be the playroom . . ."

They'd had so much hope for the future, and the house had represented the start of it. Selling it felt symbolic and, if she was honest, appropriate. Since she'd confessed her secret to Sonny five days ago, he'd been so upset with her. They'd barely said a word to each other. He'd even slept in the spare room, which was a waste of time, since Tully was still sleeping on Miles's floor (the novelty of the one night in his big-boy bed appeared to have worn off and now he was back to being a stage-five clinger). When she'd told Sonny to come back and sleep in their room, he'd said he just needed some time. He hadn't been angry—and in a way that made it worse. He was levelheaded and calm. It was the kind of mindset with which people made important, binding decisions about their lives.

"Mummy, I'm hungry," Locky said.

"I know," Tully said. "That's why we're going to McDonald's. They have yummy food."

"Smoked salmon?" Locky said hopefully. "Or pesto gnocchi?"

"No, but they have chicken nuggets," Tully said. "And burgers. And chips!"

She looked in the rearview mirror. Miles sat silently in his seat. He'd been mute since they'd left the house. Speech, it seemed, was his latest issue. These last few days, due to the broken sleep and everything else going on, she'd become increasingly snappy with him about his strange behaviors. Then, at night, when he finally fell asleep, she watched his little chest rising and falling and asked herself what kind of mother snapped at a child who was so little and so troubled.

What kind of mother was she?

Tully was just turning in to the McDonald's drive-through when her phone began to ring. The screen said it was Rachel calling, and it reminded her that she hadn't rung her sister to ask how her date had gone. It turned out she was not only failing at motherhood but sisterhood too.

"How did the date go?" she cried, before Rachel could get a word in. "I'm so sorry I haven't called! Tell me everything and don't leave out any details."

"Are you in the car?" Rachel asked.

"Yes. I'm taking the boys to McDonald's."

There was a pause. "You're taking them to *McDonald's*? Tully, are you feeling all right?"

"Aunty Rachel?" Locky cried. "Is that you?"

"It sure is," she said. "Hi, Lock. Hi, Miles."

Miles didn't respond.

"There's a photographer at our house so Mummy said we had to go for a drive," Locky said helpfully. "And a man who is selling our house."

"A man who is *selling your house*?" Rachel said.

"It's a long story," Tully said. "Probably not one to go into over the phone."

"Got it." Rachel was quiet for a minute. Hey—if you've got to be out of the house, why don't you bring the boys here and I'll make them a spinach and feta omelet."

"Yay!" Locky said. Even Miles smiled a little. "I have to say, Mummy, I didn't like the sound of McDougal's!"

22

RACHEL

Aunty Rachel!" Locky cried the moment she opened the door. He threw himself into her arms. Miles threw himself into her arms too, but silently.

"I love your tummy," Locky said, rubbing it affectionately as if it were a puppy. "It's so squishy." He pulled away and barreled into the house, followed by his younger brother.

"Thanks, buddy," Rachel called after him. She didn't bother adding, "Come on in," as it appeared that horse had already bolted.

By the time Rachel had ushered Tully inside and closed the door behind her, Miles was clambering onto one of the stools in the kitchen and helping himself to a red velvet cupcake, while Locky was jumping on the couch.

"Boys!" Tully said. "For goodness' sake! Sorry, Rach."

Rachel waved the apology away as Locky ran over to join them.

"Can I have a cupcake?" he asked, apparently noticing the smear of frosting already on Miles's face. "*Pleeeeease.*" He was looking at his mother for permission, rather than Rachel, and to Rachel's surprise Tully nodded.

"Did you want me to make the omelet first?" Rachel asked, and Tully just shrugged. It was alarming. She'd always been so controlling with the boys—what they ate, who they played with, how they spoke. For her to be suggesting McDonald's and allowing them to have a cupcake before dinner, something must be very wrong.

"Sit down," Rachel said to Tully firmly, gesturing to an armchair. "Tell me what's going on. You're selling your house?"

"Yes."

"Moving somewhere bigger and better?"

Tully laughed sadly. "Wouldn't that be nice? No."

"Okay," Rachel said slowly.

"And because I know you're too polite to ask why"—Tully lowered her voice and glanced pointedly at the boys, though it was unnecessary because they were utterly consumed by their cupcakes—"it's because we've lost our money in a bad investment."

"Seriously?"

Tully nodded.

Wordlessly, Rachel walked to the kitchen, poured a large glass of wine, and carried it back to her sister, stopping to hand the boys another cupcake each on the way past. She sat down again and instructed Tully to drink.

"Wow," Rachel said, once Tully had had a few deep gulps. "That's . . . I had no idea."

"It's a reasonably new thing. I'm still getting my head around it myself. I mean, I know it's happened, but I keep thinking that somehow we'll be able to keep the house. We'll . . . I don't know— win the lottery or something."

The lottery. It gave Rachel an idea. She walked into her bedroom, picked up the plastic bag she'd stuffed the cash into, and returned, thrusting the bag at Tully.

Tully looked at it warily. "What's this?"

"Consider it a lottery win," Rachel said. "I mean . . . it's not millions of dollars. But ninety-seven-thousand-odd dollars should help, right?"

"Ninety-seven thousand dollars?" Tully said. "Good God, Rachel. Where did you get this?"

"Found it," Rachel said. "Stuffed inside a hot-water bottle that belonged to Mum."

Tully shook her head. "What?"

"It's true," Rachel said. "Bizarre as it sounds."

"But where would Mum get this kind of money? And why would she keep it in a *hot-water bottle*?" Tully pulled out a fistful of cash and looked at it closely, as if expecting it to be fake. "Does Dad know?"

"I told him," she said. "But he doesn't have a clue where it came from either. He just told me to keep it."

"He told you to keep it?" Tully said, affronted. "Just like that? Without even consulting me?"

"I guess he assumed that you were doing okay financially," Rachel said. "As did I. If I'd known the truth, I would have given it to you immediately."

"Oh, I know that," Tully said without hesitation, and Rachel felt relieved. It was true, Rachel never knew how Tully would react to things on a day-to-day basis, but she knew that when push came to shove, Tully had her back. She was glad that Tully knew the same applied to her. That knowledge had been a strange, powerful undercurrent to her life. Rachel experienced a sudden swell of gratitude for it.

"Can we have another cupcake?" Locky called from the kitchen.

"Yes," Tully and Rachel said in unison.

Tully peered into the bag again. "What's this?" she asked, fishing out the note with her name and Fiona Arthur's.

"That was stuffed into the hot-water bottle with the cash. I don't suppose you know anyone called Fiona Arthur, do you?"

"Yes," Tully said. "She's one of Locky's swim teachers."

Rachel stared at her. "*Seriously?*"

"Yes . . . no, wait! It's Fiona *Archer*, not Arthur. I remember one of the parents commenting that she should have been called Fiona Swimmer."

"Oh." Rachel deflated. "So you don't know a Fiona Arthur? Maybe a friend of Mum's?"

Tully thought for a moment. "I don't think so."

Rachel sighed. "It's driving me mad. I searched for the name on Facebook, and it turns out there are three Fiona Arthurs in Australia. I've sent a direct message to each of them but haven't had a response."

Tully put the note back in the bag. "I get why you want to know who it is, but just because Mum wrote her name down doesn't mean she's anyone important. Fiona Arthur could be the ironing lady. Or the name of the person Mum spoke to about getting Dad's car serviced. Or a hairdresser one of her friends recommended. Or the name of a milliner who makes hats for women with large heads. Remember Mum had to get her hat specially made for the Melbourne Cup because she had such a large head circumference? You got her large head, actually."

"That's true," Rachel said. "Except that when I asked Mum about Fiona Arthur, she started to cry. And then she said, 'Stephen hurt that poor woman terribly.'"

"That's weird," Tully said. "Maybe he performed surgery on her, and there were complications?"

"Or maybe Mum was talking nonsense," Rachel said. "The frustrating part is we'll never know."

"I wish we could ask her," Tully said. "Wouldn't you love that? One more conversation where she was really with us. Where she knew who we were and who she was. Where she could access her memories and tell us what we want to know."

"It would be amazing," Rachel agreed. "Though I have to say, I think she'd be pretty happy to know that you and I were sitting here together, talking like this. She'd be over the moon."

"You're right." Tully dropped her gaze, either shy or perhaps horrified by the emotional turn of the conversation. Rachel averted her eyes too, for everyone's comfort, and that's when she noticed Miles. He was in the kitchen, still sitting on the stool, eating the cupcake directly from the plate with his mouth. It wasn't dissimilar to how Rachel had eaten the wedding cake the other day.

"Is Miles all right?" Rachel asked.

Tully glanced at him, then quickly looked away. "Honestly, I have no idea. He's been doing all kinds of weird things lately."

"Like what?"

Tully sighed, then started counting them off on her fingers. "Won't sleep in his bed. Freaks out if his hands are dirty. Scared of leaves, and sparkling water, and bananas. Only wears soft clothes. Today, to mix things up, he's a mute."

"Sounds like someone else I know."

"Who?" Tully asked, sitting forward. "Oh, me?"

"Yes! You were an utter lunatic as a child."

"Thanks a lot."

"You *were*. You had a strange eye twitch for a while. And remember when you used to pull out your hair out from the roots? And what about that time you made us all walk home from school and back again because Mum—not you: *Mum*—stepped on one of the cracks in the pavement. You were convinced that if we didn't do it, Mum would die."

"I remember that," Tully said. "Mum was dreadful at missing the cracks. She stepped on every one."

"There you go then," Rachel said. "Your son is just like you."

Tully raised an eyebrow. "A lunatic?"

"A sensitive child who feels things deeply," Rachel corrected. "I imagine there's been a fair bit of tension in your house of late, with losing the money, selling the house—"

"His mum being a kleptomaniac."

Rachel blinked. "Excuse me?"

"Oh," Tully said, "I hadn't told you that part yet, had I?"

Rachel shook her head. "No," she said, rising to her feet. "And I suspect we're going to need another glass of wine for this."

23

HEATHER

Heather and Stephen had spent the afternoon wedding planning. Or, rather, *planning* for wedding planning. They'd hired a wedding planner, an efficient woman named Eleanor who had given them a survey to complete—a multiple-choice questionnaire about the elements of their dream wedding. Heather had expected that she would complete the survey alone but Stephen had insisted that they do it together. Each time she asked a question, he frowned thoughtfully, weighed up the options, then gave his opinion, while acknowledging that, ultimately, it was up to her. It was one of those afternoons that Heather used to think were for other people.

Now, having completed the survey, they lay on his bed together—*their* bed—flicking through wedding magazines. Heather's head was in Stephen's lap. It was the first time since Heather had moved in that they'd done this, and there was something peaceful about it. She felt like the type of person she saw in the wedding magazines. Not beautiful; she didn't mean that. More . . . enviable. Legitimate. Not like a girl playing the part of a bride.

"I'm happy," she said out loud. "I'm so, so happy."

Stephen shifted so he could see her face. "Me too," he said.

They gazed at each other, caught in a blissful, loved-up bubble. Then she caught sight of the clock on the bedside table. "Ooh, it's getting late!" she said, rolling off the bed. "I need to decide what to wear."

She walked over to the walk-in wardrobe she'd designed—the one that was larger than the bedroom in her previous home. They were having dinner with Mary and Michael, who were old friends of Stephen's. Michael and Stephen had gone to medical school together and Mary had been a good friend of Pam's. There was going to be another couple there too, also friends of Stephen and Pam's. It was the first time they'd done this, and Heather was incredibly nervous.

"How about a fashion show?" Stephen said.

"All right," Heather said, reaching for her navy dress. It was silk, with a low V neckline and voluminous blouson sleeves—probably the nicest dress she owned and definitely the most expensive. It was on the short side, but she planned to pair it with T-bar sandals to give it a casual vibe. She knew Stephen liked this dress, because the last time she'd worn it he'd spent most of the night commenting on how well it fit her and how beautiful she looked.

"Remind me of everyone's names and what they do," she called to him as she stepped into the dress. "I want to make a good impression."

Stephen just laughed. "You'll make a good impression whether you remember their names or not."

Heather pulled the dress up and zipped herself into it. Then she stepped into the sandals, which were a good choice. *Yes,* she thought. *This is the one.*

"Come on," Stephen called. "Don't make a man wait!"

Heather walked into the bedroom and did a self-conscious twirl.

Stephen whistled. "I remember that dress. From our first date, right?"

"You *remembered*," she said, mock touched.

"How could I forget?" He winked, and Heather had a memory of his hands sliding up the skirt then, later, fumbling with the invisible zip. Heather had been terrified that he was going to rip it.

"I take it from your expression that you approve?"

"I definitely approve," he said, and then he winced slightly. "Although . . ."

"Although?" she repeated. She definitely didn't want any "although"s.

"Although," he said, "would it be strange if I asked you to wear something else?"

Heather blinked. "Why?"

"It's just . . . I have my own memories attached to that dress. Don't get me wrong—I love it. I love it so much I don't want share it with anyone."

"That's sweet," she said. But she was disappointed. She loved the navy dress. She felt good in it. "In that case, what should I wear?"

Stephen thought for a moment. "What about that black pantsuit with the double-breasted jacket? You know the one I mean."

Heather did know the one. She regularly wore that double-breasted pantsuit to work. It was a nice, well-cut suit. A designer label. But an odd choice for dinner, she would have thought.

She looked at him for a sign that he was pulling her leg, and found none. He was completely earnest. As if she'd be doing him the most enormous favor by putting on the pantsuit. And what else could she say to that but . . . "The pantsuit it is."

Stephen rewarded her with an approving smile.

24

TULLY

One of the cruelest things about moving house is that, in the days leading up to selling, your house will never look better. It was certainly the case with Tully's house. Since meeting with the agent, they'd repainted the interior, laid new carpet, power-cleaned the pool and outdoor area, and there were still tradesmen coming and going. They'd also had a visit from a home stylist—a thin blond woman who'd ordered them to remove two-thirds of the contents of their home so she could replace it with lovely pieces of artwork and "statement" furniture. A lot of the stuff they removed belonged to the boys, and Tully had made the catastrophic mistake of having the removalists come while they were at home.

"Not my trike!" Locky had cried, as the removalists carried away the tricycle he hadn't used in years. "Wait, that's my favorite toy!" he'd said about the bath toy that he'd never opened and that had sat in the gift cupboard ever since.

Tully had stuck to her guns and removed all the items and then bought the boys ice cream to console them. Healthy food, she realized, really was a privilege of the wealthy. When you had less help, more to do, and less money to spend, junk food was really all you had to appease tired, angry children.

They'd also brought in a garden stylist—a bohemian-looking man named Bodhi who placed ornamental rocks, garden benches, and bonsai plants around the property. Tully had been appalled at the price of it (and, frankly, at the idea of a garden stylist), but she had to admit, the garden looked bloody gorgeous.

Tully looked out the bedroom window, watching the boys bouncing on the trampoline that had been allowed to stay only if it was tucked in the far corner of the garden, out of sight. Tully could hear them shouting, "I'm going higher than you" . . . "No you're not" . . . "I am" . . . "Daddy, he said he's going higher!" It reminded her of herself and Rachel when they were younger, always fighting to be higher, or faster, or better.

"You're both going equally high," Sonny said.

Sonny had always been an exceptionally good dad. Determined not to be like his own unreliable, largely absent father, he made sure to spend time with the boys every day, and hung his parenting hat on the fact that if he said he was going to do something, he did it. (Tully, on the other hand, regularly promised the kids all sorts of things she had no intention of delivering. Her children, she'd figured out, were incredibly focused and intense, but also very forgetful, so this technique worked well, even if it was a little less noble than Sonny's.) Unfortunately, while he was spending a lot of time with the boys, he hadn't been spending time with Tully, not since she'd told him her secret. The other night, when she got home from Rachel's, he hadn't even turned around when she came to his office door to say hello. Eventually she'd taken herself to bed, stuffing the cash-filled plastic bag in her bedside table, where her stolen goods had once been kept.

Rachel, by contrast, had taken the news that her sister was a kleptomaniac surprisingly well. She'd been shocked, naturally, and had stared at Tully for several seconds. "You're a . . ."

"Kleptomaniac," Tully repeated. "It means I steal stuff. I've been doing it my whole life. Well, since I was eleven."

Rachel had lots of questions, naturally, and Tully had been happy to answer them. It had been cathartic, in a way, and Tully found herself wishing that Sonny had asked those sorts of questions instead of just cutting her off emotionally. There was something about the way Rachel spoke to her, as though she was curious rather than judgmental, that was incredibly reassuring. As a result, Tully felt closer to her sister now than she'd felt in months. Years. She might *never* have felt this close to Rachel.

Then there was the fact that Rachel had given her that money. She got out the bag of money now and looked at it.

"Where did you get this, Mum?" she whispered.

She looked out the window again. The boys were on the grass now, sprinting away from Sonny, who was pretending to be a hungry grizzly bear. She opened the window.

"Sonny!" she called. "Have you got a sec?"

For a moment, he kept on with the game, and Tully thought he was going to ignore her. But after a few seconds, he said something to the boys and, abandoning the chase, headed indoors.

"What is it?" he said, when he arrived in the bedroom.

She thrust the bag of money at him. He looked down at it and then immediately back at her, aghast. "Tully," he said. "Please don't tell me you stole this."

"Oh no . . . I didn't," she said. She very nearly laughed at his assumption, even though, she realized, it was in fact the most logical one. "Although I guess Mum might have. Rachel found it with Mum's things, stuffed inside a hot-water bottle."

"Seriously?" He looked down at the bag again. "You swear you didn't take it?"

"I swear. You can ask Rachel."

That seemed to be enough for Sonny. He nodded and looked down at the money. "How much is there?"

"Nearly a hundred thousand."

His jaw dropped. "A hundred grand? How did Pam come by that kind of money?"

"We don't know how she got it. All we know is that it was inside the hot-water bottle along with a note that had my name on it and the name of some woman called Fiona Arthur. We don't know who she is, but according to Mum, Dad hurt her in some way."

Sonny was shaking his head. "This is madness."

"I know," she said. "But Dad told Rachel she could keep the money, and when I told Rachel about our financial worries, she said *I* could keep it. I don't feel comfortable accepting it all, but I thought maybe half?" She shrugged. "I know that wouldn't solve all our problems, but every little bit helps, right?"

It took a minute, but finally he started to nod. "Yes, every little bit helps. Though I'm not sure what the bank will think when I show up with cash in a plastic bag."

"We might need to launder it," Tully said earnestly, and was delighted when Sonny laughed.

"You think Pam has given us dirty money?"

Now Tully laughed. "I don't know what that means, but I'm going to say no."

Sonny smiled. "Good old Pam."

"Good old Mum."

They were standing close together, staring down at the money. Their sides were skimming each other, and Tully could feel Sonny's body move with his breath. It was the closest they'd been in over a week. Tully felt an urge to throw her arms around him, but she held back.

"Sonny," she said, "I know you're upset with me, and I understand why. But I promise I'm going to stop stealing. I'm going to make this right."

"You need to have counseling, Tully," he said. "You've been doing this most of your life and, as you said yourself, you can't stop."

"I know," she said. "And I agree—I'll have counseling. I'll do *anything*. Whatever it takes."

"Good," Sonny said. It was hard to read his expression. For a moment Tully thought he was going to say something more, but instead he just handed her the bag of cash and walked away.

25

RACHEL

Rachel was going on a date—for real this time. She'd spent the day on the edge of nausea, her urge to cancel her date with Darcy warring with her desire to fulfill the commitment she'd made. The whole thing just felt so damn strange. After all, she had never been on a proper date. As a teen, she'd talked to boys at school, and occasionally they hung out on the weekends at the train station or bowling alley, but they'd never gone out for dinner. Never had to sit across from each other at a table and talk. This was an entirely different, terrifying beast.

When Rachel arrived at the restaurant, five minutes early, Darcy wasn't there yet. She wasn't sure if that was good or bad. She took a seat at the bar. Her shoulders felt tense, tight. In fact, her entire body did. There were some laminated menus already laid out, and she picked one up and surveyed it to distract herself. Darcy had asked her to choose the venue and she had selected a popular, midpriced Mexican restaurant, reasoning that Darcy was unlikely to be able to afford anywhere fancier on what she was paying him (though she fully intended to pay her own way). She wondered, not for the first time, how he supported himself. According to the agency she'd used to find him, he'd been unemployed for a couple of years. And though he was now working for her, he was only doing the occasional job; he wasn't earning anything like a living wage. Rachel had never cared that much about money, but one did need a certain amount to live. Maybe Darcy had another source of income? As a drug dealer, perhaps? It was yet another thing she needed to find out about him.

There was a mirror opposite her and she used it to check her appearance. She wasn't horrified by what she saw. She was wearing a black dress and a denim jacket and sandals. Her hair was tied back in a low ponytail, as usual. Rachel knew she was attractive, and carrying a few extra kilos did nothing to change that. And yet, as she looked at her reflection, she felt an intense hatred for . . . not the kilos, but what they represented. And who they connected her to.

"Hello, hello," Darcy said, appearing behind her. "You beat me here!"

"I was starting to think you were a no-show," she said with a calm she didn't feel.

Darcy sat on the stool beside her. "As if," he said. "Muffin compares to you."

Rachel couldn't help it; she snorted.

"Good one, right?" he said, grinning.

"Do you have a special interest in baking jokes," Rachel asked, "or do you simply have a perfect joke for every specialty industry?"

"I brushed up on my cake jokes recently," he said. "Like any good employee."

"For the customers?"

"Yes," he said. "But I wasted them all on the boss."

Rachel laughed. She felt her shoulders loosen a little.

"Can I get you a couple of margaritas?" the waiter asked, appearing at the end of the bar. He wore a sombrero and a stuck-on handlebar mustache and he had a broad Australian accent.

"Sure," Rachel said, after glancing at Darcy to confirm that he wanted one. "And we'd also like to order food." She looked at Darcy, perhaps daring him to object. But he was nodding.

"Good call," he said. "Let's get that out of the way so we can relax."

And with that, Rachel found that she did relax. She ordered nachos with the lot, followed by fajitas, guacamole, and shredded beef empanadas. Then, on a whim, she added a few more mains, a few more sides. As the waiter prepared to leave, she grabbed his forearm. "Sorry. Can we add the Mexican corn?"

They didn't need the corn. The table would be groaning under what she'd already ordered. But there was something about ordering it, being surrounded by it, that calmed her.

After the waiter left, she waited for the inevitable commentary from Darcy. *Wow, that was a big order,* or, *I like a girl with a big appetite.* But Darcy didn't say either of those things. Instead, he lifted his hand in one half of a high five. "Good call on the corn," he said, as she slapped her hand against his.

You're too good to be true, Rachel thought. But she must have said it out loud, because Darcy replied: "I know."

She burst out laughing. "Seriously! What is wrong with you?"

"Well," he said thoughtfully. "I do have five kids."

"Really?"

"No! But I am married."

"You are?"

He laughed. "Seriously? Of course not!"

Rachel rolled her eyes.

"Okay, listen—I live in a granny flat at the back of my mum's place." Rachel watched him, waiting for the punch line.

"That one is true," he admitted.

"Oh," Rachel said. "Well . . . there's no shame in that."

"Come on. There's a little shame." He grinned. "The thing is, it's been a funny couple of years. I've been unemployed, as you know, but I used to run a café in the city called Everything's Better Toasted."

"Good name," Rachel said.

He looked pleased. "It *is*, isn't it? I came up with it. We had a terrific spot, right near Flinders Street Station, and we did a great trade. Two years after the first café, I opened a second one a few streets away. I had plans for two more stores but then . . . COVID happened. The city emptied out overnight, and so did my clientele. We made it through the first lockdown, just. But when Melbourne had to lock down again and again, the businesses went under. I lost everything."

"That's tough. I'm so sorry."

"It really ruined me for a while." He shrugged. "I became pretty depressed. I found it hard to even get out of bed in the morning."

"Is that why you were on the long-term unemployed program?"

He nodded. "I probably could have found a job, if I really wanted one. But I was angry that I'd worked so hard for something and it was taken away for reasons completely beyond my control. I moved back to Mum's, and for a while I didn't do anything. Eventually, Mum said I had to do something or she'd kick me out. She probably wouldn't have, but I didn't want to take that chance. So now I work for you."

"But you always seem so upbeat," Rachel said. "I never would have known."

"The downside of being as charming and charismatic as I am," he said with a rueful grin, "is that people don't tend to know when I'm suffering."

Rachel smiled. "So how are you doing now?"

"Better," he said. "Definitely better. Mum was right; it turned out I just needed to do *something* to get out of my head and back into the world. But I'm sorry to tell you that I'm not the catch you thought I was."

"Who says I thought you were a catch?"

Darcy laughed raucously, and Rachel couldn't help but join in. They had finally got on top of their laughter when the waiter arrived and began unloading an absurdly large amount of food onto the table. Rachel felt the giggles start to bubble up again, even before he returned to the kitchen to get the rest.

"Can I get you anything else?" the waiter asked, when the entire bar area was covered in plates, and people were glancing over from their tables to see what was going on.

"This will do to start," Darcy said, straight-faced. "We'll let you know when we're ready for the main course."

After that, Rachel couldn't hold it in any longer. She laughed until tears ran down her face. She laughed until she forgot that the man on the beach existed, until she was just a normal woman, out on a date at a Mexican restaurant, with a very cute man.

26

HEATHER

Heather wore the pantsuit to dinner. It was, now that she thought about it, a good choice. No need to worry about bending over, lots of room to fit in dessert.

Mary and Michael's house was like something out of a fairy tale. As Stephen drove into a circular brick driveway surrounded by climbing roses, Heather gripped the bouquet of flowers that Stephen said was unnecessary. She was grateful she'd insisted, though, because it gave her something to do with her trembling hands. Yes, this was the life she wanted—civilized dinners in beautiful homes, thoughtful conversation with intelligent people. But there was also something terrifying about getting what you'd always wanted. She could've used a drink, just to take the edge off her nerves.

They were greeted at the door by both Mary and Michael, which Heather found quite charming. Was that the done thing when people had dinner parties—answering the door as a team? Heather didn't know, but she made a mental note to try it if she and Stephen had anyone over for dinner.

"Hello!" Mary exclaimed. If she had any mixed feelings about meeting her old friend's replacement, she hid it well. "You must be Heather. We're so happy to meet you."

Mary was in her late fifties, at a guess. There was no visible sign that she'd had any cosmetic work done, and she seemed to embody the idea of beauty at any age, with her shiny gray-blond hair, tailored pants and shirt, and flat shoes. She wore minimal makeup, plain gold studs, and a matching necklace. Understated. Heather felt quietly grateful that she hadn't gone for the dress. Once again, Stephen had steered her right.

Michael greeted Heather just as kindly as Mary had, and ushered them into a beautiful dining room, complete with old-fashioned fireplace, thick embossed curtains, and ornate ceiling details. The table was set with flowers and beautiful linen napery. Another couple rose to their feet as Stephen and Heather entered.

"This is Elsa and David," Mary said. "Elsa, David, this is Heather."

Elsa and David murmured politely, but unlike Mary and Michael, their manner was aloof. Their smiles were fleeting and they didn't quite meet Heather's eye when they greeted her.

"Why don't you sit down this end, Heather," Mary said. "Michael, can you get Heather a champagne?"

Heather had practiced declining a drink all day. She'd actually *googled* polite ways to do it. Google, as usual, had been quite helpful and provided her with many suggestions, including saying that she was on medication, that it "didn't agree with her," or that she was recovering from an illness. Heather's favorite, which she'd decided to use tonight, was "Just sparkling water for me" in a polite but firm voice. In none of the googled scenarios had the host just placed a drink directly in her hand, as Michael did now.

"So, Heather," Mary said, sitting at the head of the table,

"Stephen tells me you're an interior designer. I'll have to get you to come and look around this place. God knows it could use some modernizing!"

"If the rest is anything like what I've seen so far, I wouldn't change a thing," Heather said.

"That's what she said to me," Stephen said, "right before she tore the place down to the studs."

Everyone laughed.

For the next few minutes, the discussion moved in a circular fashion with ease, everyone seeming to notice when someone hadn't contributed and somehow looping them into the conversation without making them stand out or feel put on the spot. It was astonishing, being around such skilled conversationalists. The champagne went down very nicely and before Heather knew it, her glass had been refilled. Mary darted back and forth between the kitchen and the dining room, a tea towel draped charmingly over her shoulder.

"So," Elsa said, when conversation dulled, "how is Pam doing?"

"She's doing well," Stephen said. "We visited her this week, and she seemed in good spirits."

"You *both* visited her?" Elsa said.

Mary arrived with bowls of soup. "I should have checked: Do you have any dietary restrictions, Heather?" she called, setting a bowl in front of Stephen.

"No," Heather said. "None at all."

Elsa was still looking at Stephen.

"Yes," Stephen said. "Heather and I visited her together. Pam and Heather spent quite a bit of time together this past year, when

Heather was overseeing the renovations. And she's been a great support as we moved Pam into the home."

Michael was making his way around the table with a bottle of wine, filling the glasses. Elsa opened her mouth to say something else, but Mary got in first.

"Please start, everyone!" Mary said. She held out a basket of crusty rolls. "And tell us about the house, Stephen. Is it sublime?"

"Sublime is a good description for it," Stephen said thoughtfully. "Most mornings I feel like I've awoken in a hotel. It was definitely worth the wait."

"I remember sitting in the kitchen with Pam years ago," Elsa said, "while she drew up plans on a serviette. She was so excited."

"I saw her serviette plans," Heather said. "She also had a whole shoebox full of fabric, swatches, paint colors. She was a dream client in that way. She knew her style—warm, textured, ornate. Never met a throw cushion she didn't like."

This drew a laugh from the room, even from Elsa.

"I bet she'd be thrilled that her dream came to fruition, even if she wasn't able to see it," Mary said. "Are there throw cushions everywhere?"

Heather hesitated. She assumed Stephen had told them about the change in direction. She glanced at him for guidance, but he had a mouthful of bread.

"Well, in the end, we decided to go for a different style. More . . . minimalist. Clean lines." She took a quick swig of her drink. "I mean, it made sense that if Pam wasn't going to be living there, we should adapt the plans to suit Stephen's own style. I wanted him to be happy with the results."

"And evidently he is," Mary said, barely missing a beat.

"And Pam has no idea, so what does it matter?" Elsa muttered.

Silence. Stephen fought to swallow his mouthful.

"It matters," Heather said. "Of course it matters. Stephen cares enormously for Pam, and so do I."

"*You* care about her?" Elsa said. David put a hand on her arm, but Elsa shook it off. "I'm sorry, but honestly. Pam was your *client*, and not only did you fail to meet her brief, you took off with her husband!"

"That's enough, Elsa," Stephen said.

"Stephen was my client too," Heather said. "I met *his* brief."

"Enough!" Stephen said, loudly now.

The room was silent for a few moments. Even Mary couldn't seem to find anything to say. Heather looked at Stephen, but he seemed to be avoiding her gaze.

"I'm sorry, Mary, but I think we should go," he said finally.

"You don't have to," Mary said, rising to her feet. But it was clear there wasn't really another option. Elsa was planted in her seat, glaring. Her husband was sitting awkwardly beside her.

"We'll walk you out," Michael said, as Heather grabbed her purse.

At the door, they spoke in hushed tones.

"I'm sorry, Mary," Stephen said. "I thought it would be okay."

"Don't apologize!" Mary said. "It's not your fault. I have no idea what got into Elsa." Then, perhaps feeling disloyal, she added, "She and Pam were very close. I guess everyone grieves in their own way."

"It was a lovely dinner," Heather said, even though she'd barely touched the soup. "Thank you for inviting me."

"We'll do it again," Mary said. "Soon. Just the four of us."

"I'll see you at golf," Michael said, shaking Stephen's hand. "It was great to meet you, Heather. Hopefully next time will be less eventful."

Michael and Mary waved, and Stephen and Heather walked to the car.

"I'm sorry," she started, but Stephen held up a hand.

"Let's talk at home."

Heather got into the car. But as Stephen got in beside her, she felt it, that little pinch of unease she used to get when her father was on the warpath. She used to think of it as her sixth sense. It told her something was in the air. Danger.

27

RACHEL

Rachel found it hard to recall how dinner ended. At some point, the bill was paid, they'd thanked the waitstaff, and they'd wandered out into the evening together, as if it were something they'd always done. On the way back to Rachel's house they continued their conversation from the restaurant, but with new comfort, more teasing, and an undeniable frisson of chemistry.

"You know," Darcy said as they walked home, "that was the best date I've ever been on."

Rachel laughed. "Me too."

"Really?" He looked so delighted she decided not to remind him that it was her first date.

"Really."

They arrived at Rachel's house and, without discussion, went inside. Rachel located a bottle of red and some cheese, and by the time she'd returned to the living room, Darcy had moved a throw rug from the couch onto the floor.

"Night picnic?" he said.

"We definitely need more food," she replied, deadpan. "I don't think we ate enough at dinner."

It all felt so natural and normal. For the first time, instead of resisting, Rachel went with it. She poured them each a glass of wine, then arranged some cheese and quince paste on a cracker for Darcy. She enjoyed having something to focus on, something to keep her hands busy.

"Maybe you could go into business arranging night picnics?" Rachel suggested. "If you want to start a new business."

"So you like it, do you?" he said, looking pleased. "Good. I'm glad."

He put his glass on the coffee table, and smiled at her. It was a different smile from his usual, mischievous one. It sent a tingle up Rachel's spine. The kind of tingle she'd used to feel around men all those years ago, before that day at the beach. A *good* tingle.

And yet . . .

"Should I take this?" he asked, gesturing toward her glass.

Rachel let him take the glass from her and put it alongside his on the coffee table. Then he looked back at her. Paused for a beat.

He was mere inches away. She could smell his aftershave, see the little pinpricks of stubble on his jaw. He lifted her chin. It was like she was outside of herself, watching it happen to someone else. For a few seconds she actually believed she could go through with it. He was only millimeters from her face when she pulled away.

"I'm sorry," she said as she pulled away. "I can't."

28

HEATHER

Stephen was silent as he drove home from Mary and Michael's. Heather tried to talk to him a couple of times but was greeted with only one-word answers. And when she tried to put her hand on his, he gently moved his away. The tension took Heather back to a night when she was about eight, and she'd been with her parents at a New Year's Eve party. There had been two other children there: a twelve-year-old boy who'd taken cigarettes from his mum's pocket and then taken Heather behind the shed so she could watch him smoke them; and a three-year-old girl, whom Heather had played with like a baby doll until she'd finally fallen asleep on the living room floor. After that, Heather had hidden in one of the bedrooms, reading a magazine she'd found on a shelf. She'd fallen asleep there, in a corner next to a pile of coats. When her parents wanted to leave, they couldn't find her. Apparently they looked for her for hours. When they finally found her, her dad was livid.

Heather remembered the car ride, the silence of it. She could feel her mother's fear and her father's mounting rage. She knew it was all her fault. Why had she gone into that bedroom? Why didn't she fall asleep in the living room, like the little girl? A three-year-old knew better than she did. She was an idiot. And when they got home, she and her mother paid the price. As usual.

And tonight, once again, she was to blame for the evening ending badly.

"Are you okay?" she asked Stephen as they pulled into the garage.

His gaze flickered to her for a moment; then he nodded.

"I'm sorry," she said. "I shouldn't have talked about Pam. Or said that we changed the plans."

He turned off the ignition. "You can talk about Pam as much as you like, Heather. And they were going to find out about the house plans eventually. Elsa was out of line there, not you."

"Oh," Heather said, confused. "Then why are you upset with me?"

"I'm upset," he said, "because you said you weren't going to drink tonight."

"But Mary and Michael kept filling my glass."

He looked straight ahead. He was quiet for a long time, as if he was really contemplating what he was going to say next. Finally he said: "I think you have a problem, Heather."

"With alcohol?"

"Yes, with alcohol."

"But I—I didn't even drink that much." The comment might have been more convincing had it not been punctuated by a hiccup.

Stephen sighed. He opened his door.

"Stephen!" she called, as he walked into the house. She hurried after him, catching up when he was halfway down the hall.

He spun around. "What?"

But of course she had no idea what to say. She opened her mouth. Another hiccup emerged. She cursed internally.

"You didn't even drink that much?" he said, throwing up his hands.

"I didn't."

He leveled his gaze at her. "Do you know what I think? I think when you start drinking, you stop counting."

It wasn't true. Heather knew exactly how much she'd drunk. She'd had two glasses of champagne, and one glass of wine. Or maybe it was two glasses of wine? But she hadn't forgotten because she was so drunk; she'd forgotten because his friends were so adept at filling her damn glass!

"That's not it. It's just that Michael kept filling my glass."

"So what? So you just keep drinking? What if you were allergic to peanuts? Would you just eat them because someone kept serving them?"

Stephen had never got angry with her like this before. He was so close that Heather could feel his breath on her forehead. She thought of her father the night they returned from the New Year's Eve party. He'd bailed her mother up against the wall almost exactly like this. She saw a flash of her father's face, a red, contorted version of Stephen's—or was Stephen's a red, contorted version of his?

"Move back," she whispered.

"The last thing I want to do is tell you when or how much to drink, Heather," he said. "But I'm worried."

He didn't move back. Heather felt panic set in. It traveled through her belly, her chest, her lungs. She never made the decision to push him; it was as if her arm just struck out of its own volition. It happened so fast. Her arm connected; she saw a streak of red; then Stephen staggered backward. Then she pushed past him, heading for the front door. She'd barely taken a step when she felt someone grab her by the hair. She was yanked backward. Her head hit the polished concrete floor. And everything went black.

29

RACHEL

There were so many parts of that horrible day that were etched into Rachel's soul. But one of the most crushing parts to relive, even now, was the aftermath. After the man ran away, leaving her in the bushes, Rachel stood up. It felt odd, after the magnitude of what had happened, to be suddenly alone. She felt as though she were in one of those end-of-the-world movies in which the main character comes out of her home to find that everyone else has been eaten by zombies and she is the only one left. Dazed, she walked the half dozen blocks home, marveling at the normality around her. People mowing their lawns or walking their dogs. The lady across the street emptying her shopping bags from the boot of her car waved to Rachel and, on autopilot, Rachel waved back. No one gasped or stared or begged to know what had happened. People just went about their regular activities as if nothing had changed. It almost tricked Rachel into thinking that maybe nothing had.

Then she walked in her front door.

The shift in energy was immediate, mostly because Dad was there, right there in the front hall, holding a basket of laundry. He did a double take when she walked in. *Finally,* Rachel thought. *Someone sees me.*

Dad had always been able to read her; an irritating skill of his. They'd argued about it that very morning, when Rachel had asked if she could have a sleepover at her friend's place and he had (correctly) intuited that her friend's parents were going to be away and they'd be having a party. Now his irritating skill was a blessed relief. She wouldn't have to explain anything. She wouldn't have to find the words to describe what had happened, because Dad would already know.

Except he didn't know.

Instead, Dad looked at his watch, then back at her. "Call that a run? You were barely gone fifteen minutes!"

She could have just opened her mouth and told him. *Dad, I was raped.* Why didn't she? She knew he would have believed her. He would have rushed her to the hospital and called the police and stood beside her in court as she gave evidence. He would have advocated for her, protected her, done every last thing that was expected of him as a good father and then some. In the past, when she'd heard the stats of women failing to report sexual assault, she'd felt so frustrated. *Tell someone,* she'd thought. *Make the bastard pay.* Suddenly she understood. Perhaps these women had been through enough. Perhaps the murky cocktail of shame and horror and disgust that Rachel was feeling was the same one that muzzled them all?

And so, instead of telling her dad what had happened, she went to the kitchen and baked the most exquisite carrot cake with cream cheese frosting. And she ate and ate and ate until all the disgusting feelings were buried under the most exquisite, all-consuming sugar high.

Rachel was making pancakes. After last night with Darcy, it was exactly what she needed. She'd always found such comfort in making the batter, pouring that perfect creamy circle, watching it bubble up and then flipping it to see the golden yellow of the underside. Afterward, she covered the stack in sugar and syrup and berries and ate until she thought she might burst. Then she decided to make a second batch. She was pouring the batter into the pan when she heard the knock on the door.

"Rachel?"

It was Darcy. Not only did she recognize his voice, he'd also told her that he'd check in on her in the morning. Rachel should have known that a phone call was not his style.

"Will you talk to me?" he said through the door. "I don't even have to come inside. Just open a window if you like!"

Rachel put down the jug of batter, walked to the door and opened it.

"I've got pancakes on the stove," she said, returning to the kitchen. She was glad for the busywork, the excuse not to have to look him in the eye. He'd been so kind last night, so understanding, that it only made her humiliation more intense.

Darcy followed her, shutting the door behind him.

"What's all this?" he said.

She flipped the pancakes. "I'm baking my feelings."

Darcy sat on a stool. His movements were tentative, slow, as if he was worried about startling her. "Not a bad thing to do with your feelings, I guess."

Rachel shrugged. She wasn't so sure about that.

"Listen, Rachel, I'm sorry about last night . . . I mean, if I'd known you weren't feeling it, I wouldn't have tried to—"

"It's not your fault. Really. It's the classic case of 'it's not you, it's me.'"

She stacked up the pancakes on a plate and covered them in berries and syrup. With Darcy here, she suddenly felt stuffed, so she pushed them in front of him. He picked up his cutlery, but made no move to eat.

"Can I ask you something?" she said.

"Sure."

"Why did you come back here today?"

"I came back because I was hoping that you'd lain awake all night thinking about me and realized you couldn't live without me." He thought for a minute. "Also I was hungry and fancied a pancake feast."

Rachel tried to smile. "Something happened to me," she said. "When I was sixteen."

Darcy's expression changed.

"I was out jogging. He jumped out of the bushes. Don't . . . say anything. It's fine. Well, it's not fine, but that's the reason. That's why I don't date. That's why . . . well, that's what happened last night."

Darcy closed his eyes. "Rachel, I . . . I don't know what to say. I'm so sorry."

"It was a long time ago." She waved her hand with an airiness she didn't feel.

"And yet I imagine it's not the kind of thing that ever really leaves you?"

She shrugged. "I manage. Perhaps not in the healthiest of ways, but I do."

Darcy put down his cutlery. His undivided attention did something to her. For the first time ever, she felt the inclination to share more. "I don't think you'll be surprised to learn that food is my drug of choice. I eat my feelings, I bake my feelings. I order my feelings at restaurants and cafes, and through Ubereats."

"Makes sense," Darcy said.

She blinked. "What do you mean . . . 'makes sense'?"

"I mean . . . why not bake and eat your feelings? It's not the worst thing to do with your feelings, is it?"

This stopped Rachel for a minute.

"I mean, sure," Darcy allowed, "it's not ideal if you eat a wedding cake hours before it's due to be delivered. And you are a better judge of whether this is a problem or not in your life than I am. But—"

"But what?"

"From what I can see, you've done something incredible. You've not only learned to manage your feelings, you've also found a way to make a living out of it."

"It's not as simple as that," she said. And it wasn't. But also . . . it was.

There was no doubt that her food fixation had hurt her at times. It had stopped her from "sitting in the pain" and "healing" and "becoming a stronger person." At the same time, she couldn't deny that food had saved her. Over and over and over again.

"I know it's not simple," he said. "And if baking and eating your feelings isn't working for you, it might be wise to try a different form of therapy. I just mean, don't beat yourself up for single-handedly saving yourself with the tools you had available to you. Where I come from, that's called survival."

Rachel felt a rush of emotion. Tears came to her eyes and she tried hard to blink them away. When she failed, she took a deep breath and walked around the counter to stand right in front of Darcy. With him sitting on the stool and her standing, they were the same height. "A different kind of therapy?"

"I was thinking of counseling," he said, as she leaned toward him. "But we could try this."

"Let's try this," Rachel agreed. And after that, they didn't talk anymore.

THE WEDDING

The ambulance wails as it tears away from the chapel. I wonder if the sirens indicate hope? After all, if a person—or persons—had been declared dead, the ambulance wouldn't be in any hurry, would it?

The wedding cars remain out in front of the church, empty now, and useless. It makes me think of tables that will be set somewhere, the canapés and fish and chicken that will never be eaten. Police stand around in clumps, talking to guests and taking down names.

Standing on the street outside the chapel, I listen as new theories are advanced. Most people now think it was Heather who was injured, rather than Stephen. It does make sense. After all, it was a young woman's scream that we'd heard. Then again, there were quite a few young women in the vicinity when it happened.

"Did you see how miserable his daughters looked?" he says. "Like they were at a funeral rather than a wedding."

"But trying to be supportive of their father," another woman adds. "Those girls have always adored Stephen."

The ambulance had parked at the side door of the chapel to avoid the crowds, so no one had seen who had been ferried away. The family, too, had all disappeared; presumably they were on their way to the hospital as well. As for the guests, no one seems in any great hurry to leave. I suppose they'd planned to be spending the afternoon and evening at the wedding and so have nowhere else to be. One man suggests everyone head to the local pub for drinks and to wait for news together.

Obviously I'm not going to do that, but I'm in no hurry to leave either, now that I've had to give my details to the police. That was something I'd hoped to avoid, but the damage is done now. So I stand among the knots of people, trying to look like a concerned friend.

"I think Pam went for Heather," a middle-aged woman in a pink skirt suit says. "Yes, she has dementia, but she was always pretty savvy. I mean, who could blame her? The woman was marrying her husband, for God's sake."

"Ex-husband," the man standing beside her points out.

"How would she know that? She couldn't possibly have consented to the divorce; she's not exactly of sound mind, is she?"

"Which one is it, Daph? Is she savvy, or not of sound mind?"

"Both!" Daph sounds indignant. "Savvy but not of sound mind. Shut up, Greg."

"It could have been one of the daughters," Greg says. "Trying to take out the wicked new stepmother."

Greg is enjoying the drama a little too much, and apparently Daph thinks so too because she elbows him in the guts and he makes an *oof* sound.

"I hear Rachel made the wedding cake," another guy in the same group says. "So it won't be her. If she wanted to kill Heather, she could've just poisoned the cake."

"But then she would've poisoned everyone, you dill."

"Oh yeah."

"The poor bloke probably had a heart attack," Greg says. "All that sex with a younger woman . . . gotta be bad for the heart."

"Greg!"

"What? It would be ironic, wouldn't it? Heart surgeon dies of a heart attack?"

All around me, people are having similar conversations. The consensus is that it was either the bride or groom who was injured. Most people blame Pamela, and it is, I suppose, the logical assumption. She has dementia, she may have got confused or violent. But I don't think it was Pamela. Not that she wouldn't have had cause to do it; I myself was certainly tempted, more than once. But I'm starting to think it was the daughter, the one who bakes. She was the glue that held the family together. Walking down the aisle, she looked like she carried the weight of the world on her shoulders, and little wonder after the pressure cooker they'd all been in this past year. Yes, my money is on her.

30

HEATHER

Heather sat on the edge of the bed with her elbows on her knees, staring at the floor. Her head throbbed, despite the two ibuprofen she'd taken. Stephen must have put her to bed last night, because she didn't remember how she'd got here. His side of the bed was made, so clearly he'd slept somewhere else, but she knew he was in the house. She could *feel* him.

She'd packed a small overnight bag—toothbrush, toothpaste, pajamas, a change of clothes—and it sat at her feet. She had to leave. What choice did she have? The irony was that this was exactly what she wanted to avoid. This was why she'd re-created herself! For a nicer life, yes; a life where she didn't have to worry about money. But more importantly, for a life where she didn't have to be afraid in her own home.

She wondered if she should call someone to be here, just in case. But who? She'd never had many friends and she'd lost contact with the few she did have after she started dating Stephen. She was far too ashamed to call her work colleagues for this. And it wasn't as if she could call Rachel or Tully. She was on her own. Like her mother had been, in the end. It was thinking of her mother that finally got Heather into a standing position. She wasn't going to be a battered wife, like her mother. She was going to ensure a different fate for herself.

She threw her bag over her shoulder and walked out of the bedroom, down the hall and stairs, and into the living room. Stephen was sitting at the breakfast bar with his back to her.

"I'm leaving you, Stephen," she said.

He turned to face her.

"Oh my God. What . . . what happened to your face?"

He had a black eye. He also appeared to have a deep scratch under the eye that was bruised.

He blinked slowly. Suddenly her fear of him hurting her seemed ridiculous. In fact, seeing Stephen now, it felt laughable that she'd even had that fear in the first place.

"Stephen?"

He took off his glasses. That's when she noticed they weren't his usual glasses but a spare pair he kept in the bedside table. "I'm sorry," he said. "I'm just not sure if you're joking or not."

Suddenly Heather wasn't sure either.

"You don't remember what happened last night?"

"Yes," she said, though she was starting to doubt herself. "You were upset with me for drinking at the party. We had an argument. I tried to leave, and you grabbed my hair and . . ."

She trailed off, trying to remember. She knew she'd gone down. After that she didn't remember anything.

Stephen was still looking at her, confused, as if her face were a maths problem he was trying to solve.

"I don't know," she said finally.

"Do you want to sit down?"

"No. Just tell me."

Stephen nodded. "Well, as you say, we came home and we argued. Evidently I got too close to you. I apologize for that. I didn't realize you were feeling so hemmed in until you shouted for me to move and then punched me."

"I *punched* you?"

Stephen smiled thinly. "Knocked the glasses clean off my face. I think that was what caused the scratch." He pointed to the mark under his eye. "Then you took off. I was going to let you go; you were very upset. Then you slipped. You went down hard and hit your head. I sat with you for a couple of hours down here, in case you were concussed. Eventually I took you upstairs and put you to bed."

Heather tried to line up this version with her own memory.

"What did you think happened?" Stephen asked.

Heather had no idea anymore. "I know that we argued, and then I was on the ground. I assumed . . ." She trailed off.

"That *I* did it to you?"

"Yes," she admitted.

He looked, among other things, very sad.

"I'm sorry," she said quickly. "I . . . I don't know what I was thinking. I just . . ." Heather suddenly felt at a loss. "I don't know."

"I might be way off," he said, after a long pause, "but I wonder if this might have something to do with your dad."

Just like that, an image of her father popped into her head. He was holding her mum by the throat, pressing her against the wall.

"Yes," she said. "I think it might."

Stephen exhaled. He looked like he wanted to reach for her, but then appeared to think better of it. "Heather," he said, "you need to understand that I will never lay a hand on you in violence. I don't hurt women. I don't hurt men. I'm a doctor. I have taken an oath to do no harm."

Heather nodded. How stupid she had been. *Of course* Stephen would never hurt her. He was a good man. A family man. A *doctor*! The idea that he would be physically violent was preposterous. She let her bag slide off her shoulder and onto the floor. "I'm sorry. I don't know what's wrong with me, Stephen. I feel like I'm going mad."

"You're not going mad," he said.

But she must have been. Because if she wasn't going mad, it meant that Stephen was a monster. A monster who, in the next few months, was going to become her husband.

31

TULLY

Her psychologist was a *man*. Tully had spent the first fifteen minutes of her appointment marveling at that, which equated to about fifty dollars. Probably not the best use of their money, especially at the moment. Sonny had made the appointment for her. For the past week he'd been either reading a book, listening to a podcast, or watching a documentary about kleptomania. As it turned out, he'd crossed paths with a lot of psychologists when they'd given evidence in court, and apparently Dr. Shearer was one of the best.

When Sonny suggested Dr. Shearer, Tully had pictured a woman. A forthright woman in her mid-forties with short hair and a well-cut blazer. A lesbian, perhaps. *Call me Amanda*, she would say, and then she and Tully would exchange small talk about where she'd bought the well-cut blazer. Instead, Tully sat face-to-face with an older man. He was probably in his late sixties, with a shock of white hair, an open-necked shirt, and corduroy trousers. A man who hadn't, thus far, asked her to call him Alan.

"Anyway, I think I've talked enough for now," he said. "Why don't you tell me a little about you?"

"Well," Tully said, "as my husband told you, I've been shoplifting since I was a little girl . . ."

"He did tell me that, and I understand that's what brought you here today, but before we get into the specifics I'd like to know a little backstory. I understand you have two living parents, one sister, is that correct?"

"Yes," Tully said. "Although Mum has dementia."

"I'm sorry to hear that."

"And Dad is getting remarried soon, to a woman my age."

"That must be hard," Dr. Shearer said sympathetically.

There was something about the sympathy that made Tully want to share more. She decided Dr. Shearer might be all right, even if he was a man.

"On top of that, my two-year-old son won't sleep in his big-boy bed and refuses to eat anything he's touched with his hands!"

It was addictive, Tully realized, getting this stuff off her chest. She was starting to feel positively giddy with it.

"*And* my husband lost nearly all of our money in a bad investment!"

Dr. Shearer scribbled something on the notepad in front of him. *Make them pay up front*, probably. Then he looked up. "You certainly have a lot going on. What about support? Who do you turn to for support during all of this?"

"Sonny, usually. But he's not speaking to me much these days."

"What about your sister? Are you close?"

Tully hesitated. "If you'd asked me a few months ago, I'd have said no. But things have been better between us lately. As children, we were super competitive with each other. I wanted to beat her at everything."

"Why do you think that was?" Dr. Shearer said.

Tully didn't know. Suffice to say, she didn't care about beating Rachel at anything now.

"Go back to your childhood," Dr. Shearer said. "This stuff is actually very important. What happens in our childhood shapes us—our ability to relate to people, to manage our emotions, to control our impulses. There'll be a reason you felt competitive with your sister as a child, just as there'll be a reason that competitiveness has subsided."

Tully thought harder, trying to unearth some significant childhood memories. Funnily enough, all the ones that presented themselves featured her dad's voice.

Come on, Tully! You can beat her. She has the strength but you're faster.

You can ride your bike faster than that. Rachel can do it and she's younger than you.

Rachel climbed that tree all the way to the top. How high did you climb?

Sure, he'd been a competitive dad, but Tully had been fine with it, because he was usually on her side. Often, during a race, he'd even maneuver himself in front of Rachel to slow her down. Once, he even tripped Rachel when it looked like she was going to beat Tully. Later, when Dad was putting her to bed, they'd laughed about it. Tully felt like it was a little secret between them. A few weeks later, though, Tully found she didn't find it so funny. Because, that time, she could have sworn that her dad tripped *her*.

32

RACHEL

Rachel was delivering a cake to a client. She liked to do that from time to time—it made her nostalgic for the early days of her business, when she used to personally deliver every item to the client. And there was no doubt she felt a certain spring in her step today. She and Darcy had spent most of the previous few days kissing like teenagers. That was as far as she was ready to take it— which felt embarrassing and strange for a thirty-five-year-old woman, but Darcy seemed perfectly happy with the arrangement, so for now Rachel wasn't going to question herself. She also wasn't going to question the fact that, after he left this morning, she opened and finished a small block of chocolate.

Where I come from we call that survival.

Today she was delivering a birthday cake in the shape of a football. Rachel had assumed it was for a child until she received the instructions from Nancy, the man's wife. *Please write: Happy 72nd birthday, Jimmy.*

"I take it Jimmy is a football fan?" Rachel asked, when Nancy arrived at the door. There was, Rachel noticed, no sign of a party underway.

"He most certainly is," Nancy said. "He played for the Hawks for seventeen years. But that was a long time ago."

"No way! I'm a Hawks fan."

"Naturally—they're the best team," Nancy said with a wink. She opened the box. "Ah, look at this. It's perfect. He'll love it."

"Are you having a party?"

"Well, no. Jimmy isn't a big fan of crowds these days. He has dementia, you see."

"I'm sorry to hear that."

Rachel thought about adding that her mum did too, but she held it back. So often when she told someone about Mum's dementia they interrupted, desperate for her to know about their mum, their friend, their husband who also had it. Sometimes it was nice to keep the attention on the person who was sharing.

"We think it was the football," she said, lowering her voice. "So many falls and knocks to the head. I can't even count the number of times he was in hospital for concussion."

"And you think that caused the dementia?"

Nancy shrugged. "They don't know for sure. But there *is* a proven link between repeated head trauma and dementia later in life."

"Really?" Rachel thought of her mother. The head injuries she had sustained over the years from various trips and falls. *I'm so clumsy,* Mum always used to say. *Always tripping or stumbling on something.* "I didn't know that."

Nancy smiled sadly. "You see a lot of these ex-sportspeople developing symptoms in their fifties and sixties. They think they're invincible when they're young, but then it turns out they aren't."

"I know what you mean," Rachel said, then added, "I hope Jimmy enjoys the cake."

Nancy thanked her again, and then shut the door. But as Rachel made her way back to the car, she realized something. Despite her mother being notorious for clumsiness, Rachel had never seen her stumble. Not once.

33

HEATHER

Look, Miles!" Stephen said. "Bluey has come to your party!"

Stephen pointed at Sonny, who was encased in an inflatable dog costume and waving a giant hand at the dozen little party guests, who were exhilarated at Bluey's arrival. Miles was not exhilarated. He let out a piercing scream and cowered behind Stephen, his little arms wrapped around his grandfather's knees as he shrieked, "No Bluey! No Bluey!"

It was Heather's very first kids' birthday party. She'd been looking forward to it. She'd spent days researching the perfect present before deciding on a wooden fire station, complete with fire trucks, firemen, and a pole (though now she was wondering if she should have got the Bluey paraphernalia she'd seen at Big W for a quarter of the price).

Pam was at the party too. Stephen had insisted. "Why should she miss out on her grandson's third birthday party?" he said.

The girls had been less enthusiastic about Pam's attendance. Tully had worried it might be unsettling for Pam, and Rachel had worried Pam might upset the kids. And, admittedly, there'd been a moment upon arrival when Pam had accused Sonny of stealing her handbag (calling him a "shifty son of a bitch"). But now that she'd settled in, Pam did seem to be coping pretty well. When the little children came up to her to show her something or hand her a piece of food they were finished with, she just smiled and patted them on the head.

Heather had to admit the party was more low-key than she'd expected. She'd heard so much about the designer toddler parties people had these days, the ones that looked like they belonged on Pinterest rather than in real life. This, apart from its beautiful setting—Sonny and Tully's home—was refreshingly simple: a dozen kids running about on the lawn, a man in a dog suit, party games and a piñata (filled with actual lollies rather than nutritious snacks). There was no official party entertainer, no designer goodie bags, no painstaking decorations beyond balloons and a generic cardboard HAPPY BIRTHDAY banner. The food table boasted party pies, sausage rolls, fairy bread, and a fruit platter. The only thing faintly fancy about the party was the cake, prepared by Rachel, in the shape of the dog—Bluey.

"What's the problem, buddy?" Stephen said to Miles when the boy continued to scream. "I thought you loved Bluey."

"No!" Miles cried. "Too big! Bluey go away!"

Tully appeared, directing Sonny to the far end of the garden, and Stephen squatted down in front of Miles. "I see what you mean," Stephen replied seriously. "Then again, you're pretty big too. You're three now, don't forget. And I think you've grown a bit taller since I last saw you." While he was talking, Stephen swept Miles up and planted the boy on his shoulders. "See? Look how tall you are. You're even taller than Bluey!"

This did the trick, sort of. Miles stopped screaming, although he continued to look wary. Stephen was the perfect grandfather, Heather decided. The perfect dad. The perfect doctor. Now she just needed to be perfect too.

There were a few glasses of champagne dotted around the coffee tables, but by and large, it was a dry party. Heather was fine with that. She hadn't touched a drop since the night she punched Stephen and she didn't plan to. As ashamed as she was by what had happened the night of the dinner party, it had proved to be a turning point for them. Since then, things had been good. Calm. Lots of evenings in watching documentaries and cooking very basic meals in a very un-basic kitchen. They'd even had a lunch date with Mary and Michael—just the four of them this time—and it had been an unmitigated success. Afterward, when Heather commented on how lovely it had been, Stephen had replied, *And that is how lovely everything can be.* He stopped short of saying, *if you don't drink,* but Heather had heard the subtext.

"The cake looks amazing," Heather told Rachel.

Rachel smiled. "I haven't made Bluey before. But I like a challenge."

"Stephen's birthday is coming up," Heather said. "I'll have to get you to make his cake."

"Stephen likes mud cake," Pam said to no one in particular. She was still seated on her chair just a few paces away. They all looked down at her in surprise.

"You're right, Mum," Rachel agreed. "Chocolate mud cake is Dad's favorite."

Rachel and Tully squatted down in front of her. They moved carefully, hesitantly, as if they feared any sudden movement might break the spell.

"What's your favorite?" Rachel asked her.

"Glazed lemon cake," Pam said without missing a beat.

The girls laughed. "That's right," Tully said. "You love lemon cake."

As they started venturing to other foods—favorite breakfast, favorite snack—Locky wandered over and started playing too. You couldn't have scripted a more lovely scene. Stephen was right, Heather realized. *Of course* this was the right place for Pam. She was exactly where she should be.

As if on cue, Stephen came over with a bright-eyed Miles still perched on his shoulders. "Is it time for the Bluey cake?" he asked. "I'd like an ear, please."

They all looked up, even Pam.

"I want an ear!" Miles cried.

"There are two ears, baby," Tully said, getting to her feet.

"And since you are the birthday boy," Stephen said, removing Miles from his shoulders and setting him back on his feet, "you can have first pick."

Miles grinned and gave Stephen a high five.

Pam stared at Stephen, her nose scrunched, as if she'd smelled something that had gone bad.

"Look out for that guy," she said, pointing at Stephen.

The warning was delivered in a quiet moment, when the music was between tracks and the lion's share of the kids had gone inside to scavenge from the party food table.

"What guy?" Tully said. "You mean Dad?"

But Pam wasn't listening to them; her gaze was still on Stephen. "He made my life hell," she snarled. "I should've left him years ago." She spat.

"Yuck, Grandma," Miles said.

Stephen patted Miles's head. "It's all right, buddy. Grandma's just a little confused."

"How convenient," Pam said.

Stephen opened his mouth, but before he could speak, Sonny appeared in his Bluey costume again and Miles let out a particularly shrill scream that had everyone wincing.

"For Christ's sake," Stephen said to Sonny. "Will you take off that bloody suit? You're terrifying the poor kid."

"Go on, Sonny," Tully said, standing. "I'll bring the rest of the kids in for pass-the-parcel."

Everyone shuffled toward the house, grateful, Heather assumed, that they could move on from the awkwardness of Pam's comments. But after everyone was inside, Heather noticed Rachel was still by her mother's side, looking at her mother closely. After several seconds, she glanced back toward the house. She was staring straight at Stephen.

34

TULLY

"What do you mean you took them?" the lady behind the counter of the department store said to Tully.

Dr. Shearer believed that returning as many stolen items as she could was an important step in Tully's recovery. She wouldn't be able to return every item, as a lot of things had been thrown out, given away, or donated, but he suggested she start by choosing items that she had taken recently, ones that would still be stocked, and the ones that were most valuable. The goal was both to take responsibility for what she had done and to make reparations to the store where possible. Tully hadn't been keen on the idea, but she'd made a commitment to do whatever she had to do to heal.

Sonny, too, had mixed feelings about the exercise. *As a lawyer,* he said, *I'd recommend against it. If one of the shop owners calls the police, you could end up with a criminal record. But as a husband, I see that it's important for your recovery, so I think you should do it.* He added that, as a lawyer, it was a bad idea for him to go with her.

And so Tully had had to swallow her pride and ask the one other person in the world she could tell without being entirely humiliated. Rachel.

"You need to *what*?" she'd said when Tully called her.

"Return my stolen items," Tully explained. "I think it's shame therapy. I must atone for my sins."

"And what's my role?" Rachel asked. "Am I your witness?"

"Yes," Tully said. "And maybe my accomplice, if I have to evade arrest."

Up to this point, the day had not been as bad as Tully had imagined, especially with Rachel coming along for the ride. In fact, it was almost fun, in a perverse kind of way. They'd visited six stores so far, bearing items to return. From the elderly woman who patted her hand and said, "I stole the most beautiful pair of earrings from a boutique in Paris once; I still have them somewhere," to the baffled woman at the hardware store who kept repeating, "A screwdriver? You took a *screwdriver*?" everyone had seemed happier to gloss over it and move on rather than make Tully feel bad. But the lady at Myer—Judy, according to her name tag—didn't seem to have got the memo.

"Do you mean you *stole them*?" she asked, mortifyingly loudly.

"Well . . . I didn't pay for them," Tully said quietly, turning to glance at the woman who'd just lined up behind her, holding a four-pack of tea towels and a cheese board in her arms.

"You mean you forgot?"

Tully wanted to nod. *Yes, yes I forgot. Here you go, I'll pay now. Do you take Visa?* But that was not part of the deal. When Dr. Shearer first raised the idea, Tully had suggested leaving the goods in front of the shops in the middle of the night, or returning them by post, but neither of those ideas equated to "taking responsibility," which the psychologist insisted was the point of the exercise.

"No, I didn't forget," Tully said quietly. "I made a decision to take them without paying."

"So you stole them?" Judy said, impatient now.

Tully looked at Rachel. So far her sister hadn't had to speak at all, but she had come into each shop with Tully and stood beside her as she made her confession. It had been surprisingly fortifying, having her there.

"Yes," Tully said. "I stole them."

"I'm going to have to speak to the manager," Judy said, before picking up the phone and explaining the situation loud enough for most people in the vicinity to hear. When she'd hung up she said, "My manager is calling the police. Can you please wait over there?"

Tully and Rachel stepped to the side, and Judy gestured to the woman with the tea towels to step forward and began scanning her items.

Tully felt a panicky feeling start in her chest. She'd known this was a possibility. "Some people might not be forgiving," Dr. Shearer had said. "They might decide to take legal action against you, which they are within their rights to do. You have to accept that. That's part of taking responsibility too."

Tully tried to imagine going home and telling Sonny that she had been charged. It would be a disaster for him. For one thing, they couldn't afford a fine or legal representation. For another, having a wife with a criminal record would look very bad for a criminal lawyer. And she couldn't even bring herself to think about jail time. She'd done some googling and found out that, given the value of the items she'd taken, she could be imprisoned for a maximum of two years. Even though it was warranted and she deserved it, what would she say to Locky and Miles? How could she bear to be parted from them?

"Is that really necessary?" Rachel said, stepping forward. "She has the items here, they are undamaged. She has brought them back of her own accord."

"My manager said this is the procedure," Judy said.

"Look," Rachel said, lowering her voice, "my sister isn't well, okay? She's a kleptomaniac. She doesn't *mean* to steal. She doesn't need these items. Even if she did, she had the money to pay for it!"

"I'm sorry," Judy said, not looking sorry. "There's nothing I can do."

Another customer approached and Judy began to serve her.

Tully looked at Rachel.

"Let's make a run for it," Rachel said, deadpan.

It was one of those bizarre moments when they both started to laugh. It bubbled up from within, a little at first, and then more, until suddenly they were both roaring. At that moment, the manager appeared. She looked to be all of nineteen, with skintight black pants and a white shirt tied in a knot at the front. According to her name tag, she was Jazmin.

Judy nodded at them. *They're the guilty ones,* her nod said.

Jazmin, who had been looking quite authoritative, appeared a little less sure of herself.

"Uh . . . follow me, please."

Tully and Rachel nodded solemnly and followed Jazmin down a narrow corridor to a small windowless office. It was funny how far she'd fallen. Normally, Tully felt right at home in Myer. The marketing was tailored to people like her. The clothes—for both adults and children—were aimed at people like her. The salespeople smiled at her when they saw her, confident that she belonged. Now she was in a back room. She felt like one of those people on *Border Security* who'd been detained for trying to enter the country without a visa.

"Does this remind you of *Border Security*?" Rachel asked.

"That's *exactly* what I was thinking," Tully replied.

They waited in the windowless room for what felt like an eternity. It must have been part of the process: trying to "sweat them out."

"Do you think someone's going to come in with a spotlight and a glass of water?" Tully asked her sister. But Rachel's gaze was faraway, her mind somewhere else.

"It was weird, what Mum said at Miles's party, don't you think?" Rachel said. "About how Dad made her life hell and she should have left him years ago?"

"It *was* weird," Tully agreed. "But not true, obviously. You don't think she meant it?"

It took Rachel a long time to respond. So long that Tully turned to her and repeated, "You don't think she meant it?"

"No," Rachel said hesitantly. "I mean, I don't think so. But . . ."

"But what?"

"I guess I keep thinking about it in the context of the money. If Mum wanted to leave Dad, maybe . . ." Rachel paused.

"Maybe what?"

Rachel looked at her as if assessing whether Tully was up to hearing this. The answer must have been yes, because she continued, "I was going to say, it's almost as if she was saving to run away."

Tully gave a little scoff, as though the very idea was unthinkable.

Which, of course, it was. Mum and Dad had been married for thirty-eight years. They were a solid couple. Mum would never have wanted to leave him. He was her soul mate. "You can't possibly believe that," Tully said, right as the door opened and the police strolled in, with Jazmin on their heels.

"Which one of you is Mrs. Harris?"

Tully shot to her feet. "Me."

She looked at the police officers, trying to get a read on them. She'd ascertained from *Law & Order: SVU* that there were two types of cops: the thirsty-for-an-arrest type, who liked to make an example of people; and the lazy type, who couldn't be bothered with paperwork. Tully prayed for the latter, but it was hard to tell at a glance. One was a young man, probably in his twenties; the other was older, in his fifties. He had a kind, lined face. There was a fuss around who would sit where for a moment, before the older cop, who introduced himself as Sergeant Paul Harvey, offered to stand. He was the one who did the talking.

"I understand that there has been a shoplifting incident, is that correct?"

Tully nodded.

"And the items in question are a game of Uno, some Post-its, and a . . . pencil?"

"A pen," Jazmin said helpfully. "Four-color."

The police officer ignored Jazmin. "So the total value of that is . . . what, around ten dollars?"

"Twelve dollars fifty," Jazmin said.

"And, Mrs. Harris, you came here today to return the items?"

"Yes," Tully said. "And to apologize."

"I see." He focused on Tully. "Mrs. Harris, the punishment for larceny in Victoria for an offense like this is up to two years imprisonment. You may also be fined up to ten thousand dollars and have a criminal record. Do you understand that?"

Tully felt her cheeks heat up. "Yes."

The police officer looked at Jazmin. "It does seems like a severe punishment for twelve-fifty."

Jazmin didn't look like she thought so.

The police officer waited for a few seconds, then let out a loud sigh. "May I make a suggestion?"

Everyone, including Jazmin, nodded.

"I get the impression, from the fact that Mrs. Harris has returned the goods, that she is sorry for what she has done. We don't see that sort of thing in our line of work as much as I'd like to. I believe that Mrs. Harris understands the serious nature of her crime, and I hope the severity of the punishment will deter her from committing theft in the future. So, given the negligible value of the goods, my recommendation would be to return the stock into the system and let that be the end of it."

Jazmin opened her mouth. "Well I'd really need to check with—"

"If your supervisor has any problem with what I've suggested, please let them know that I would be happy to speak with them about it." He handed Jazmin his business card and nodded to his partner to stand. "Mrs. Harris, I will be making a note of this incident, which means that if you offend again, you will not be let off so lightly."

"We understand," Rachel said.

"Good. So I won't be seeing Mrs. Harris again?" he asked, but it appeared to be a rhetorical question, because the police officers left without waiting for a response.

Tully was glad that she hadn't been forced to answer the sergeant. Because the truth was, she could already feel the tension building. And when the tension rose, there was only one thing she could do to ease it. . . .

35

RACHEL

Tully was quiet as Rachel drove her home from the shopping center. It was fine with Rachel; she'd had enough drama for one day. For a while there, she'd thought she and Tully might end up in the back of a police wagon on the way to jail. It felt like the kind of thing that should have happened to them as teenagers. It occurred to Rachel that, in a way, she was having a lot of those teen experiences now, in her thirties.

"I have something for you," Tully said as they pulled into Rachel's driveway. Tully had driven to Rachel's place this morning and her car was parked out the front.

"What?"

Tully reached into her giant tote—the tote that had carried her stolen goods—and pulled out the bag of cash.

"You've been carrying that around all day?!"

Tully shrugged. "Who knows? We might have needed to bribe our way out of something." She grinned.

Rachel gaped at her. "We were with the police five minutes ago! How would you have explained it if they'd found it?"

"You would have come up with something," Tully said, unperturbed. "Anyway, this is your half."

"You keep it," Rachel said. "You need it more than I do."

"No," Tully said, thrusting it into Rachel's hands. "This half is yours. Mum would've wanted it that way."

"Fine. Well, thank you, I guess."

They both went quiet.

"Anyway," Tully said. "You never told me about your date with Darcy."

Rachel pulled up the handbrake. "Actually, it went pretty well."

"It did?"

Rachel laughed. "Yes."

Tully looked delighted, but also a little confused. "So . . . you simply waited until you'd found the most exquisite man alive before starting to date? Is that it?"

It was a fair question. Rachel had never elaborated on why she didn't date—not to anyone. And her family—Mum, Dad, and even Tully, mostly—had respected that. But maybe, with this new closeness between them, it was time to open up a little more to Tully.

"Why don't you come inside and I'll tell you the whole story?" Rachel said.

Tully's eyes widened. "About Darcy, you mean?"

"Yes," Rachel said. "Darcy . . . and all the things that came before him."

Tully nearly fell over in her eagerness to get out of the car.

36

HEATHER

It had been a month since the ill-fated dinner party at Mary and Michael's. Mostly Heather blocked that night out, pretended it never happened. She and Stephen carried on as usual, doing pleasant things like going out for lunch or visiting galleries or planning the wedding. She had to admit, the lifestyle of being coupled and childless was hard to beat. They were slaves to nothing and no one. Stephen had booked a beach house for the summer, big enough for Rachel and Tully and her family to come down and stay for as long as they wanted.

"The best bit," Stephen had said, "is that when the noise becomes too much, we can head down to the beach for a walk or go to the pub for an early dinner, and leave the parents and kids to it."

Heather couldn't wait. It would be just like the Christmas she had with Lily's family when she was younger. Except this time she wouldn't be the hanger-on, a guest. She would be in the master bedroom. It was *her* family.

Now she sat on the bathroom floor, but this time, she didn't have a drink. It was midafternoon and Stephen was at the hospital.

It was the first chance she'd had to be alone in days. It had been a momentous week. Stephen's divorce to Pam had been granted. Stephen had been appropriately reflective about it, and even spent the afternoon in the nursing home with Pam the day it came through. He really was hard to fault. That was what made her other thoughts about him so . . . confusing.

There had been an incident the night before. One of the charities that Stephen was on the board of had a cocktail party in the city. Stephen had gone straight to the function after work at the hospital, so Heather had met him there.

On arrival, a man at the door held out a tray of colorful cocktails. Heather had glanced around for Stephen before accepting one, which made her hate herself a little bit. After all, she didn't need his permission. Drinking a cocktail didn't mean she had a drinking problem. The only person who seemed to have a problem with her drinking was Stephen.

And so, with the cocktail in hand, she made her way across the room. She found Stephen holding court among an eager audience, telling a story about a group of doctors who'd started a flash mob when he was on his way into surgery that morning. Heather caught his eye as she approached, and he put his arm out to her.

"I don't know if everyone has met Heather, the lady in my life," he said proudly.

Heather smiled and waved at the familiar and unfamiliar faces.

Stephen looked happy, but his gaze had lingered for a second or two on her glass. For the next two hours, she sipped the same drink, ready to respond to any of his assertations that she was drunk. She hadn't had anything else to drink. And still the drive home had been tense.

"I only had one drink, Stephen."

"I didn't say anything."

"But you were thinking it. You have your worried face on."

"I don't have my worried face on. I didn't say anything, Heather. I don't know why you're sniping at me like this."

Sniping? Was she?

When they got home, Stephen went straight to the bathroom for a shower. After a few minutes of stewing on what she'd done, Heather decided to join him. It would be just the thing, she realized, to smooth things over between them. It was steamy in the bathroom, and she couldn't see very well, but then the shower door opened and Stephen's arm shot out. Her legs shot out from under her, and she fell, landing hard on the tiles.

"Are you all right?" Stephen said, as he picked her up. "Did you hurt yourself?" Heather shook her head, even though her back and legs were throbbing.

"It's slippery in here," he said, chidingly. "That's why I tried to grab your hand."

She didn't even try to argue with his version of events this time. She knew better.

He was right, and she was going mad.

Still.

Heather had been thinking a lot about what Pam said that day at Miles's party. That Stephen had made her life hell. Just the ramblings of an ill woman, probably. Unless . . . it wasn't? Heather was almost certain that Stephen was the good guy, the upstanding doctor, the loving husband and father that he seemed. There was only the tiniest doubt in her mind. It was minuscule really. Still, she needed to get to the bottom of it, and fast.

Because her period was late.

37

RACHEL

On Thursday, Rachel received a reply from Fiona Arthur. Or, more accurately, from Fiona's son Derek, who managed her Facebook account since Fiona was ninety-three now and lived in a nursing home. Derek didn't know of any connection between his mother and Rachel's. His mother lived in Far North Queensland, for one thing, and the Astons had neither lived nor holidayed there. Also, she was more than a quarter of a century older than Stephen and Pam. Rachel had to conclude that it wasn't her Fiona, which was beyond frustrating, because it was starting to feel like Fiona Arthur was Rachel's last hope for finding out why her mother was hoarding money.

Since she still hadn't heard back from the other two Fionas, Rachel decided to try her mum again. Since Miles's party she couldn't stop thinking about how she had looked right at Dad and told him he'd made her life hell. Logically, Rachel knew her mother wasn't in her right mind—indeed, she'd accused Rachel of stealing from her several times—yet, in light of the money she'd found, Rachel thought it was worth trying one more time.

"Hello, there," Mum said cheerily when she saw Rachel standing in the doorway.

"Hello," Rachel replied. "You look nice today."

In fact, she didn't look that great. Her shirt had a soup stain on the front and her fly was undone. But Mum didn't seem bothered, so Rachel didn't feel the need to point it out.

She took a seat in the spare chair. Normally she'd lunge straight into small talk about the weather or what she'd been baking— nothing that required too much input from Mum and certainly nothing that required much recollection. Rachel had learned that her mother found this kind of conversation soothing and it usually made for a harmonious visit. But today she couldn't help herself.

"Do you know who I am?" she asked.

Mum looked at her thoughtfully.

"I'm Rachel," she said, when her mother didn't reply.

"My daughter's name is Rachel," Mum said. "I have two daughters. Rachel and Natalie."

"Yes!" Rachel said. "That's right."

Mum smiled. "Do you know them?"

"Yes," she said. "I also know your husband Stephen."

Mum's smile stalled.

"I've never liked Stephen much, I must admit," Rachel continued, with a sick sensation of betrayal. "I always had a funny feeling about him. It's hard to explain."

Mum glanced around cagily, then lowered her voice. "Who have you been speaking to?"

"No one."

"Because I told Diana to leave it alone. She was always pestering me about Stephen, asking where I got this bruise or that."

"Diana Rothschild?"

"Yes. Pest of a woman."

Diana Rothschild was one of Mum's best friends. She'd been a bridesmaid at Mum's wedding.

"Diana thought Da— . . . Stephen had given you the bruises?"

"Yes."

"And had he?"

"Of course not."

Rachel would have found it reassuring had Mum not looked so confused and frightened.

"Are you sure, Mum?" Rachel said. "Are you sure Stephen never hurt you?"

Mum shook her head and her gaze slid away from Rachel. A moment later, she looked back. "He's married, you know."

"Who?" Rachel said.

Mum rolled her eyes. "Stephen, obviously."

Rachel took a moment to consider that. "Who is Stephen married to?"

Mum leaned in close, lowering her voice. "Her name is Fiona Arthur."

38

TULLY

Tully had always thought that her wedding was the day she reached maximum levels of manic. Even the half a Valium she'd taken that day had barely taken the edge off. She'd barely managed to sit still while she had her makeup done, and she'd stuttered her way through her vows. But she'd now realized she had a new, hidden maximum level of anxiety reserved especially for the auction of her beloved home.

If only she had some Valium handy today.

Tully had always thought it was a particularly sadistic practice of Australians, selling their homes by public auction. She yearned to be one of those people she saw on the American property shows where a "Realtor" passed on an offer that the vendors could choose to accept or reject after thinking it over or sleeping on it. The Australian way seemed unnecessarily savage, both for the buyer and the seller, forcing people to compete to be the winner when the hammer went down.

It was a bright, blue-skied day, and most of their neighbors were milling about the Harrises' front yard as if it were a garden party. Half the preschool mums were there in their activewear, with prams and coffee. Men in sportswear were shaking hands with acquaintances they'd encountered unexpectedly. Tully saw a woman from her Pilates class (Celia, whom Tully always referred to behind her back as Snobby Celia) greet a friend with a double air kiss. The friend looked familiar, but Tully couldn't quite place her. Tully knew of only two seriously interested buyers; everyone else had just come along to be lookie-loos. Tully herself had done this very thing at countless auctions. Looking into other people's homes was a particular pleasure of hers. Often, before bed, she scrolled through realestate.com.au on her iPad just looking at beautiful houses. Sonny called it "property porn." She'd gone to half a dozen auctions in her local area, simply because she'd always wanted to see the inside of a particular house, or to get an idea of her own house's worth. It had felt so normal when she'd done it. Now that she was on the other side, it felt vaguely grotesque.

Tully's family were all here, and she felt a wave of gratitude. Dad had greeted her with a kiss on the head and a handshake for Sonny, and Heather had brought her a tiny rabbit foot for luck. Tully thought it was a sweet gesture but also kind of disgusting— yet she gripped that little foot with all her might.

Rachel had arrived a few minutes ago with freshly brewed coffee for Sonny, chamomile tea in a thermos for Tully (because the last thing Tully needed was caffeine while she was so hyped up), and homemade apple cinnamon muffins for everyone (which Tully actually stress-ate, for once). Rachel was garnering even more surreptitious glances than usual, which may have been due to the fact that for the first time in forever she was wearing her hair out. Tully couldn't stop thinking about what Rachel had told her the last time they talked. She had been *raped* when she was sixteen. It felt un-imaginable that she had been carrying that secret around all these years, never telling a soul. Several times this week, as Tully reflected on it, she became so angry, so utterly furious, that her entire body began to shake. Now though, alongside the horror, Tully felt a wave of hope—that now that Rachel had shared this, maybe she'd have the chance to heal. Maybe they both would?

"Ladies and gentlemen," said the auctioneer, a good-looking young man in a supertight navy suit. "We are getting ready to kick off the auction!"

The chatter of the guests at the garden party died down.

He went into his spiel about the "blue-chip" area, the good schools, the shops nearby, the proximity to the city and the Bo-tanic Gardens. Tully looked around the Lycra-clad crowd. Who was going to bid? she wondered. Around these parts, people did bid on houses while wearing Lycra. Around these parts people had the kind of money that meant they could decide to buy a house on a whim on the way to the dog park. It wasn't beyond the realms of possibility, at least.

The auctioneer had been quite enthusiastic when he talked about sales prices the first time they chatted. In fact, some of the numbers mentioned would have been enough to wipe out most of their debt and put them back on the path to starting again. But as the open houses went on, the numbers had grown more and more conservative. By this morning, when they were trying to agree on a reserve, the numbers were looking downright depressing.

"The market has softened in the past few weeks," the real estate agent had said. "We need sellers to be realistic."

"I understand," Tully had said at the same time as Sonny had asked, "How realistic?"

The auctioneer's introductory spiel took a comically long time, leaving Tully to wonder how many of these the guy did per day. Did he ever get the houses mixed up? Or did he refer to all the properties as being located in blue-chip areas with great schools? After an eternity, he finished up by reminding everyone that a house of this caliber didn't come up very often before asking for opening bids. Tully squeezed the rabbit foot so hard that if it hadn't already been detached from the rabbit, it would be now.

The silence was deafening.

The auctioneer had warned them that this would happen. No one ever wanted to make the opening bid, and they'd likely have to offer a vendor bid in order to get things going. And that was exactly how it went. Except the vendor bid didn't get things moving either.

Tully didn't dare look at Sonny.

The auctioneer seemed unfazed. He just continued with his spiel like the cocky little fucker he was, throwing in a few words about the marble benchtops, custom cabinetry, double garage, and heated swimming pool. But at the end of it, when he called for bids—crickets.

"Come on," Sonny said under his breath, sending Tully's anxiety into a tailspin. If Sonny was getting anxious, it meant things were bad. Even the cocky, tight-suited auctioneer was looking a little dejected. Then, just when Tully thought her anxiety couldn't get any worse, she realized where she knew the woman standing by Celia from. She owned the little shop up on High Street . . . Sophie! She was the woman who'd caught Tully stealing from her shop. Tully made the connection a split second before Sophie raised her hand and made a bid on Tully's house. Not a great bid, mind you. An insultingly low bid, in fact. But fifteen minutes later, it was the bid that bought their house.

Snobby Celia cheered. Sonny swore under his breath. Tully studiously ignored Sophie and focused on smiling and waving at people who traipsed across her front garden and back out onto the street to continue with their mornings.

Irritatingly, Celia was one of the last to leave.

"My sister Sophie bought your house!" she said to Tully excitedly. "She wasn't even seriously looking, but when there were no bids she thought, *What the hell? I'll throw my hat into the ring.* Lucky for you, I suppose."

Tully kept the smile pasted onto her face, when on the inside all she could think was: *Your* sister? *Your sister is the lady from the shop? And now she's bought my house?* Tully stared at Celia, trying to read from her face what her sister might have told her. From their brief interaction, Sophie certainly seemed more discreet than Celia. And sisters could have different sensibilities; look at her and Rachel.

"Well," Tully said, "I hope she loves it. We had a lot of happy years here."

"I'm sure she will," Celia said, and then Tully saw it in her eyes. A hardening. A *knowing.* "After all, she got it for a steal."

39

RACHEL

Rachel had just fed Darcy a dinner of lamb moussaka and salad followed by a traditional Greek dessert of *galaktoboureko*, and they'd drunk a bottle of red wine. Now they were lying in each other's arms on a blanket on the floor. Rachel had expected that in this situation she'd be thinking about *that day*, but as Darcy's kisses moved from her mouth to her neck, she found it couldn't be further from her thoughts.

"Come here," Darcy said.

Rachel laughed. "I don't think I could get much closer to you."

"Try."

Rachel did. She was amazed to find that she felt safe. It was just so unexpected. For nearly twenty years, Rachel had equated being in close proximity to men with being powerless and terrified, but this felt . . . different.

"Can I do . . . this?" Darcy asked, taking the strap of her top between two fingers and sliding it down her arm.

Rachel nodded. His face was so serious, she felt an odd urge to laugh.

A few moments later, he did the other side. Her top came off, and her bra. She removed Darcy's shirt. He had the most magnificent pectoral muscles. Wordlessly, they wriggled out of their pants.

"Do you want to . . ." He gestured toward the bedroom.

"No," Rachel said. She was afraid that moving would break the spell. "Let's stay here."

Darcy was tentative to begin with. Rachel didn't know when the tentative part ended, but she knew it was okay with her. It bore no resemblance to what came before it . . . or anything else. It was like chocolate fondue. Like a mild opiate. The deepest, most intense pleasure. To compare it to what happened on the beach would be ridiculous. Like comparing soft cheese to a car axle. So it was a surprise that afterward, as she lay with her cheek against Darcy's chest and his hand running lightly up and down her spine, her mind turned back to the day on the beach.

"What are you thinking about?" Darcy asked. She was lying with her head on his chest. They were relaxed and sated and tangled in the blanket.

"I was just thinking that I . . . I wasted so much time."

Darcy rolled onto his side and propped himself onto an elbow. "Maybe. But we're here now."

"Yes. I guess I'm just kicking myself that I didn't get here sooner. I didn't realize how healing it would be, telling someone what happened."

Darcy stared at her. "You mean, you've never told anyone? Not even your parents?"

"No," she said. "It sounds weird, I know."

"Not weird. But you must have had a reason. "Explain it to me."

"Actually, I'm not sure I can. I remember seeing Dad the moment

I got home from the attack. I wanted to tell him . . . I was about to. But I couldn't bring myself to say the words."

"Why not?"

Rachel pulled the blanket up around her. "Lots of people don't report rape. Some statistics say up to ninety percent of rapes go unreported."

"I've heard that," Darcy said. "But I just assumed that meant they weren't reported to the police, not that they were never spoken of at all."

Darcy spoke gently, without judgment. And yet Rachel felt found herself feeling defensive. "Well," she said. "My instincts told me to leave it, okay?"

Darcy had a strange look on his face. He shifted on the blanket, conspicuously silent after all his questions.

"What?" Rachel said. "You think I was wrong not to say anything?"

"Look," Darcy said carefully. "I would never presume to know what was right or wrong for another person, particularly a woman who had been raped."

"But . . . ?"

"But," he said, "You say you have a close, loving family. So I guess I'm wondering why your instinct was to hide the truth from your dad."

And that was the moment Rachel started wondering the same thing.

40

TULLY

Tully should have seen it coming.

It had been a stressful week. Since the day of the auction she'd been in a bit of a downward spiral. The fact that Snobby Celia knew about her shoplifting meant it might as well have been written in the sky. Yesterday at Pilates, the room had gone silent when Tully walked in. And the moment she walked out at the end of the class, the whispers started up again. Tully could have survived the whispers at Pilates—after all, once her membership expired she wouldn't be able to afford to renew it anyway—but a few of the ladies from Pilates were also preschool mothers, and a day later the whispers were happening there as well. Tully understood. A few months ago Tully would have delighted in this kind of scandal herself. How fast things could change.

On top of all this, her relationship with Sonny was still on shaky ground. The fifty-odd thousand dollars she'd given him had gone some distance toward smoothing this ground, but the fact that their house hadn't fetched the price they'd been hoping for served to undo most of this good. Add to this the fact that Dad had set a wedding date with Heather and Tully had taken up permanent residence on Miles's floor during the evening hours, and suffice to say, there were a lot of emotions swirling in her mind when she was in the baking aisle at the supermarket.

This, she presumed, was what brought on the urge to take the bottle of vanilla extract. Whatever it was, as soon as her fingers closed around the smooth glass bottle, everything else faded away. Her handbag sat in the basket in the front of her trolley in the spot where the boys sat if they were with her. It would be so easy. She just needed to lean forward as if about to put the bottle in the trolley but drop it into her bag instead, like she'd done so many times before.

After her last session with Dr. Shearer, Tully had started on SSRIs, as well as a drug called naltrexone, which supposedly helped to control impulse-based behavior. Fat lot of good it was doing her. Beyond that, she'd been given some "exercises" to do if she found herself in this situation. The first was the most ridiculous of them all. *Breathe.* Good one, Doc, she'd wanted to say. She needed to shoplift *in order* to breathe, that was the whole point! She didn't tell Dr. Shearer this, that would be rude. Who was she to point out that the technique he'd spent his whole life studying was useless? Instead she'd just nodded and smiled . . . even muttered, *Breathe! What a wonderful idea.*

The next step was to remove herself from temptation. This was important, apparently. *Don't remove the temptation,* the psychologist had said. *Remove yourself.*

It won't be easy. In fact, it will feel entirely unnatural, he'd warned. *It might mean leaving the store. It might mean starting a conversation with someone when you least feel like it. It might mean drawing attention to yourself. Inviting attention. A circuit breaker, so to speak.*

The pressure inside her was building. Tully tried reminding herself of the guilt she would feel afterward. Lately, the guilt had become even more debilitating than the urge itself. Not to mention the terror of getting caught. After the incident at the department store, the police had put a note on her record, which meant that if she was caught shoplifting again, she would be prosecuted. She imagined having to tell Sonny she'd been caught. She imagined the boys finding out. Their friends' parents gossiping about it.

Her grip tightened on the bottle as she held it over her bag. Then, at the last minute, she dropped it onto the floor, hard.

"Whoops," Tully said as it smashed into pieces.

Three women nearby looked away from the shelves to the broken bottle. One of them was a woman about Tully's age with twin toddlers strapped into a double pram and a newborn dangling from a pouch on her chest. "Oh, phew," she said. "I thought one of my kids did it!"

"Me too," muttered another woman, whose little boy kept kicking a ball despite her begging for him to stop.

"I'll call an attendant," said the third, a helpful woman in her seventies, carrying just a small basket.

All of them smiled at each other. And Tully felt something, a tiny thing, release in her.

"Thank you," Tully said. "That would be a great help."

She couldn't wait to tell Dr. Shearer.

41

RACHEL

Rachel stood on her father's doorstep holding a box of red velvet cupcakes with cream cheese frosting. She knew Dad wouldn't be home; he always cycled on Saturday afternoons. That was why she'd chosen this time.

Heather looked surprised when she answered the door.

"Oh," she said. "Hi, Rachel."

"I brought cupcakes," she said brightly, opening the box. "To celebrate you setting the wedding date."

Heather was wearing jeans with a hoodie that belonged to Dad and she looked tired, as if she'd just woken up. "That's very sweet of you, but your dad isn't home. He's gone cycling."

"That's okay," Rachel said. "You and I can hang out."

"Oh," Heather said. "All right. Well . . . why don't you come on in."

Rachel followed Heather into the kitchen and took a seat at the counter. The place was immaculately clean, apart from a half-drunk bottle of wine on the counter, probably from the night before.

"Cup of tea?" Heather said.

"That would be lovely," Rachel replied.

Heather wandered around the kitchen, opening two cupboards before finding the correct one. There was definitely something off about her. She rubbed her stomach absently while she waited for the kettle to boil.

"Are you feeling all right?" Rachel asked.

"Fine," Heather said. She got out the teabags. "Regular tea or herbal?"

"Regular," Rachel said. "With a splash of milk. Have you done any wedding planning?"

Heather looked up, pausing from the tea-making a second. She seemed apologetic. "Listen, I'm sorry about how we announced setting the date. It must have seemed very insensitive, us bringing it up straight after the auction."

"You didn't bring it up," Rachel said. "It was Dad."

"Well, yes." She smiled. "But I did tell him it wasn't the best idea."

Rachel feigned a grimace. "I bet he didn't like that. He doesn't like to be told, does he?"

Heather looked uncertain. "Well . . ."

"I imagine he was pretty angry about what Mum said at Miles's party too. About making his life hell?"

Heather put the teabags in the mugs. "That *was* a bit weird, wasn't it?"

"I thought so. And it's not the first time Mum's said it, either. She keeps saying things like that—about Dad hurting her."

"Really?"

Rachel nodded. "I mean, she's not in her right mind clearly. I would totally discount it, if not for . . ." Rachel trailed off.

Heather was watching her intently now. "If not for what?"

"If not for the hot-water bottle."

The kettle boiled but Heather ignored it. "The *what?*"

"Didn't Dad tell you? I found a hot-water bottle stuffed with cash in with Mum's things. Nearly a hundred grand! No one knows where she got it. If she had been putting it away, she must have saved for ages."

"She stashed a hundred thousand dollars in a hot-water bottle?"

"I know, right? I've been scratching my head over it. But then, after Miles's party, I wondered . . ." Rachel trailed off again.

"Wondered *what?*"

"I don't know. I'm probably way off. But she said Dad made her life hell. Maybe she was going to use the money to leave him?"

"You think?"

Rachel shrugged. "It seems bizarre to Tully and me, as we've never seen any evidence of him being cruel to her. But I guess things can happen in private? Behind closed doors?"

Heather had paled a shade or two. Her hand touched her stomach again and Rachel started to worry she might be sick.

"Anyway, I'm not worried," Rachel continued. "If Dad was cruel to Mum, it's not the kind of thing that's a one-off. So, if Dad happened to be some kind of abusive monster, *you'd* definitely know about it, right?"

"Right," Heather said softly.

"And Dad has never . . . hurt you, right?"

Heather paused. She placed her hands on the counter, then dropped them back to her sides.

"Heather?"

But it was too late. Rachel had wanted a firm decisive no.

A quick no. She hadn't realized how much she had wanted it until that very second. "No," Heather said finally. "Of course he hasn't."

Rachel wanted to be reassured by the answer. The problem was, the pause had said it all.

42

HEATHER

Heather had gone back and forth on what she was doing. Back. Forth. Back. Forth. The proverbial pendulum. She was fairly certain it was a bad idea. She'd been working so hard to keep herself together, and a meeting like this could definitely push her over the edge. At the same time, since her visit from Rachel, she'd become increasingly desperate to get to the bottom of things. And she knew of only one person who could help her do that.

The drive took over an hour, and after that she underwent the extensive process of being scanned, searched, and directed to leave valuables in a locker. By the time she moved into the visiting area, she was already exhausted. There were about a dozen men in the room, which was about the same size as a high school classroom. Also as in a high school classroom, each man sat at a small desk, and the desks were spaced about a meter or so apart.

It took Heather a moment to locate him in the room, and when she did, she did a double take. He looked so much older. Smaller too. Admittedly it had been nearly a decade since she'd last laid eyes on her dad, and he'd spent the entirety of that time in prison, which she imagined would age a person. He was almost completely bald now. His liver-spotted head was misshapen and ugly. Wiry gray hairs grew out of the V of flesh that was exposed at the collar of his shirt. It helped her nerves a little, seeing him look so pathetic. Had he always looked like this? Or was it just his freedom that had made him look so terrifying?

He whistled when he saw her. "La-di-da . . . look at you."

She wondered what he meant. Heather had dressed down, in jeans, a black turtleneck sweater, and sneakers. It was astonishing to her that he could think she looked fancy. Maybe it was just his trademark way of insulting her without actually insulting her.

"Look at *you*," she replied neutrally, sitting down.

She hadn't contacted her father since the night he killed her mother. She'd been living in Melbourne for a few years by then, and hadn't seen either of them for months. In fact, the last time she'd seen her mum, she'd been drinking on the floor of the bathroom. Not wine anymore; she'd moved on to gin. Her dad had been the same. Heather (and her mother, clearly) had given up hoping that things would ever be different. "It's just your father," she would say, when Heather asked her about it. "He just gets funny sometimes." So when Heather received the 3:00 A.M. phone call to tell her that her mother had died by strangulation, she didn't feel shock. Why should she? Her father had been promising he'd do it for years.

For a while, she thought she might have to go to court to give evidence, but in the end she didn't have to. So, she hadn't gone to court, she hadn't gone to the prison, hadn't even picked up the phone. As far as she was concerned, it was convenient that her father was locked up—she wanted to leave that part of her life behind. If only that had been possible.

"I was surprised to hear you were visiting," he said.

"Not as surprised as me."

He laughed at this heartily, even as Heather remained stone-faced.

"To what do I owe the pleasure?" he asked, extending his legs out in front of him and crossing them at the ankle. He sounded chipper, upbeat. As if, by visiting, she'd finally cracked, just as he'd always known she would.

"I wanted to ask you something," she said, since they didn't have time to waste. They had twelve minutes from start to finish; the guards had been very specific about that. No time for getting reac-quainted.

That was fine by Heather. Fine by her dad too, it seemed. "Shoot."

"Why did you beat Mum?"

"Ah." He smiled. "So it's one of *those* visits."

Heather felt the first tingles of impending rage.

"I didn't know you were such a cliché, Heather. I thought you were more interesting than that. Been to see a therapist, have you? They said you needed to confront me? I think that's wise. I was telling your mother for years you needed therapy."

Heather snorted. "Yes. Because of *you!*"

"Yes, well, maybe you're right," he agreed, spitting on the floor.

Heather stared at him. "Were you always this vile?"

He grinned, catching the eye of another inmate and offering him an eye roll. Heather wondered what she was doing here. Then she remembered.

"I am writing an article about abusive relationships," she said. She knew her dad would like that; he enjoyed notoriety. "You won't be surprised to hear that you feature quite heavily."

His grin extended.

"I'm looking for insights into what makes a man abusive. What brings on a violent episode? What do they tell themselves to justify it? Did you ever just deny that you did it at all?"

This flummoxed him a little. Perhaps she'd used too many big words. But he appeared to be considering her questions. She guessed no one had asked him anything so specific about himself in years.

"Well, let's see," he said, after several seconds. "Why was I violent? I was violent because I wasn't appreciated. I worked hard to provide for you and your mother—a bit of gratitude would have gone a long way. Your mother was always making a fool of me. Running off with other blokes. Getting drunk and flirting. That made me wild."

It took every ounce of self-control Heather had not to pull his argument apart, starting with the fact that he'd never worked a day in his life, unless picking up unemployment benefits was a job. As for her mother running off with other blokes, Heather wasn't sure if this was true or not, but it was certainly something he'd always said. If it bothered him so much, you'd have thought he might have left her, but instead he stuck around, just flinging the accusation at her whenever they argued.

"As for denying it, that would have been futile—your mother wasn't likely to forget what I'd done."

"Did you ever try to make out that Mum had caused her own injuries?"

That stopped him for a moment. But only a moment. "Well . . . in a way, she did cause them. Like I said, your mother asked for it. She made a fool of me. Got off with half the neighborhood, did you know that?"

Even as he said it, his blue eyes flashed. It sent a chill through Heather.

Suddenly, the idea that she could ever have got anything useful out of him felt utterly ridiculous. Stephen and her dad were in different leagues. Stephen was smart, sophisticated. Her father was a buffoon. Even if they did have violence in common—*if*—it was ridiculous to think that the reason for it would be similar. It had been a mistake coming here.

"Well," she said. "That was . . . helpful. I think it's time I was going."

"Fine by me," he said, though he seemed a little less cheery now. He probably hadn't had a visitor for a while. "Though this visit was novel, I'll admit. Something to break up the day."

"I'm glad you enjoyed it," Heather said with a thick layer of sarcasm.

She made eye contact with the guard, who stood and walked slowly toward them. At the last moment, she looked back at her dad.

"How can you tell if a man is violent?" she asked.

"Ah," he said, grinning again. "Got a new fella, do you?"

The guard reached the table. "You can exit via that door," he said, pointing to the door through which Heather had entered. "You come with me," he said to Dad.

As the guard led him away, her father twisted so she could see his face. "There's one way to know for sure," he called over his shoulder.

"What is it?" Heather asked.

"Provoke him."

And then the heavy door slammed shut between them.

43

RACHEL

I know who Pamela Aston is. I used to be married to her husband Stephen.

Rachel was making brownies when she saw the name Fiona Arthur appear on her phone's screen. Even then, it took a few minutes for her to absorb it. It had been a few weeks since she'd reached out to the three Fiona Arthurs via Facebook, and she'd all but given up hope of ever hearing anything more than *Sorry, I think you have the wrong person.*

Now, she picked up the phone and read the message again.

I used to be married to her husband Stephen.

Immediately Rachel recalled her conversation with her mother. Wasn't that what she'd said? That Dad used to be married to a woman called Fiona Arthur? But if that was the case, why hadn't Dad ever mentioned it?

It didn't make sense. They weren't exactly a conservative family; Rachel and Tully would have coped with an ex-wife. Lots of Mum and Dad's friends had divorced and remarried—heck, Rachel's school friend Georgia's parents had divorced, married other people, and *then* got back together. Mum and Dad had laughed about that (most people did, including Georgia's parents). So why would Dad hide Fiona's very existence?

Meeting in person had been Rachel's idea. After going back and forth via Facebook Messenger and getting only one- or two-word responses, Rachel had decided that this wasn't going to be the best forum for getting the information she needed from Fiona. The other woman had been cagey with her personal information, seeming reluctant to reveal where she lived, which was why Rachel had suggested a public venue.

Rachel hadn't been to this café before. It wasn't particularly nice. It had big glass windows along one wall, offering a view of the car park. That could have been an advantage—enabling her to watch Fiona's arrival—if Rachel had known who she was looking for. But Fiona had a picture of a sheepdog as her Facebook profile pic, and her account was private. Rachel had told Fiona she would be wearing a green dress but Fiona had provided no corresponding information. In her mind, Rachel was picturing someone her mother's age, but who knew?

They had agreed to meet at 11:00 A.M., and at twenty past, Fiona walked in. Somehow Rachel knew immediately that it was her, and she stood and waved.

"So sorry I'm late," Fiona said as she slid into the seat opposite. "I went to the café across the street by mistake."

"No problem," Rachel said. She gave Fiona a quick once-over, noting that she did indeed seem to be around her mother's age, perhaps a touch younger. She was nicely dressed, with a short gray-blond bob. "I just ordered a coffee. Would you like something?"

"Water will be fine," Fiona said, folding her hands together on the table. Rachel noticed a tissue peeking out of her sleeve. She had a forthright way of talking that indicated she was a no-nonsense sort—or perhaps she was being brusque to hide the fact that she was nervous.

"All right," Rachel said, her voice sounding similarly brusque. "I'll get straight down to it then. As I mentioned via Messenger, I'm Stephen and Pamela Aston's daughter. My mother, Pamela, has advanced dementia and is in a nursing home, and when we were clearing out her things I found a large amount of money stuffed into a hot-water bottle. There was also a piece of paper in the bottle with my sister's name on it—and your name."

"*My* name?" Fiona's surprise appeared genuine.

"Yes. I'd never heard your name before, so I asked Dad and he said he didn't know anyone called Fiona Arthur."

Fiona raised her eyebrows. "He said that?"

Rachel nodded. "And yet, you're saying you and Dad used to be married. Do you know why he would lie?"

Fiona took a sip of water. "I'd say that's a question for your father, Rachel."

The waitress arrived and set Rachel's coffee down in front of her. Rachel ignored it. "Do you have any idea why Mum would have written your name on that piece of paper?"

"No," Fiona said. "None whatsoever."

"I thought perhaps Mum might have found out about you somehow and that's why she wrote it."

Rachel might have been imagining it, but at this Fiona looked faintly amused. "I think it's unlikely."

"Why?"

"Because your mum didn't 'find out' about me. She knew about me before I knew about her."

Rachel took a minute to digest that. "You mean . . . Mum and Dad had an affair? While you were married to Dad?" Rachel couldn't imagine it. Her parents were both such upstanding citizens. The idea of their relationship starting adulterously didn't compute somehow.

"It was a long time ago," Fiona said. "We don't need to rehash it all."

It was hard to rehash something that you'd only just learned, Rachel thought. But she decided to park that for now.

"Okay, but Mum must have been thinking about you to have written your name. She wasn't in touch with you in the last few years, was she? Even the last ten years, say?"

"Not in the last thirty-five years," Fiona said.

She looked as though she was being truthful, but who knew? Dad had lied about knowing Fiona. Mum had never mentioned that Dad had an ex-wife. What were they trying to hide?

Rachel must have looked upset, because Fiona softened.

"Listen, I'm sorry to hear about your mother, Rachel, I truly am. But I'm afraid I don't have any information that will help you. I don't know why Pam wrote my name down. Perhaps she was just confused?"

"Yes," Rachel said. "Perhaps."

"My advice would be that you speak to Stephen. He might have a good explanation for everything." She paused a second before adding: "He usually does."

Fiona asked if she could help Rachel with anything else, and when Rachel declined, she stood and made her way to the door. But after she left, Rachel realized she'd forgotten one very important question. She threw some cash onto the table and ran after Fiona, catching up with her in the car park. Fiona was getting into a blue sedan.

"One more question," Rachel said, panting. "This might sound a little strange but . . . did my dad . . . hurt you?"

Fiona held her gaze for several moments before responding. "Yes, Rachel," she said. "I'm sorry to say, he did."

Fiona waited a second or two, perhaps for any further questions. When Rachel remained silent, she nodded, shut her car door, and drove away.

44

HEATHER

Stephen stood in the front hall, dressed head-to-toe in Lycra. His bike was already on the front lawn. He went cycling every Saturday afternoon with his doctor friends and claimed it was the reason for his good mental health. He'd been looking forward to this particular ride, as he'd had a tough week. He'd lost a patient, which was always difficult, but this one had been a child. "He was just a year older than Locky," Stephen told her when he came in that night, tears welling in his eyes. He'd shaken it off after a minute or two and then quickly excused himself to take a shower. As Heather lay on the bed, listening to the sounds of the shower, she asked herself: *Could this man hurt me? Surely not.*

Now that she was eight weeks pregnant, though, she needed to be sure.

"I'm off," he called from the foyer. "I'll see you in a few hours."

"Oh," she said, following him. "Are you going for a ride? I thought we could spend some time together today."

Stephen frowned. "But Ian's already on his way."

"He won't mind, will he? It's not like you cancel on him regularly."

Stephen was utterly thrown. He glanced from the bike to Heather and back again. "I wish you had said something earlier, Heather. This is . . . awkward."

It was, she knew, her opportunity to renege. *Just go,* he wanted her to say. *We can do it another time.* But she couldn't. She needed to be unreasonable. She needed to *provoke him.*

"I'd really appreciate it," she said.

"Fine," he said. "I'll call Ian."

He wasn't delighted at the prospect. In fact, he seemed down-right irritated. It wasn't the first test, after all. This week alone, she'd arranged to meet him for lunch and then failed to turn up (she said she forgot and left her phone at home). She'd left an empty bottle of red wine in the recycling (which she hadn't drunk), and when he'd asked she said she'd shared it with a friend, and sorry about the stain on the arm of the sofa. She'd also dropped one of his hundred-dollar wineglasses on the concrete floor, shattering it into a million pieces. Every time she'd done something to press his buttons, he'd been calm and considerate. She'd decided if he passed this last test, she'd tell him about the baby. It would, after all, be the biggest provocation of all.

While Stephen called Ian, Heather went to the kitchen and pulled two wineglasses from a high cupboard.

"So," she said, when Stephen returned, "shall we have a glass of white or red?"

Stephen looked at her. It was an assessing look. "Nothing for me," he said finally. "It's a little early."

"Fair enough," she said, peering into the wine fridge. She picked out a bottle—a good one. When she stood, Stephen was right behind her.

"Heather."

He reached around her and took the bottle from her hands.

"Hey!" she said crossly. "I was going to drink that."

"Look at me," he said, spinning her around. "What's going on?"

She feigned confusion. "What do you mean?"

"You know what I mean. Something has been off with you for a while now."

She tried to take the bottle back from him, but he kept it out of her reach. She let out a groan of frustration. "Nothing is wrong, Stephen! I just want a glass of wine. Give me the *bottle*."

She lunged for the it, once, and then again. She could feel that Stephen was beginning to tire of her. First the bike ride, now this. This was not how he planned to spend his afternoon. It wouldn't take much now. His feet were bare, she noticed. She stepped forward, and pressed down hard.

"Ow," he cried. "Jesus, Heather!"

That was it. It was like the flick of a switch. She saw in his eyes what was going to happen. One minute they were standing in the kitchen, the next her back was to the fridge and his hands were around her throat. The bottle of wine smashed.

"Stop," she tried to say, but her voice was squashed by the pressure of his hands. A shiver traveled the length of her spine. What had she *done*? She'd been baiting Stephen for weeks, trying to provoke this very result. Now, she might get the proof she wanted. But it would be over her dead body.

She gurgled and gasped, staring into Stephen's eyes, which looked different now. Bluer. She could feel his thumbs against the cartilage in her neck, pressing until her body was cold and her head swam. He seemed to be doing it so easily.

"Stop," she tried again, but he didn't. She thought of her mother.

This was how she'd left the world, with hands around her throat. Heather had pictured it so many times, the fear in her mother's eyes before she became slack and slid down the wall. Now, she wouldn't have to picture it. She would experience it. And so would her baby.

The *baby*.

"I'm pregnant," she whispered. It was so quiet, she wasn't sure he would hear her, but a moment later he released her. Heather slumped to the floor. She landed in spilled wine and broken glass.

45

TULLY

M iles," Tully said. "Sit on the potty."

"Nooooooo," he cried. "I not like the potty."

"Why don't you sit on it and I'll put the TV on," Tully pleaded. "And I'll give you a chocolate!"

"NO! NO POTTY!"

It was all Tully's fault. Yesterday, when Miles taken himself to the potty unprompted, Tully had had the audacity to think that it might be a good time to start potty training. Now she understood how stupid she'd been. Even if they weren't in the middle of a financial crisis, marriage trouble and moving house, any idiot would have realized that Miles would develop a phobia of his potty. Why wouldn't he, when he developed a phobia of everything else!

"Fine," she said. "Put your nappy back on."

"No nappy! I not like nappy."

Tully swore under her breath. Half the house was packed up in boxes. The only things that remained were their clothes and some staging furniture that was getting collected tomorrow. The last thing Tully needed was for Miles to take a dump on the Persian rug. They could barely afford the bill for staging let alone an additional cleaning fee. Not that Miles gave two hoots about what they could afford. He leaped now, bare-bottomed, onto the L-shaped couch. Tully was chasing after him when her phone beeped—a text message from Michelle.

> Hey babe. Listen, I wanted to let you know, I heard some preschool mums talking about you. They said you shoplifted from that homewares shop in Armadale. I told them it was ridiculous, don't worry. Where do people even get this stuff?

Michelle finished the message with the emoji of the woman in the purple dress holding her arms out in confusion.

Tully threw down the phone and fell onto the couch beside Miles. So this was it. Her fears had been realized. There was, she supposed, some sort of comfort in it. Now she had nothing else to lose. Her marriage was a shambles, her youngest child was broken, and she'd been humiliated in her community. Really, what else was there?

The doorbell rang and Miles jumped, naked, from the couch and started running for the door. "Wait!" Tully called. "Don't answer the door. Wait for—"

But Miles didn't wait. Apparently answering the door naked didn't feature on his lengthy list of phobias. Luckily it was only Rachel. By the time Tully got there, Rachel was already holding Miles on her hip.

"I did poop on the potty," Miles told her, beaming.

"Clever boy," Rachel said. "Now, let's play hide-and-seek. You hide, I'll count. Go!"

Rachel put him down and he ran off happily toward the living room. It was like he was a different child. Why was he such an angel for everyone else?

"I think Miles hates me," Tully started, but before she could finish, Rachel took her by the arm and led her past mountains of boxes into the reception room off the foyer.

"I found Fiona Arthur," Rachel said.

Tully frowned. "Wait. Who's Fiona Arthur again?"

Rachel lowered her voice. "The woman whose name Mum wrote down."

Miles appeared in the corner of the room, made a shushing gesture to Tully, and tucked himself behind the curtains.

"Oh," Tully said. "Yes! Of course. Fiona Arthur!"

"Well . . . it turns out she was Dad's first wife."

Tully blinked. "But Dad doesn't have a first wife. Except Mum, I guess."

"That's what I thought too."

"So who told you he did? Fiona Arthur?"

"Yes."

Miles started to move impatiently behind the curtain.

"Hmmm," Rachel said loudly. "I wonder where Miles could be. Could he be under the table?"

Miles giggled loudly.

Tully said, "Well, she must be lying."

"But why? What would she have to gain by lying? Besides, I met her today, Tul. And she was credible. Apparently Mum and Dad met while he was married to Fiona, and Dad left her for Mum."

"She said that?"

"She did."

Tully's mind was boggling. Even without everything else going on in her life right now, she wasn't sure she could wrap her head around this. "But if that's true, why didn't Dad tell us?"

"I have some theories. The leading one is that Mum was saving money to leave Dad."

"What?" Tully said. "Why would she want to leave Dad?"

"This is going to sound crazy," Rachel said, "but I'm starting to suspect that Dad is abusive."

Tully opened her mouth to refute this claim, but before she could speak, Rachel held up a hand. "Why don't I tell you my reasons?"

Tully didn't respond, which Rachel must have taken as a sign to continue.

"First, Mum has suggested it more than once when I've been to see her. She's called him a sadistic bastard, and at Miles's party she warned us to look out for him and said he'd made her life hell. And I know Mum says all sorts of things—that's why I've never taken it seriously. But there's more."

"Like what?"

"Mum's dementia. Remember how perplexed the doctors were when she was diagnosed so young with no family history of the disease? Well, I've been doing some research and apparently there is a strong correlation between multiple head injuries and dementia."

Tully felt the beginnings of a headache coming on. She pressed her fingers to her temples. "So you're saying what? Mum got dementia because Dad beat her up and gave her head trauma?"

"She did get injured a lot while we were growing up. Remember all those times she had a sprained ankle or a dislocated finger?"

"Mum was very clumsy."

"So she used to say. But I don't have a single memory of her falling over or injuring herself while she was with me. Do you?"

Tully thought about that. A memory came at her—a summer

holiday when she was a kid. They were at the theme park in Arthurs Seat, doing a big tree-climbing tour. Mum had been a natural
at it. She'd danced along the branches, clambered up and down
ropes, and ridden the flying fox zip line to the end. She'd beaten
them all, including Dad.

"No," she said. "Now you mention it, I don't remember any incidents."

"All of that could be explained away, though, if it wasn't for what
Fiona said," Rachel added. "She told me he hurt her."

"So you're saying—"

"If Mum wanted to leave Dad, she would have needed to save a
lot of money. She didn't have any of her own. She didn't even have
a bank account. She might have been saving it for years."

They looked at each other for a long time.

"But do we really think Dad is abusive?" Tully said finally. "Dad?
Our dad?"

Rachel started to respond, but then she got distracted. Her gaze
darted to the corner of the room. "Uh . . . Tul?"

"What?"

"I think Miles just took a dump on the rug."

Tully closed her eyes.

46

HEATHER

Heather sat in the passenger side of Stephen's Porsche. Stephen kept shooting her pensive looks from the driver's seat. Perhaps he was worried about what she might say when they got to the hospital. If so, he needn't have worried. She wasn't going to tell anyone what had happened; she had too much shame for that. But she wasn't going to put up with it either. She'd seen Stephen's true colors now, and she'd made her decision.

Before they'd got into the car, he'd mopped up the blood, checked her arm for glass, and then wrapped it in a clean towel. She'd fallen hard, landing right on the smashed glass. Stephen thought one of her cuts might need stitches.

As they drove to the hospital, he was every inch the concerned husband, as if her injuries had been sustained as the result of a random accident rather than at his hand. Highest on his list of concerns was what she'd told him right before he let her go.

"You're really pregnant?"

Heather kept her eyes forward. "Yes."

"But . . . I thought you were on the pill?"

"I am," she said. "But I was on antibiotics a couple of months ago, so maybe it happened then. I've heard that antibiotics can lower the effectiveness of the pill. And I had that stomach bug a few weeks back—maybe I vomited up a pill? I don't know! It's a bit late to worry about that."

"Yes," he said. "Yes, you're right."

They lapsed back into silence. It occurred to Heather that she probably should have taken an Uber to the hospital. She also should have packed a bag. She didn't want to have to return to that house after this.

"I'm leaving you, Stephen," she said finally.

Stephen glanced away from the road in apparent surprise. "What?"

"What do you mean *what*? Do you really need me to explain it?"

He looked back at the road. "I'm afraid I do."

"Fine," she said. "I'm leaving because I won't allow myself to be abused a moment longer."

"Abused? Heather, what are you talking about?"

She shook her head. She wasn't going to fall for this again. "I was sober this time, Stephen, so you can't say I was drunk and confused."

"I can assure you I wasn't going to say that," he said. "Heather, can you tell me what you . . ." He paused, shook his head. "Can you tell me what you think happened back there?"

"You were there!"

"Humor me," he said.

"Fine." She glanced at him warily. "I told you I was having a drink and you pushed me up against the fridge and strangled me.

"When I told you I was pregnant you let me go, and I fell into a pile of broken glass."

Stephen was quiet for several seconds. "That's what you think happened?"

"No," she said. "That's what *happened.*"

He didn't respond.

"What's your story then?" she asked, as they pulled into the hospital car park.

"My *story?*" He laughed, but there was no humor in it. "I was trying to talk to you. I tried to take the wine bottle from you and you screamed at me. You dropped the bottle and it broke. Then you slipped in the wine on the floor. I grabbed your arm to try to stop you but you landed in the glass."

She shook her head. "That's not right. You strangled me." She lifted her hands to her throat where his hands had been. "You had your hands around my neck and I . . . I . . ."

Stephen pulled up the handbrake. "If I had my hands around your neck, Heather, where are the marks?"

Heather pulled the rearview mirror toward herself and peered at her reflection.

She couldn't see any marks, but it was dark in the car. She twisted her head back and forth.

"I'm worried about you, Heather," he said. "I think you might need to speak to someone."

Heather continued to stare at her neck in the mirror, suddenly less sure of herself. That, she realized, was why she didn't want to tell him she was pregnant. Stephen was so clever at getting her all turned around. At least with her father she knew for sure she was dealing with a monster.

"Let's just go get these stitches," she said, and she got out of the car and slammed the door.

47

TULLY

Why wasn't he wearing a nappy?!" Sonny cried, when he found Tully on her hands and knees, scrubbing the rug. "It's going to need to be professionally cleaned now. This is going to cost a fortune."

"Maybe not," Tully said, sitting back to survey the damage. "I think I've got most of—"

"God, Tully. It's just one bloody thing after another with you!"

"It's not like *I* took a dump on the rug!"

"You were in charge of him!"

"How was I supposed to know he was going to crap on the rug?"

After she'd recovered from the initial trauma, Tully had tried to find out the answer to that question herself. She hadn't yelled or even voiced frustration; she'd merely squatted down to Miles's level and said, "What happened, buddy?"

"I not know," he'd replied.

"An accident?" she suggested.

He'd looked at her with the sweetest, most earnest expression. "Not an accident."

Tully nodded. "Sometimes people do things on purpose and they don't know why. Sometimes even I do that."

"You do?"

She nodded. Then, in the most classic example of child randomness, he threw his chubby little arms around her neck.

Tully wasn't sure what she'd done right, but for some reason, she felt proud of that parenting moment. She hadn't felt anything resembling pride for months. And now Sonny had come along and ruined it.

"You know what?" she said. "Forget it. You're here now—you deal with it!"

She threw down the sponge, stood up, and walked out the door, even as Sonny shouted after her that he was sorry. She needed to get away. There was too much on her mind. Dad had another wife before Mum. Dad might be an *abuser*. Mum might have been saving money to get away from him. It felt like everything that she'd trusted to be real and true had turned out to be a mirage and now she didn't know what or who to believe.

She drove to Bunnings.

As she entered the hardware store, it was as if she'd slipped into a parallel universe. She was above herself, watching as she perused each aisle. At her last session, Dr. Shearer had asked her to describe the feeling she got before she stole something. To her surprise, she'd managed to articulate it fairly well.

"It's like that moment when, after being on keto for three weeks, someone walks past you in a food court carrying a baked potato with sour cream and bacon. You can try to think of other things, but thoughts of that potato haunt you day and night. You can try to satisfy yourself with a bit of chicken or an egg, but you know you're kidding yourself. The fact is, the moment you saw that potato, a clock started ticking until the moment you'd eat it. In most cases, it's better to just eat it and be done with it."

Now, in aisle 37, Tully stood in front of a wall of spray paint. She wanted all of it. Everything. She wanted . . . the baked potato.

Her mind was a tumble dryer of thoughts and feelings. The obvious answer was that Rachel was wrong about Dad. Indeed, her theory was nothing more than a cobbled-together jumble of insinuations from less-than-credible sources. But there was some stuff that was hard to explain away. Like the fact that Dad had kept his previous wife a secret. If she really was his wife.

Tully took one tin of spray paint and shoved it into her bra.

As she walked the aisles, memories filled her mind—snapshots, really—of moments with Dad. Moments when he'd been short with her. Moments when he'd pitted her against Rachel for no apparent reason. Moments when he was unnecessarily mean, or rough, or unfair.

Tully strolled down the next aisle. Garden lamps. Two of them went into the legs of her stretchy pants. She still couldn't breathe. A tin of chalk paint went up her sweater. A Phillips screwdriver down the back of her shirt. A packet of thumbtacks into her pocket. Some 3M hooks in her undies.

People around her were watching, obviously. She looked like a Michelin man, bulging with goods. Tully didn't care. A little boy around Miles's age pointed at her and laughed, and his mother grabbed his arm and dragged him away. Tully didn't care about any of it. All she cared about was the release. The sweet, sweet release of potato after weeks of chicken. Nothing else mattered until she'd finished the last bite.

When she couldn't physically carry another item, she strolled toward the exit. When the manager approached, she wasn't even surprised or upset.

"Excuse me, ma'am," he said politely. His name badge read TRENT, ASSISTANT MANAGER. "Can you show me what you've got down your shirt and your pants?"

"I'm sorry," Tully said, still walking. "I can't."

"In that case, ma'am, I'm going to have to detain you while I call the police." He gestured to a colleague of his, a woman. "Rhiannon will take you to my office to wait for them."

"You can't detain me," Tully said. "It's against my human rights."

As a lawyer's wife, she hated herself at this moment. Sonny and Tully routinely chortled about the rights people seemed to think they had. But it was enough to make Trent, Assistant Manager, unsure of himself.

"We have several witnesses, including staff, who saw you putting items inside your clothing," Trent said. "Which means we *can* detain you."

"How?" Tully said. "Because you're not allowed to physically put your hands on me . . . that's assault."

She wasn't sure what she was doing. Going mad, probably. It was as though she was in some suspended version of the real world, in which she could say whatever she wanted and do whatever she wanted. She strode toward the exit. "Bye, Trent."

The police pulled into the car park as she got into her car. She watched the officer walk to the front door and then watched Trent point to her. By the time Tully was reversing out of her parking space, another police officer was tapping on the driver's-side window.

"I'm going to have to ask you to get out of the car," the officer said to her, when she refused to open the window.

"I'm sorry," Tully called, not stopping. "I'm late to pick up my son."

"I am asking you TO STOP AND GET OUT OF YOUR CAR," the policeman repeated, raising his voice.

Tully turned up the radio and drove away.

48

HEATHER

Seventeen stitches," the young ER doctor told Heather. Actually he told Stephen, and Heather just happened to be there to hear it. The doctor had practically swooned when Stephen walked in— all the hospital staff had. It was as if Mick Jagger, or Barack Obama, or Jesus Christ had showed up in the ER. Heather had to confess that seeing him like this, so admired and revered, made him more attractive in her eyes. He stood taller, his eyes shone brighter. He was so comfortable in this environment, nodding at other doctors and waving at nurses and administrative people. Everyone knew him. Everyone. Heather had been seen right away, a perk of his position in the hospital. She had been examined, scanned, stitched, and cleaned up and they'd only been here a little over half an hour.

What would all these people think, Heather wondered, *if I told them what you'd done to me?*

"How is the pain?" the doctor asked.

"It's a little sore," Heather admitted.

"I can give you something for that."

"Oh no," Heather said quickly. "It's nothing I can't manage."

"Are you sure?" the doctor said. "You don't need to be a hero."

"I'm fine," Heather assured him. "But thank you."

"All right then, I'll leave you to get dressed." Heather had changed into a hospital gown for her scans. "If you are worried about anything at all, of course you can come back. But I'd say you're in good hands with Dr. Aston."

Stephen thanked the young doctor and he left the room. When he was gone, Stephen turned to her. "He's right about the pain, Heather. You don't need to be a hero."

"In case you'd forgotten," Heather said, "I'm pregnant."

"I hadn't forgotten," he said patiently. "But there are medications which are safe to take while pregnant."

Heather hesitated. Her arm *was* throbbing. "Really?"

He smiled. "Trust me. I'm a doctor."

Stephen left her in the room and disappeared to find painkillers. While he was gone, Heather tried to make sense of everything. Stephen had strangled her . . . hadn't he? She had felt his hands around her neck, saw him staring into her eyes. But even now, when she looked at her reflection, there were still no marks on her. How was that possible? Was she going mad?

Stephen was gone a long time. Long enough that the scenario had gone around in her head several thousand times, and it still wasn't any clearer. When he returned he had two pills in his hand, one long and the other round. He also held a plastic cup of water.

"Are you sure these are safe?" Heather asked.

"One hundred percent certain," he said. "That's what took me so long—I had to find my obstetrician colleague to make sure."

"Thank you," she said, softening a little.

He put a hand on her leg. "You might not believe this right now, but I do want the best for you, Heather. I'm not sure what's going on, but I think that now there's a baby in the picture, we need to trust each other and know that we are in this thing together. Do you think that you can do that?"

Heather didn't know what she thought. All she knew was that the pain was getting worse, so she took the pills from him and swallowed them both in one large gulp.

49

RACHEL

As Rachel stood on her father's doorstep, she felt quite nervous. She was empty-handed this time. It felt unusual, and yet she didn't think it was the kind of visit that warranted cupcakes.

"Rachel," Dad said, when he opened the door. "This is a surprise."

"Well, you always drop in on me unannounced, so I thought it was time I returned the favor."

Dad looked tired, and not ecstatic to see her, but he opened the door wider and Rachel stepped inside. After trying and failing to reach him by phone the night before, she had woken up determined. She was going to confront him. She *had* to. And she would do it face-to-face.

"Is Heather home?" she asked, taking a seat on a barstool in the kitchen.

"Yes, but she's sleeping. We'd better keep our voices down."

Rachel looked at her watch. "Still sleeping at nine o'clock?"

He looked at her quizzically. "It's Sunday morning, Rachel. Some people like to have a lie-in."

"Not you," she said, pointing to the jogging outfit Dad was wearing.

"No, not me." He sighed, falling onto the stool beside her. "So . . . what's up?"

"What's up," she said, "is that I wanted to talk to you about Fiona Arthur."

There was that flicker of recognition again. "Rachel, I told you—"

"—that you didn't know who she was, I know. But I met Fiona yesterday and she said she used to be married to you."

The look on her father's face was surprisingly rewarding. Annoyed, but also cornered. "You met Fiona?"

"*That's* all you're going to say? Not, 'Sorry I lied to you'? Not, 'Rachel, I can explain'?"

He massaged his temples. "I wasn't aware I had to share every aspect of my life with you, Rachel."

She stared at him. "You don't. But I'm not sure why you would lie to me when I asked you a direct question."

"I'm sorry. It is a part of my life that I intended to keep private, that's all. I didn't know how important it was to you."

"It's only important because her name was written on a piece of paper inside that hot-water bottle of Mums!" she cried. "I've been trying to work out why Mum was saving all this money, and you had an essential piece of the puzzle and didn't tell me."

Dad had the decency to look contrite. "I'm sorry," he said. "Where did you find Fiona?"

"On Facebook."

"Of course on Facebook." He sighed. "Rachel, I really wish you hadn't reached out to her."

"I wish you had told me that she used to be your wife!"

"It's complicated, okay? Believe me, I had a good reason to keep it to myself."

"She said you abused her."

Dad gaped. "She said I *abused* her?"

Rachel thought back to the language Fiona had used. "She said you hurt her," she corrected.

Dad rose from his stool. "And you took that to mean I *abused* her?"

Irritatingly, this caused Rachel to falter. "Well . . . how else would I take it?"

Dad looked positively stricken. He stood up and walked over to the kettle as if to switch it on, but then turned and walked back to her. "Do you really think that of me? That I could abuse someone? Your mother?"

"I don't. But . . ."

"I don't know what is going on in this family. It's like no one knows me at all."

"What does that mean?" Rachel said.

Dad stared into space for a moment. It was uncomfortable, seeing him like this. Normally Dad was calm, in charge, in control. It had shaken him, having her question him like this. But after a few moments, he appeared to make a decision. He returned to the barstool beside her. "I did hurt, Fiona, all right? We were married for three years. We tried for a baby the entire time but she just couldn't fall pregnant. She was older than me, and her time was running out. We'd been starting to look into other options when I met your mother."

"While you were married."

"Yes. She and Fiona were friends, believe it or not. We were all friends. But when Fiona started to go into a black place, I fell in love with your mother. Eventually, I left Fiona. I have always felt dreadful about it, even though I never regretted my decision. It left Fiona in a pretty awful position. I don't suppose she would have been able to have children after that . . . Did she mention anything about children?"

"No."

He nodded. Rachel had to admit, he was doing an excellent job of feigning concern.

Finally he sighed. "Look. Your mother and I felt ashamed about how things had happened. She never even told her own mother—you know Gran would have been mortified if she thought Pam's relationship began in sin. And we both felt terrible about the way we'd hurt Fiona. I guess we didn't want you kids to know how our relationship started. But if she insinuated that I physically hurt her . . ."

"She didn't. That was my takeaway."

"Your *takeaway*! Rachel, can you please explain why in the world you would think that? Have you ever known me to be abusive? Have I ever laid a hand on you or your sister?"

"No," she said. "But Mum . . ." She stopped, finding she could barely project the words.

Dad waited. "Mum what?" he prompted, when she didn't continue.

"Mum was always getting injured."

A long silence. Dad kept blinking and screwing up his face as if he just couldn't process what she was suggesting. "And you think . . ."

"I'm trying to piece things together, Dad!" Rachel burst out. "You lied about an ex-wife who tells me you hurt her terribly. Mum left a hundred grand hidden away with a note with your ex-wife's name on it. Now, whenever I visit Mum, she says something awful about you. And I've started remembering all her funny little injuries—her falls, her knocks on the head, her broken bones. What am I supposed to think?"

"Not *this*!" Dad bellowed, clearly forgetting to keep his voice down. It reminded Rachel about Heather.

"Heather is a heavy sleeper," Rachel commented.

"Yes, well, we had a late night," Dad said.

There was something about the way he said it that piqued Rachel's interest. He had a flush of . . . guilt or something. "Did something happen?" Rachel asked.

"Heather had a fall. She cut her wrist and needed stitches, so we were at the hospital late." His face was resigned, as if he knew how she would read this. "It was an accident, Rachel," he said. When Rachel didn't reply he added, "You don't believe me." It was a statement rather than a question. There was something heartbreaking about it.

"It's just . . . a lot of accidents," she said.

Dad nodded. "So your theory is that I abused Fiona. Then I left her for your mother, whom I also abused. And now I'm abusing Heather. Is that right?" He watched her, as if waiting for a reaction, but Rachel didn't give him one. "So tell me this: How is any of it related to a hot-water bottle full of cash?"

"I think Mum was saving up to leave you," Rachel said. "She would have had to save for a long time, since you only ever gave her housekeeping money. But then, as her mind started to go, she forgot about the hot-water bottle."

"And Fiona's name was in there because . . . ?"

"I don't know. Maybe she wanted to reach out to her?"

"As fellow abused former wives of Stephen Aston?"

"Why not?" Rachel said. "She needed support from someone."

Dad lowered his head into his hands. "Well, it sounds like you've made up your mind. What is it you want from me?"

"I want the truth, Dad," she said. "All I'm asking for is the truth."

50

HEATHER

Heather was lying in bed when she heard the raised voices. It sounded like Rachel, which was strange for a Sunday morning. She lay there for a while, to give them privacy. The last thing they would want if they were having a disagreement was Heather showing up.

She rolled over in bed. Her wrist wasn't hurting anymore. The pills Stephen had given her seemed to have taken care of that. She'd slept well too. She hadn't even got up to pee—which was a first since she'd become pregnant. It was amazing how different things could look after a good night's sleep.

Just after 9:30 A.M., Stephen poked his head around the door. "Heather? How are you feeling?"

Still lying flat, she did a scan of her body. "My wrist feels better. I just feel a little . . . achy. Like I ate something bad."

"You had those pills on an empty stomach," he said. "I'll make you some toast."

Stephen returned a few moments later with the two pieces of sourdough spread with jam.

"Was that Rachel I heard before?" Heather asked, as he sat on the end of the bed.

Stephen nodded. "She dropped by. She's going through a strange time at the moment."

"I'm sorry," Heather said.

"I am too. I worried so much about Tully when Pam got sick. Rachel always seemed so competent, so emotionally in control. *I* went to her for support, for heaven's sake. But I don't think she's coping as well as I'd thought." He sighed. "Anyway, don't you worry about that. How are *you* feeling?"

"Fine, just . . . still not feeling the best. I need to use the bathroom."

Heather walked into the bathroom. It was bizarre, eating toast made by her abuser. Sharing a bed with him. Talking to him about his daughter. She was so distracted about the strangeness of it that when she sat on the toilet, she almost didn't see the blood. It was just a tiny bit; the barest stain. Only when she saw it did she register the low, dull ache in her lower belly and back. The absence of nausea. The fact that last night had been the first night she hadn't needed to get up and use the bathroom during the night. She took some paper and wiped. This time the blood was darker.

Heather thought about the painkillers Stephen had given her before they left the hospital.

"Heather?" he called. "Everything okay?"

51

TULLY

Tully's marriage was over. It was, she realized, just the last item on the never-ending list of things she'd lost. Her mother. Her father. Her dignity. Now Sonny. He'd been unhappy with her for weeks, even when she was trying her best not to steal. There was no way he would stay with her now.

She was at the police station around the corner from the hardware store, and Sonny was on his way to get her. It was one of those old-school police stations with a small foyer, a desk, and a window that slid open. She was in a tiny interview room alone, because she'd refused to give a statement. She knew things didn't look good for her. The police had CCTV footage of her taking the items.

The shame had taken longer than normal to come, perhaps due to the shock of the arrest, but now that it was here, it was epic. And not only did she have the shame of the theft, but also of being caught. What was wrong with her? Her whole life her family had joked that she was mad. Was she? Not just a little peculiar, a little quirky, but downright crazy? Perhaps she'd be admitted to some kind of asylum? Maybe, while mounting her defense, Sonny would enter a plea of insanity to keep her out of prison? The horror and shame of that was tempered only by the idea of a stint in a cool calm hospital with clean lines and muted furniture. Meals delivered and "talk therapy." She'd probably befriend a whole lot of wackos in there. Maybe she could write a book about it? A memoir of her experiences in a sanatorium. It could be a career to help her get back on her feet once she was discharged.

She was startled from her fantasy by Sonny's arrival. She heard him before she saw him. "Sonny Harris. My wife Natalie is—"

"Through here," the guy at the desk said, and then the buzzer sounded, the one that had buzzed to let Tully through. Men were so dry in terms of greetings, Tully thought.

A moment later, Sonny stood in the doorway to her little room.

"Have you admitted to anything?" he asked.

She shook her head.

"Given a statement?"

"No."

He nodded, looking relieved. Then he turned to the police officer. "Is my wife under arrest?"

"We haven't arrested her," he said. "But we have CCTV footage that leaving the store with goods concealed under her clothing, plus two witnesses. And the items amounted to nearly a thousand dollars, so it will go to court. This is your notice to appear." He handed the paperwork to Tully.

Tully tried to read Sonny's expression. He didn't look angry exactly, nor did he look forgiving. He just looked . . . tired. "Is she free to go?" he asked.

"She is," the policeman said.

Tully followed Sonny out of the room, through the buzzing

door, across the foyer, and out into the car park. They were almost at the car when he grabbed her arm, spun her around.

"Tully," he said. "What happened?"

"I can't stop," Tully replied, starting to cry. "Even though we're standing here outside a police station. Even though you're probably going to leave me and take my children away. Even though I'm a laughingstock in my community. Sonny, I can't stop." She was sobbing now, so hard she had to stop for breath. "I don't know what to do."

For a moment, Sonny stared at her, genuinely shocked. Then something changed in his expression. Tully saw the precise moment he got it. It was like a dawning, an awakening. Finally, he understood how powerless she was.

"All right," he said, putting his arms around her and letting her sob into his chest. "Shhh. It's going to be all right."

52

HEATHER

Heather and Stephen had just returned home from the hospital, the second visit in twelve hours. She lay in bed, staring at the wall.

"An anembryonic pregnancy," the doctor had said. "Also known as a blighted ovum."

The doctor explained that an anembryonic pregnancy meant the sac and placenta had grown, but the baby had not.

"It's like the body was tricked into thinking it was pregnant," he explained. "It stopped your periods, started creating the hormones, but eventually your body figured out it had been tricked and that's why you started bleeding. It could never have been a baby."

This information, which perhaps should have come as a comfort to Heather, felt like more of an assault. Not only had she lost the baby, she'd never been pregnant in the first place. She'd been tricked. Her body had been tricked. Why hadn't she and her body been smarter? It brought on a fresh wave of tears.

"I'm so sorry, Heather," Stephen said.

Now, he sat on the side of their bed, the epitome of a man in pain. It was as though the fact that he hadn't wanted this baby—the fact that he'd been involved in the death of this un-child—didn't matter now that it hadn't been a real baby anyway. And perhaps that was the case? Did it matter if you killed a person who was already dead to begin with? Heather didn't know anymore.

"I'm so sorry," he repeated. "I know what a loss this must be."

"For me," she said.

She winced at the sound of her own voice. It sounded flat. Toneless. Lifeless.

"I won't pretend that having a baby was something I wanted," he said. "But I didn't want it to end this way."

"How did you want it to end?"

He sighed. "I don't know how to answer that."

She rolled over onto her back and looked at him. "Tell me the truth," she said. "Those pills . . . did they bring on the miscarriage?"

He reared back, as if not quite believing what he was hearing. "I can't believe you would ask me that."

"You didn't want a baby," she said. "It makes sense."

He peered at her, like he was trying to read the fine print at the back of her eyeballs. "Heather, people don't drug women they love to make them have miscarriages, even if they didn't want the baby. That is just madness!"

She held his gaze. "Is it?"

He threw up his hands. "I don't know what to say. Get some rest. I'll come back and check on you in a little while."

And he left.

She had to admit, it had worked out well for him. The baby was dead, and he didn't even have blood on his hands. Now he got to play the role of the grieving father-to-be. It was *perfect*.

Heather must have fallen asleep, because when she woke up, it was to a knock at the door. By the time she opened her eyes, there was a head poking around the corner.

It was Mary. Stephen's friend Mary. The lovely dinner party host, Mary.

"Sorry to barge in, I just wanted to give you these," she said, opening the door wider to reveal a large bunch of flowers.

Heather started to sit up, but Mary held up a hand. "Stay where you are. You need to rest. Do you mind if I come in?"

Heather shook her head. Oddly, she felt glad to see Mary. There was something comforting about her neatly bobbed hair, her crisp white shirt, and the scent of her perfume. Like she was being looked after by a warm, very competent mother or nurse.

Mary sat on the edge of the bed and laid the flowers gently on the bedcovers. "I heard about your loss. I'm so, so sorry."

She did indeed appear to be sorry. The genuine emotion on Mary's face undid Heather a bit.

"Oh, sweetheart," Mary said, and then, like it was the most natural thing in the world, she wrapped her arms around Heather, enveloping her in her comforting scent. "I know. It's awful. Go ahead and cry."

It was unimaginably gratifying to hear someone give her permission. It turned on a tap that Heather couldn't seem to turn off. When she finally managed to, several minutes later, she felt a little embarrassed by her outburst.

"I'm so sorry," she said. "I'm not sure what—"

Mary held up a hand. "Don't you apologize. You've suffered a terrible loss. Your hormones will be going crazy. It's absolutely normal for you to feel this way."

"Is it?" Heather said.

Mary nodded with wonderful certainty. "I'm not sure if Stephen told you, but I'm a psychologist. I actually worked in pregnancy loss and infertility for many years, so I'm very familiar with what you're going through. I've also experienced two miscarriages myself."

Heather and Mary talked for over an hour, about the women Mary had seen in her practice, about the two babies Mary lost, about the emotions Heather would go through in the coming weeks. Heather couldn't remember the last time someone had spent this much time with her, devoted to her, caring for her. There was something about it that made her feel both vulnerable and powerful.

"Thank you so much," Heather said, when Mary looked at her watch and commented on how the time had flown. "I didn't realize how much I needed to talk about all of this."

"Everyone needs to talk sometimes," Mary said. She stood up, reaching for her handbag. "If you ever wanted to talk to anyone in a professional sense, I'd be happy to recommend a colleague of mine. No pressure. You might be fine. But the offer is there if you need it."

If she had been sent here to see if Heather was crazy, she'd concealed it well. Heather felt completely disarmed. She actually thought she might take Mary up on her offer of a referral to her friend.

"Thank you, Mary," she said. "Maybe I will."

Mary smiled, putting her bag over her shoulder. "Well. I'm here if you need me. *Please, please, please* don't hesitate to contact me if you need anything at all. Promise?"

Heather smiled. "Promise."

Then, in her most disarming move yet, she leaned forward and kissed Heather's head.

"Mary?" Heather called after her, when the older woman was almost out the door.

"Yes, my love?" she said, turning.

"Do you think Stephen is a good man?"

A pause. Heather scanned her face for surprise at the question. And she did find a little. But within a second or two Mary's comforting knowingness was back. "I think he's a very good man. And he cares a lot about you, Heather."

Heather nodded. She trusted Mary. And if Mary said Stephen was a good man, he was. That was the end of the story. She guessed she'd have to contact Mary's friend after all. Because the jury was in . . . and she was clearly crazy.

53

TULLY

Sonny handed Tully a cup of tea and sat down beside her on the floor. The room felt large and echoey without furniture. She and Sonny had been talking for hours, about everything. They'd talked about Dad and Heather, about Fiona Arthur, about the possible abuse—which Sonny didn't believe. They talked about what happened to Rachel when she was sixteen. They talked about the kleptomania and the hold it had over her. They talked about Tully's fears about Miles.

Now, Tully sat with her back against the wall and sipped her tea. The boys were in bed, or "on their mattresses" to be more accurate, now that the beds had been taken away. Sonny had put them to bed single-handedly, much to Tully's frustration.

"What is wrong with me?" she demanded. "Why is Miles perfect for you but not for me? For me, he doesn't eat, he doesn't talk, he doesn't sleep. He shits on the carpet!"

"Maybe because he feels safest with you?" Sonny said. "Maybe with you he feels like he can finally let his guard down."

For some reason this brought tears to Tully's eyes.

"Everyone needs someone with whom they can let their guard down," Sonny continued. "That said, you're right, this has been going on for a while. Maybe it's time to get some outside help."

Tully nodded. "Yes. For me and Miles both."

Sonny placed his tea on the floor beside him. "I wish I'd known how much you've been hurting, Tully. I knew you were upset about your mum. And I assumed you weren't coping too well with your dad remarrying. But you never talked about it, and I was so busy with trying to sort out our financial situation . . . And I can't even begin to think about the kleptomania. To know that you've been doing this for as long as I've known you and I didn't notice . . ."

"I didn't let you notice."

"Why didn't you?" Sonny asked. "You used to be honest with me once, didn't you? At the beginning of our marriage, I loved how vulnerable you were with me. Remember that time you split your pants at the theater but you still wanted to go to drinks afterward so I spent the whole night standing right behind you so no one would see your bottom?"

"You were very unreliable," Tully said. "Every two seconds I felt a breeze and turned around and you were gone."

"And remember right after we were married when you dyed your own hair and it turned orange?"

"There was nothing funny about that," Tully said, appalled. "I had to wait two weeks for an appointment to get it fixed!"

"And during that time, whenever you left the house you wore a woolen hat with all your hair tucked underneath it, which made you look like a homeless bald lunatic! But you insisted it was better than orange hair."

"The hat was a fashion statement," Tully muttered.

"One of the things I love about you is how kooky you are. Or at least you used to be. But I've seen it less and less. Since we had the boys, it's been all routines and schedules. You seemed like you had everything under control—always talking about your 'game face' and 'no chinks in the armor.' But I guess I missed the fact that you didn't have it all under control. You've been handling all this stuff by yourself. No wonder you needed to find ways to cope."

"Thank you for saying that," Tully said. "It means a lot."

For a moment they were silent.

"Look at us, sitting here on the floor!" Sonny said, with a sad laugh.

"I kind of like it," Tully said. "It reminds me of when we were starting out and we didn't have so much to lose."

"I guess we've come full circle," Sonny said.

Tully shook her head. "Actually, now I have everything to lose. You. The boys."

"You're not going to lose us," Sonny said.

"I always thought I came from this ideal family. Mum and Dad and Rachel, I mean. I prided myself on it. Now I can't think of a more dysfunctional one."

"There can be pride in dysfunction, Tully," Sonny said. "If anyone can find pride in dysfunction, it's you."

"But what if it's more than dysfunction? What if Rachel's right and Dad was abusing Mum? What if he's abusing Heather now?"

"If that's the case," Sonny said, "then that's the next challenge we'll confront. But you can drop your game face now. I don't want to see your game face again."

"What about chinks in the armor?" Tully said.

Sonny smiled. "The chinks are my favorite thing about you, Tully. From now on," he said, "I want to see every last one."

54

HEATHER

Heather had seen Mary twice since she'd come to visit that day—not as a counselor, but as a friend. It felt so good to be able to talk, really talk. It was during one of those conversations, which Mary had said she would keep completely confidential, that Heather confessed the reality of her childhood. Mary had taken it surprisingly well. She didn't seem disgusted. Not even particularly shocked. And Heather was starting to realize how much she was projecting her expectations of a violent, destructive relationship onto a healthy one.

"We are all products of what we experienced as children," Mary had said. "Our childhood helps form the way we view things. Certainly, if you experience trauma as a child, it can lead you to believe that trauma is life and that you will never be, and indeed don't deserve to be, safe from it, even in your own home. But in your case, you *are* safe from it, Heather. It's those childhood demons that you aren't safe from. You need to address them."

And so that was exactly what Heather was doing.

Heather's psychologist was a very beautiful, very well-dressed woman in her midfifties. She had the faintest trace of a Russian accent, and a matching difficult-to-pronounce name starting with an H. "Everyone calls me Inna," she said. "You're welcome to do the same."

"Thank you," Heather said. "You can call me Heather."

"I've read the notes that you provided before you came in today. You had an extremely traumatic childhood, Heather. It's amazing you are coping as well as you are."

Heather smiled shyly. "I wouldn't say I'm coping all *that* well."

Inna crossed her legs. "Tell me about that."

And so Heather did. She told Inna about her drinking, about the miscarriage, about the "abuse."

"Tell me more about the abuse," Inna said. "I'm particularly interested in why you are so certain you are imagining it."

"Well," Heather said, "there have been several incidents where I've been injured. Once I fell down the stairs. Another time I landed in broken glass after I could have sworn Stephen strangled me."

Inna regarded her closely. "You say *you could have sworn*. But now you don't think that was the case?"

"No. I think I imagined the incidents."

Inna took a moment to digest this. "Did you have any injuries?"

"Yes. But I'd been drinking during nearly all of these incidents, and I don't have a great recollection of them. I may have been responsible for my injuries. There have also been times when I should have been injured . . . and I wasn't. Like the time I thought Stephen strangled me, but I didn't have a single mark on my neck afterward."

"Interesting." Inna made a note in her notebook. "And you said that your father strangled your mother? That's how she died?"

Heather nodded.

"What does Stephen have to say about this abuse?"

"He's horrified. He said that he would never lay a finger on me."

"And what do you think?"

"I . . . I think I believe him," Heather said. "I think maybe I internalized some of the brutality I saw against my mother and imagined it was happening to me instead. Is that possible?"

Inna appeared to consider this for a moment. "It's not my area of expertise, but I do know there is some overlap between the parts of the brain that perceive and the parts that imagine. I heard of a study done recently about how external stimuli can distort memories and even produce new, seemingly accurate memories. So in short, yes, it's possible. My question to you is, *is* that what is happening here?"

Heather thought about that.

"Don't think about it," Inna said. "Answer me from your heart, because that is where the answer lies. You know the truth better than you think you do."

Heather looked deep inside to her heart of hearts. It turned out Inna was right. The answer was right there.

THE WEDDING

After one guest's suggestion that we adjourn to the pub to await news, some of the guests go home, but most join the foot traffic to the Half Moon. As I walk, theories surround me.

"Apparently Pam had an *episode* in the chapel," a woman says. "You saw how agitated she was. Tony's father was the same when he was alive. The dementia made him violent. Once, he pushed Tony into the wall. And he was such a sweet man before!"

I hear that Pam was both the perpetrator and the victim, that

Stephen had had a heart attack, and that Tully had had an anxiety attack. Someone swears they saw one of the little boys trip and hit his head. Yet another person says a fight broke out between the daughters. It's funny how desperately the brain will seek an answer if it doesn't have one. Not knowing is not a restful state. I know this. I have never felt less rested, more agitated, than I do right now.

At the Half Moon, we are ushered into a function room. I wonder who among us had the connections to organize this. Waiters have already set up tables and a couple of waitstaff are circling with wine. This is a wealthy group, I realize. Someone will probably quietly go and take care of the bill. Or several people will argue for the right to pay it. Strange beings, these upper-middle-class men.

I decline a drink and make my way to the bathroom. A bit of a queue has formed and I stand in line behind a woman holding another woman's hat and talking to her friend while she's in the stall.

"I just hope Stephen's okay," the woman holding the hat says. "He's such a sweet man."

"I always had a crush on him," the woman behind the door said.

"Like everyone else," the woman with the hat said.

"He was always so in love with Pamela. I was actually surprised to hear he'd met someone else while she was still alive. I mean, Heather is beautiful, and seems to be very nice, but it just didn't seem like something Stephen would do. Not that I knew him that well," she added quickly. "But there are things you can tell about a person."

The toilet flushed a few seconds later, and the second woman appeared. She was probably in her midforties, pleasant-looking, with a round face and a swinging ponytail.

"I knew him well," I hear myself say. "And in fact, taking up with Heather was far more in character for him than you might think."

55

TULLY

It was the night before the wedding. Heather definitely looked happy. Tully had spent much of the evening watching her, and this fact seemed indisputable. It was a warm evening and they were on the rooftop terrace of an Italian restaurant. Heather was dressed in a white pantsuit, tanned and shiny from all her pre-wedding treatments. At intervals, she looked adoringly at Dad. It was nice, as everyone else in the room was looking at Rachel's staggeringly good-looking boyfriend, whom she'd brought along as her date.

This was the rehearsal dinner, as it were, although they hadn't rehearsed anything. Dad and Heather had been to the church earlier in the day, but Tully and Rachel hadn't been invited to that part, even though they were supposedly going to be "bridesmaids."

"Have you got some peach taffeta for them to wear?" Dad had said to Heather, when she'd asked them, a few weeks back.

Heather had just smiled. "They can wear whatever they want."

Heather hadn't been much of a bridezilla about the wedding, Tully noticed. The opposite, in fact. She seemed eerily calm. Calm enough that Tully started to believe that maybe she was telling the truth when she said Dad wasn't hurting her. Tully envied that sort of calm.

Two weeks ago, she and Sonny had moved into a small but comfortable rental home in a less-fashionable part of town. They'd removed the boys from their fancy private preschool and sent them to the community kinder instead. And she'd taken Miles to see a child psychologist, a highly recommended but unorthodox young man named Lionel who wore bright orange sweaters and glasses like Harry Potter's. Miles instantly adored him. After the initial session, Lionel's preliminary diagnosis was that Miles was a highly sensitive little boy who suffered from anxiety. He had a lot of tools to help, he said, and he thought Miles would benefit from their sessions. Tully thought of what Rachel had said: *Your son is just like you.* Sonny agreed that she was right to seek help for Miles. It made Tully feel good to be right about something.

Another upside of this was that while paying for Miles's appointment, Tully overheard the office manager saying they were looking for a new receptionist. While Tully didn't have any experience in reception, it turned out she was excellent at selling herself and by Miles's next session she'd landed herself a job. She hadn't asked if there was a staff discount for employees' children, but she intended to.

All of these life changes hadn't been without their adjustment periods, but so far Tully had managed to get through it without stealing anything. It was imperative, her lawyer told her, that no further charges were laid against her before her court date. She still saw Dr. Shearer once a week—also important when it came to her court date. Sonny and her lawyer seemed to think that she had a good chance of getting off with a fine and perhaps some community service. But it was essential that she didn't steal again. Which was all well and good, but it was proving to be a daily battle, one she had to fight each time she went to the supermarket or the newsagents, and now, with the wedding coming up, Tully felt stretched and weary. Every day, she feared, would be the day she would snap.

"I don't like this sausage roll," Locky said, holding out a half-chewed canapé.

"Oh," Tully said. "Well, there's a rubbish bin over—"

"Here," he said, depositing it in her hand and running away.

It had been Dad's idea, of course, that they should bring the boys tonight. They were family. Quite frankly, Tully would have preferred to enjoy her champagne in peace while the boys were at home with a babysitter, but that didn't appear to be an option. Across the room she watched Locky give Rachel a high five before disappearing under a tablecloth.

Rachel had been quiet this evening. Tully was worried about her. Even with her gorgeous new man on her arm, she still seemed . . . off. It was something to do with the way she looked at Dad. Since her meeting with Fiona Arthur, she'd become obsessed with the idea that Dad was an abuser. Tully herself had got caught up in it for a while, but as the weeks went by, it felt less and less feasible, especially tonight. Currently Dad was chatting to Sonny, with Miles sitting high on his shoulders, his hands covering both of Dad's eyes. Dad was in his element here, surrounded by his family. Tully wondered now how she could ever have thought him capable of hurting anyone. She chalked it up to grief. It was amazing the things grief could do.

Miles released his hands from Dad's eyes, and he made eye contact with Tully. He lifted Miles off his shoulders, handed him to Sonny, and then made his way toward her.

"Hello, sweetie," he said. He took a seat at the table beside her. "How are you doing?"

"Fine," she said. "It's a lovely night."

"It sure is. And it will be a great day tomorrow. For the whole family." Dad smiled, but his eyes were cautious. "Speaking of family, I've been thinking . . . maybe we should bring Mum to the wedding tomorrow."

Tully blinked. "*My* mum?"

He chuckled. "Well, my mum probably won't be able to make it."

A group of people walked past and Dad shook a few hands and patted a few backs. Then he returned his attention to Tully.

"I don't understand," Tully said. "Why would you want Mum at your wedding?"

"I know it sounds strange, but I've talked about it with Heather and she agrees. Your mother is a part of this family. That didn't change when we divorced. And you know how much your mum loves parties."

Tully thought of last Christmas. Mum had just moved to the nursing home and it had been a shocker of a few months with her getting confused and agitated. But Christmas Day itself, Tully had to admit, had been nice. They'd eaten lunch in the dining room with the other residents, and when the music started, Mum danced. It was lovely to see her like that.

"Maybe it's selfish, my way of wanting to believe she's happy for me, but I'd love to see her enjoying a party one last time."

Tully shook her head. "It's just such a strange idea, Dad."

"I agree. It's totally bonkers. But so what? I think we need to give up on any idea of what is normal or expected. That horse bolted for this family long ago." Dad laughed and so did Tully, a little. "We need to do what feels right for us, for Mum, and for the family. That includes you. And so I'm asking you . . . would you like Mum there?"

Tully thought about it. Part of her liked the idea. Mum did love a party, and maybe having her there would make Dad's remarriage seem like less of a betrayal.

"I guess I'd be okay with it," Tully said eventually. "I don't know if Rachel will feel the same though."

"You leave Rachel to me," Dad said with an air of confidence.

"All right," Tully said. But she wasn't sure his confidence was warranted.

56

RACHEL

Rachel and Darcy stood on the terrace, clutching their champagne glasses. It wasn't, on reflection, the perfect meet-the-family occasion. Rachel actually felt as if she was at a fundraiser for a local preschool or a work function. Sure, her dad was there, and Sonny and Tully and the boys. But the rest of the guests—mostly work colleagues of Dad's and Heather's—were strangers.

There were waiters circling with canapés, but they were few and far between. Heather had mentioned that there would be some "more substantial" food later, whatever that meant. Normally, on a night such as this, Rachel would have found the lack of information about, and control over, food unbearable, but tonight she felt okay about it. She put part of it down to the man standing by her side, but the greater part, she knew, was the fact that she'd finally started talking about what happened to her—first to Darcy and then to Tully. She had a long way to go, but last week she'd even booked an appointment with a therapist to do some more talking about it. One day, with enough talking she might even be able to manage her feelings without food. If not, she was okay with that too.

"Sorry, sweetie," Dad said, coming to stand by her side. "I haven't had much of a chance to chat to you. This is for you, Darcy." He handed the other man a beer. "I'm so glad Rachel brought you along tonight."

"It's great to be here," Darcy said.

Dad clinked his drink against Darcy's. "So," he said, after taking a sip, "I understand you're doing some work for Rachel?"

"Yes," Darcy said. "I'm one of her delivery boys. Part of her conglomerate."

Rachel restrained herself from jumping in to say that he'd actually run his own café *and* he'd just last week launched an Everything's Better Toasted food truck, but she decided against it—partly because she didn't want to apologize for Darcy, and partly because she knew Dad would have no issue with Darcy being "just a delivery man." Dad was old-fashioned in some ways, but he wasn't the type to get all "you're not good enough for my daughter." If Rachel liked him, that would be good enough for Dad. It was this kind of knowledge that made it so hard to reconcile herself to the idea that her dad was an abuser.

Over the past couple of months, she'd forced herself to consider the fact that she might have gone a little bit mad and created this idea that her dad was abusive from nothing. She'd vacillated between believing that yes, of course she'd only imagined it . . . and a little glimmer of fear that she'd been right all along. She'd also been forced to accept that, even after tracking down Fiona Arthur, she would probably never know what Mum's money was for—if it was even for anything at all. If nothing else, she'd found out that Dad had been married before. Thanks for that little nugget, Mum.

There was a loud crash from the other end of the terrace, and they all looked over to see the two little boys' heads next to an upturned table. Sonny put down his beer and started toward them.

"I'll go give Sonny a hand," Darcy said, placing his beer on a low table. He'd been playing with the boys earlier, while half a dozen women looked on, salivating. It was another feather in his cap that he was a natural with kids.

Rachel and Dad remained where they were. A moment of awkward silence passed between them. Rachel surveyed the people standing around them, but she felt Dad's eyes on her.

"He seems like a nice guy," Dad said finally. "It's nice to see you with someone."

"It's nice to be with someone," Rachel agreed, smiling at someone walking past.

"He's being good to you?"

She nodded, sipping her champagne.

"It's a good time for our family," Dad said. "There's only one thing that would make it even better."

Rachel looked at him at last. "And what's that?"

"If I could make things right with you." Dad's voice shook just the tiniest bit. "I'm sorry things have been strained between us these past few months. I should have told you about Fiona. I wish I had."

"Dad—" Rachel started.

"I've made mistakes," he said over the top of her. "But you can't really believe that I would hurt your mother, can you?" His tone was pleading.

Dad held her gaze for several moments, before his face fell.

"I just wish I understood, Rachel. Why would you start thinking this now? Did I ever lay a hand on you or your sister?"

"No," she said.

"Did your mother seem unhappy in her marriage to me?"

Rachel thought about that. Her parents had had their moments, but overall the answer was no: Pam hadn't seemed unhappy. Her mother adored her father. Rachel had never known her mother to shrink away from Dad or be afraid to voice a contrary perspective. They always seemed like a strong couple who respected each other's opinions and beliefs, even when they differed. That was what made her suspicions now so confusing.

"Listen, I know you want to figure out what that hot-water bottle money was for. I'd like to know too. I wish we could just ask your mother. There are a million times every day that I'd like to ask your mother something. I'd like to know if she remembers who I am, and if she knows who Heather is. I'd like to know if she understands how much we all love her. But there's so much in this world that we will never know, Rachel."

He sounded so sad, it stirred something in Rachel. Something intangible and slippery—a little like doubt. After all, it *was* possible that she'd got the wrong end of the stick. It was possible that she'd let her desire for closure, an answer to the mystery, cloud her judgment. It was possible that, just as Tully was shoplifting all over town, this was her way of grieving her mother.

It was possible.

"It might be too much to ask," Dad said, "but more than anything I'd love to hear you say that you believe I'd never hurt your mother. The idea that you think I could, it just . . . it keeps me awake at night."

Me too, she thought.

"I don't want you to say it if it's not true," he said. "But if it *is* true, it would mean everything to hear you say it."

Around them, the party hummed on. A waiter offered a guest

a canapé. Someone tittered with laughter. And they were inside a little bubble right in the middle of it all. Dad looked like he might cry. Rachel wanted to say it more than anything. The instinct to please her father ran deep, even now. She opened her mouth, tried curving it around the words she needed to say. But no matter how she tried, she couldn't bring herself to utter them.

57

HEATHER

This was her life, Heather thought. This was her *life*.

She was sipping champagne and nibbling canapés and laughing. The restaurant was fancy, but low-key. The guests were interesting and intelligent. The family was here, even the little boys, who tore around the place creating happy mischief. Stephen had invited some colleagues, all very nice people who congratulated her and wished her well. Mary, who'd become something of a close friend these past couple of months, was here too.

She'd continued her weekly counseling sessions with Inna, which had been wonderful, even though they had taken their toll. She was delighted to realize that her husband-to-be was not abusive, but at the same time it was hard not to be able to trust herself. If she was capable of getting something so wrong, how could she ever trust herself again? It was a perfectly normal fear, according to Inna, who assured her it would pass. The main thing was that she had things clear in her head now. Her father was a bad man. Stephen was good. The falls, the trips, the miscarriage—they were accidents. Stephen would never hurt her. He would never hurt anyone.

"Can I have everyone's attention, please?"

Heather looked around. Stephen was standing on a chair, gesturing for guests to pay attention. When he caught Heather's eye, he looked a little guilty. He'd promised not to give a speech. Heather didn't like the attention. At the same time, she knew she'd have a hard time keeping him quiet. It was a social occasion, and social occasions always brought out the emotion in Stephen.

"It is a delight to have you all here tonight," he started. "If you're here, it means that, whether you are an old or new friend, you're among my and Heather's nearest and dearest. We have had a rather . . . unconventional courtship. And I'll admit it's one that took me by surprise." At this he looked directly at Heather and smiled so warmly, she found it hard to think of anything but how lucky she was. "I have been very fortunate in my life. I've known a lot of joy. A couple of years ago, I thought my time for joy had ended. And I was okay with that. It seemed fair, after all the happiness I'd had, that I should know suffering. Now I find that I have a new chapter ahead with this amazing woman . . . I don't even know how to express my gratitude. So"—he gestured to Heather—"I'd like to raise a glass to my lovely wife-to-be, Heather Wisher. Tomorrow, Heather Aston."

Heather drained her champagne and collected another glass from a circling waiter.

"Heather Aston," everyone chorused.

Stephen climbed off his chair and came to her side. He pressed his lips against her forehead and she leaned against the solid mass of him. In the past few months, he'd become such a haven for her. Such a comfort. A week ago, after discussing it with Inna, she'd told him the truth about her parents. Inna had convinced her that Stephen wasn't going to change his feelings for her over it, and after a while she'd come to believe that. Still, she'd been unprepared for his response.

"I was wondering when you'd tell me."

Heather had stared at him. "You knew?"

He smiled sadly. "Your mother was brought into the hospital I worked at all those years ago. Doug Wisher's name was spoken for months at work. When you told me your surname and said that your parents had died, it wasn't hard to work out who you were."

"But why didn't you say anything?"

"I knew you'd tell me when you were ready."

Heather couldn't get her head around it. "You weren't worried about getting involved with a woman whose father killed her mother?"

"Only insofar as it was affecting you. Which it seems it has been these last few months. I'll admit, I was a bit heavy-handed when it came to the alcohol. I read that your dad was a drinker, and I worried about what that might mean for you. And then, when you started to have the violent episodes and were accusing me of hurting you, I worried more. I assumed you were projecting things, but I didn't want to push you to face anything you weren't ready for."

"You really are an amazing man," she said.

But it turned out that she wasn't the only one with a confession to make, and Stephen had something he wanted to get out into the open.

"I was married before Pam," he told her. "To a woman called Fiona Arthur.

"It was a long time ago, while I was in my twenties. Pam and I never told the girls about it, but they found out recently, so I told them. Now that they know, I wanted you to know too."

Heather had been surprised to learn there'd been a wife before Pam, but after the confession she had just made, she had to admit it paled in comparison. And there was something about sharing these secrets that made her feel closer to him.

"I just need you to know that you are safe with me, Heather. I would never hurt you. I promise."

"I know," she said.

And as she stood in his arms the night before their wedding, she did.

58

RACHEL

"Are we having a picnic?" Mum asked, looking at the manicured grass. It was the fourth time she'd asked in as many minutes. And, indeed, it would have been a lovely day for a picnic. The sun was shining, the sky was blue—it was a perfect spring day.

"Yes, Mum," Rachel said, and Mum beamed. She'd always loved it when she was right about something (even when she wasn't). The first time she asked, Rachel had explained that they were going to a wedding, to which Mum had of course asked, "Whose wedding?," and Rachel had looked at Tully and they'd both come up blank.

Mum was in a cheery mood, her spirits lifted perhaps by the sunny day and all the people dotted around the grass. As Dad said, Mum had always liked a party. Maybe Dad was right. About everything.

"Time to go in," Tully said, when the last of the guests had entered. Heather hadn't arrived yet, and they thought it would be wise to get Mum into the chapel before she saw the bride and asked who she was. They'd decided they weren't going to do the traditional walk down the aisle with Heather, and Rachel was grateful for that. It was going to be a strange enough day without that ceremony, and everyone decided Rachel and Tully would be far more useful looking after Mum.

Still, like good bridesmaids, they'd paid Heather a visit that morning and found her with the typical nerves—her brow a bit sweaty, her hands shaking. Rachel was glad Heather hadn't insisted that she and Tully wear elaborate matching gowns and have their hair and makeup done. Instead, Rachel had done her own makeup and chosen her own outfit—a long navy-blue dress with cap sleeves and an empire neckline. She had to say, she felt quite beautiful.

"Showtime," Tully said.

Tully entered the chapel first, and Rachel followed with Mum on her arm. It wasn't a formal procession, thank goodness. The music didn't change and people didn't stand. But most of the guests were already there, and they turned and smiled. The chapel was tiny, and people were stuffed in cheek by jowl. Still, Rachel had to admit it looked beautiful. The flowers were tasteful. There was a harp playing softly.

Mum waved to people as Rachel walked her down the aisle, as if it were her own wedding. It was funny—Rachel had definitely not been a fan of the idea of bringing Mum today, but it was actually rather a lovely touch. Periodically, Mum glanced at her, as if for reassurance, and Rachel smiled back. She didn't know if Mum recognized her today, but she knew Mum felt secure with her, and that was enough.

Rachel saw Darcy in the crowd. She was grateful he had come. Part of her thought it would be better to leave him out of it, to let her muddle through this peculiar family situation on her own, and yet there was definitely a comfort in having someone there to support her. Things had been good between them. With Darcy, she felt like she'd taken back her sexuality from that man on the beach and reclaimed it as her own. She accepted the bad things that had happened to her, as well as the good that had come from it.

They reached the altar and Rachel tried to guide Mum to her seat, but Mum continued walking toward Dad, beaming at him with recognition.

"Well, hello," she said, heading straight for him.

Rachel felt the room hold its collective breath.

"Mum," she started, but Dad just held up a hand, stopping her.

"Hello, Pamela," he said to Mum, holding out a courtly arm. "Don't you look beautiful? May I take you to your seat?"

"Aren't you a gentleman?" she said with a giggle.

Dad walked her to the front pew, and she sat beside Rachel. Rachel had to hand it to her father; the crowd loved it. You couldn't wipe the smiles off their faces.

He'd only just returned to his position at the altar when the music changed. Everyone rose. Mum stood too, looking eagerly toward the back of the room. Rachel casually took hold of her hand to prevent any more unauthorized movements.

Heather appeared, looking radiant. Her dress was off-white, an A-line with a floor-length embroidered veil. She'd decided to walk herself down the aisle, since neither of her parents were alive. There was something dignified and elegant about it.

Dad looked as proud as can be, flanked by Miles and Locky, who were looking very irritated to be in suits and kept pinching each other. Dad was every bit the image of a man in love. Mum too watched Heather coming up the aisle with a smile. When she noticed Rachel watching her, she leaned over. "Doesn't she look lovely?"

"Yes," Rachel agreed. "She does."

Heather arrived at the altar and the guests took their seats. Everyone except Mum. Rachel tugged on her hand. "Sit down, Mum."

But Mum just stood there.

"Mum," Rachel tried again quietly. She could feel a hundred sets of eyes boring into the back of her head. "Mum, can you please . . ."

But her mother shrugged her off and walked toward the altar. Toward Dad.

59

HEATHER

Heather felt unwell. Part of it was wedding-day jitters, the other part, perhaps, the drinks she'd had last night to calm her nerves. Still, she'd managed to get herself dressed and ready this morning without having a breakdown. She'd practiced her deep breathing in the car on the way over. She'd smiled at the happy faces of the guests (mostly strangers) on her way down the aisle. Then she'd seen Stephen . . . and all her nerves faded away.

Until Pam joined them at the altar.

"Hello, Pam," she said uncertainly. She could feel the tension in the room. Stephen looked apologetic.

For a moment, Heather didn't know quite what to do. Then she noticed Pam looking at her posy. "Would you like these?" Heather said, holding them out to her. "They match your outfit beautifully."

Pam beamed. "You think?"

"Definitely."

"That's very kind." Pam took the flowers and happily returned to her seat.

Crisis averted.

"All right," the celebrant said, sounding relieved. "Let's do this, shall we?"

The celebrant started by welcoming everyone. Then she went on to share some observations about love. As she talked, Heather felt Stephen's eyes on her. Kind eyes. She was doing the right thing, she was sure of it. Almost 100 percent sure. This was her fairy tale. She was having her happy ending.

She'd had a call from her dad last night. It was the second call he'd made since her visit. "Nothing else to do," he said the first time, when she'd asked why he was ringing. "Pretty boring in here." They didn't have long to chat; within a few minutes a recorded announcement informed them that the call would end in sixty seconds. In that first brief call she'd told her dad that she was an interior designer (and then she'd had to explain what that meant). Then, last night, she'd told him she was getting married. He'd been excited to hear that.

"A doctor," he said, then whistled. "Good work, Heather."

It was good work, she supposed. A girl like her, clawing her way from the bottom of society's ladder to a higher rung. No thanks to him.

The celebrant began the vows with a call for the rings. Stephen produced them from his own pockets, after announcing that he hadn't trusted his best men (Miles and Locky) with the honor. Everyone laughed.

As they continued with the proceedings, Heather noticed that Pam was starting to look a little restless. Rachel and Tully were doing their best to settle her, but eventually Stephen gestured at them to let her be. Immediately, Pam was out of her seat. She headed toward the altar determinedly. She looked like a woman on a mission, Heather thought. . . .

60

TULLY

Tully liked to think she'd become pretty zen since she'd started therapy, but she had to admit this whole affair was pushing it. It was supposed to be a wedding, for heaven's sake! Instead she felt like she was herding cats.

Dad had insisted on having Locky and Miles as his "best men"— which was all glory and cuteness for him, all pain-in-the-arse for her. She was the one who'd had to strong-arm them into tiny little dinner suits and then forbid them to play on the grass. She was the one who had little fingers poking her in the butt during the service asking if they could go outside and play and, also, were there any snacks? And, as if this circus wasn't enough, now Mum was wandering around the altar while the entire congregation ignored Dad and Heather's exchange of vows and watched her with bated breath, waiting for her to do something.

It wasn't civilized, Tully thought. This was why people liked civilized things.

Mum was standing at the altar now, holding Heather's bouquet. *What are you thinking, Mum?* Tully wondered. *Do you know what is happening? Are you aware that you are being usurped before your very eyes?* Tully wasn't sure. Mum had seemed perfectly happy at first, but she was definitely getting a little restless now. She placed her flowers on the altar table, and picked up a large candlestick. The celebrant looked a little nervous about it, but it appeared everyone had decided to pretend nothing unusual was happening. How very middle-class of them.

"I now pronounce you husband and wife," the celebrant said finally. "You may kiss the bride."

There was an outburst of cheers as Dad and Heather shared a (thankfully chaste) kiss. It startled Mum, who looked around worriedly, wielding her candlestick. Dad and Heather beamed and waved at the crowd, until the celebrant invited them into the sacristy to sign the register. They were followed by the little boys, who took off at a run. Rachel and Tully went after them, collecting Mum along the way and taking her with them, for her own safety as well as everyone else's.

"Congratulations," Tully said to Dad in the sacristy. Heather was already signing the register. It was a small room and the boys were all but bouncing off the walls.

"Thanks, sweetie," Dad said. He seemed pleased but also a little distracted by all the commotion. "Can you—"

"I'll deal with the boys," Tully said, but unfortunately it was easier said than done. She looked to Rachel for help, but her sister was trying—and failing—to prize the candlestick from Mum's grip. Each time Rachel reached for it, Mum swung it this way and that, as if it were a game. The boys thought this was wonderful and tried to join in, ducking and weaving around her. Tully wondered if Dad was finally rethinking his "family is everything" stance. Locky took a flying leap, his elbow narrowly missing his grandfather's groin.

"Tully," Dad said, the first hints of impatience starting to show.

She nodded, although in the back of her mind she was thinking, *You're the one who wanted them here.*

Rachel reached for the candlestick again, but this time Mum lifted it high in the air.

Dad sighed audibly. It was getting quite raucous now and the celebrant was looking nervous as she bent to sign her portion of the register. Miles stayed by Mum's side, leaping uselessly at the candlestick, while Locky strategically climbed onto a chair and jumped. Mum, perhaps anticipating another grab at her treasure, jerked it away—straight toward Locky's head. Tully let out a squeal. Fortunately, Dad managed to get there first.

For a moment it was calm. Tully exhaled with relief. Locky, unaware of his near miss, rolled around on the floor with his brother. Dad held the candlestick out to Rachel, and that's when Tully noticed Rachel had an odd look on her face.

Tully looked at Dad. He stood behind Mum, holding the candlestick in one hand and restraining her with the other. But there was something not quite right about it. It was the way a guard would detain an escaped prisoner, or a policeman would seize a dangerous criminal—not the way a man would hold his confused, middle-aged ex-wife. His arm was wrapped around her neck, pulling her up so her chin rested on his elbow. In wrestling, it would have been called a chokehold.

Horror spread through Tully. Dad was rigid with the effort of holding Mum, even though she was not even trying to pull away from him. And his face—it looked almost as if he were . . . enjoying it.

"Dad," Tully started, but she didn't have a chance to finish the sentence because Rachel chose that moment to seize the candlestick and lift it high above Dad's head.

61

RACHEL

The grotesque thud of the candlestick connecting with Dad's head was unlike anything Rachel had ever heard. But even worse was the feeling of his skull crumpling. He hadn't blocked, he hadn't braced; his body went limp the moment Rachel released the candlestick. Mum, free of his grasp, walked away from him with incongruent casualness. Perhaps it resembled the way she'd wanted to walk away from him for years.

Rachel had known, the moment Dad grabbed her. The way he held her—it wasn't the way someone should hold another human being; certainly not someone they loved. It was what she'd been waiting for: confirmation that'd she'd been right about him all along.

The celebrant, who'd been signing the register, jerked upright and, seeing Dad lying in a pool of blood, let out a cry. "What happened?"

No one replied, even as she dropped to her knees at Dad's side and tried in vain to find a pulse. There was something hypnotic about the way the blood seeped into the fabric of her white pantsuit.

Outside in the chapel, the harp played softly and the sound of people making small talk hung in the air. Locky and Miles lay giggling on the floor, unaware of the catastrophe that had unfolded meters away.

Tully and Heather appeared entirely frozen. Perhaps they were having the same realization as Rachel had had. *So it's true.* You *are the reason we are like this.* Tully with her neuroses. Rachel's self-destructiveness. Heather's shaking hands. Mum's dementia. Dad had made them believe that they were crazy to question him, but he had finally revealed his true colors.

Mum sat on the floor now, a few paces away, her hands over her face.

The boys paused in their wrestling when they saw the blood.

"Does Grandpa need a Band-Aid?" Miles asked.

That snapped everyone into action. The celebrant stood and ran out of the room. The harp stalled.

"Is there a doctor in the house?" she called.

62

TULLY

There was a doctor in the house. In fact, there were several. They hurried into the sacristy, removing hats and suit jackets. A man got there first, but he moved aside when an older female arrived.

She kneeled beside him. "Has someone called an ambulance?" she asked calmly.

"I'm on the phone to them now," Sonny said.

Tully hadn't realized he was standing beside her until that very moment. Holding the phone to his ear with one hand, with the other he ushered the boys away and into the care of a couple of wedding guests whom Tully didn't recognize.

"I need something to stop the bleeding," the woman said, as several more doctors arrived and Tully, Rachel, and Heather were all pushed back, out of the way. Heather was bone white and shaking. Rachel was still. Unnaturally so.

"What happened?" Sonny asked, his phone still pressed to his ear. "Who saw it?"

He looked at Tully. Tully had seen it, of course. She'd seen Rachel bring that candlestick down on Dad's head with what looked—and sounded—like incredible force. But she also saw what Dad had done to Mum a moment before that. And she had a feeling that, if Rachel hadn't done it, she would have.

Another doctor pushed past, carrying what looked like a woman's shawl, presumably to help stanch the bleeding. The movement jolted Tully from her frozen state and she stepped forward.

"Mum hit him," she said in a loud, clear voice. "With the candlestick. It was an accident. She . . . she was playing a game with the boys."

She didn't glance at Rachel, despite feeling her sister's gaze on her. She didn't look at Heather either, too afraid of what she might see.

Sonny nodded and spoke into the phone.

"No," Rachel said weakly. "Sonny, it was—"

But her voice was lost in the din, and Sonny was entirely focused on Tully.

"Where did she hit him?" he asked. "What part of the head did she connect with?"

"This part," Tully said, pointing to the back of the skull.

"Sonny," Rachel tried again. "It was—"

"—horrible," Heather said. "But let's not get into it now. We need to give them space to work on your dad."

Sonny turned and headed back into the throng to report the information to the doctors, as Mum came and stood with her daughters and Heather. Through the window, Tully could see the guests filing out of the chapel through a side door. She heard the siren of the approaching ambulance. She heard the doctors working on Dad.

The commentary between them was short and clipped. She heard one of them say, "He's not breathing. Can anyone get a pulse?"

Tully listened hard.

There was no response.

63

HEATHER

The hospital was buzzing. Two uniformed police stood at the end of the hallway, waiting to take them all to the station to give statements. Heather sat on the floor with her back against the wall, the hem of her wedding dress gray with dust and grime and blood. Her wedding shoes lay beside her. Three people had offered Heather a seat, but she'd shaken her head without even looking up. She *couldn't* move—it was taking all of her energy to merely exist. Was this what shock was like? In theory, she should have been in shock before—when her mother died or when her father was convicted of her murder—but neither of those experiences felt anything like this. That was a thin, reedy feeling, an empty quiet that preceded a storm. This was all-consuming pain—a loud, raging inferno that threatened to burn her to the ground.

She, Tully, Rachel, and Pam had followed the ambulance to the hospital, with Sonny driving. Sonny had planned to drop Pam back to the nursing home on the way, but one of Stephen's colleagues had called Rachel and told them to come to the hospital right away.

Now they were in the hallway in their wedding clothes, waiting. For what? Heather wondered. She'd seen Stephen. She knew the news wasn't going to be good. The question was . . . did she even want it to be?

It was a strange feeling, finally having her answer. All those months she'd doubted herself. All that counseling. The visit to her father! All to convince herself, and everyone else, that she was crazy. How had she fallen for it? The moment she saw Stephen holding Pam, she knew. They all knew. And yet, if Rachel hadn't brought the candlestick down on his head, she felt certain Stephen would have talked her out of what she knew. For that reason, she wouldn't let anything happen to Rachel. It could have been her that did this to Stephen. Perhaps it should have been.

"Heather," Tully said.

Heather managed to lift her head. Rachel and Tully had been joined by two doctors. One of them, she noticed, had blood on the paper booties that covered his shoes.

"Can you stand up?" Tully asked.

Heather shook her head.

"Let me help you," Sonny said, and he pulled her to her feet.

"You're Stephen's wife?" one of the doctors asked.

"Yes," Heather said, wondering if that was true. They'd exchanged their vows and signed the papers, so she supposed it was.

"I'm sorry to tell you," he started.

Even before he finished the sentence, everyone was crying. Everyone except Pam, who tugged on the doctor's arm and asked, "Can we go back to the picnic now?"

It was meant to be their wedding night, Heather thought, as she stepped out of her dirty wedding dress and laid it over a chair some hours later. Stephen had booked a hotel room in the city for them tonight. They'd sent their overnight bags there this morning. Heather imagined the bags sitting in the unoccupied room. Stephen's toiletries, his clean underpants and folded T-shirts and jeans. They'd been planning to stay in the city for two nights. Stephen hadn't been able to take any time off work, so they were going to have their honeymoon later in the year. On a yacht in the Whitsundays, if you don't mind.

Heather was too tired to shower or even wash off her makeup, so she just found one of Stephen's tracksuits in the wardrobe and pulled it on with a pair of his socks. She'd expected to wear something quite different tonight. She imagined Stephen's face, seeing her appear in his tracksuit. He'd almost certainly smile. Her favorite of his smiles: the one that was a little perplexed, but very fond. A paternal smile, she realized. Perhaps she did have father issues after all?

She lay on the bed and, finding that even climbing under the blankets was too much of an effort, pulled the throw rug over her. It was amazing, the effect a father had on a person. A father was the benchmark that told you what to expect. What to accept. And, perhaps most importantly, what to *believe* about yourself. Her father had taught her to expect nothing and to accept less. And he'd taught her to believe that she *was* nothing. Maybe she'd come to Stephen thinking that he could overturn this belief for her?

If so, he had—ironically—succeeded.

FIONA ARTHUR

AFTER THE WEDDING

I have news," a man at the next table down from me says. He rises from his chair and glances around, commanding the attention of the guests who'd come from the wedding.

I shuffle forward. I've been standing at a cocktail table, nursing the shandy I'd ordered an hour ago, waiting for this moment. I'd thought to leave several times, but the idea of going home without knowing what happened was simply unfathomable. I'd managed to avoid the lion's share of the small talk by looking distraught. Once you're a woman of a certain age, people tend to treat you as if you're fragile. The other guests have smiled kindly at me in passing, but no one has drawn me into conversation, which is fine by me.

"What is it?" someone at the back asks.

"It's Stephen," the man says. "He didn't make it."

A wave of emotion sweeps the room. Not tears. Not dramatics. A deep, heavier type of emotion. Men lower their eyes. Women sit back in their chairs. People glance from one to the other as they absorb the news, sighing deeply. I survey my own feelings but find myself padded by a thick layer of shock.

After a few moments, the chatter starts.

"It's awful," someone says.

"Tragic. And on his wedding day!"

"Do we know what happened yet?"

"Just that it was an accident. His family are with him at the hospital."

Everyone nods at this. This is good news. Surrounded by family fits the narrative everyone wants for this situation. At least, it fits much better than the possibility that one of the family members caused the harm.

A group of people return from the bar holding bottles of red wine. Pinot, apparently. Stephen's favorite. The waiters follow with wineglasses and everyone is instructed to fill their glass. When all our glasses are full, a man about Stephen's age stands.

"I'd like to raise a toast to Stephen," he says solemnly. "A good man, who lived a great life."

"To Stephen," the crowd repeats, nodding respectfully.

"To Stephen," I say quietly. "May that bastard rot in hell."

64

TULLY

Mum didn't come to the funeral. Under the circumstances, it didn't feel like the greatest idea. Dad would probably have been disappointed about that. Tully had to say, there was a bit of a thrill in being able to disappoint him from beyond the grave, after what he'd done.

She and Rachel and Heather occupied the front pew of the church. People gave them a wide berth—offering just a polite smile or brief condolences—which was fine by Tully, but also a little disconcerting. It took her a little while to realize that in fact there were only a few faces she recognized in the crowd. Mary and Michael, Elsa and David. Most of the others were colleagues or old uni friends of Stephen's—people Tully might have met once or twice but whose names she would struggle to conjure up. How often had she taken pride in how wonderfully civilized her family was, how they knew the right way to behave, the right way to do things? It turned out they were so civilized they didn't have a huge number of good friends.

It was a funny thing, attending the funeral of a man everyone thought was a hero. Several people volunteered to speak when Rachel, Heather, and Tully said they were too traumatized. All were good, competent speakers. They put on a good show. Which was appropriate since, as it turned out, putting on a good show was all Dad really cared about.

Heather was clearly uncomfortable in her role of grieving widow. Several times when people approached to offer their condolences she said, "Well, we really weren't married all that long." Once she even said, "Offer them to Pam, she was his real wife." Her odd comments were attributed to grief and shock or, later, at the wake, alcohol.

There was plenty of that; they'd made sure of it. It was the one thing they'd all agreed on when they'd met to organize the wake. It was at Dad and Heather's house, and there were plenty of capable people, like Mary and Elsa and a swarm of Mum's friends, who'd offered to order the canapés, the flowers, even clean the house for the occasion. They'd taken the ladies up on all their offers, but Tully, Heather, and Rachel insisted on purchasing the alcohol themselves. It had been a surreal experience, the three of them wandering around the bottle shop, each with a shopping cart, tossing bottles of booze in without thought or hesitation. Every now and again one of them looked at their cart, and then the other two, and decided they didn't have enough and went back for more.

Eventually, when the wake was over and the guests had departed, Tully sat in the living room with Rachel and Heather and the gigantean pile of booze and they had to concede that they might have gone a little over the top.

"We can return it," Tully suggested.

"We'll get through it," Heather replied.

She opened a bottle of red and filled up their glasses. Tully's was still half full of white, but she just shrugged and drank it anyway.

"A toast," Heather said, raising her glass. She sounded different, her accent a little broader, her words less carefully enunciated than usual. Probably the alcohol. "To shitty fathers."

Tully looked at her. "Your dad was shitty too?"

She swallowed a large mouthful of wine. "Still is."

"But I thought he died?" Tully tried to recall the circumstances of his supposed death. "In a . . . a car accident?"

"I just said he died because it sounded less shameful than saying he was in jail," Heather said. "But there's no point in lying now, is there?" She smiled, one of those heartbreakingly sad smiles. "He killed my mum. That's why he's in there."

Tully sat up. For the first time all day, she put her drink down. "Wow. Heather, I'm so sorry."

Heather waved this away. "He was always abusive. For as long as I could remember, I was afraid of him. He could be nice, sure, but I never knew when he would turn violent."

"That's awful," Rachel said, also sitting forward.

"Were you afraid of Stephen when you were growing up?" Heather asked.

"Not at all," Tully said. "That's the strangest part. How could we not have known?"

"I suppose some people are masters at keeping it hidden," Rachel said.

"It's a trait of Dad's that we inherited, Tul."

"But not anymore," Tully said.

Rachel and Heather nodded. "Not anymore."

65

RACHEL

A MONTH LATER . . .

Hi," Rachel said from the doorway of Mum's room.

Mum looked over at her blankly, which was a little frustrating, as it was the third time Rachel had visited in as many days. Since Dad's death, she found she couldn't stay away.

The day after the wedding, they'd all had to go to the police station to give statements, except Mum, who had been declared unfit by the forensic medical officer. They'd all consistently said that Mum had been the one to swing the candlestick, apart from the celebrant who said she'd been too busy signing the register to notice anything, and a hearing had determined that to be the case. It was possible that the prosecution could still charge Mum with something, but Sonny explained that even if they did, it was unlikely Mum would live long enough to face it. The event had made the papers—GROOM DIES AT THE ALTAR—but it had been written up as an accident; the story was that he'd slipped and hit his head. It was preferable to "groom murdered by daughter who then blamed killing on ex-wife with advanced dementia."

The wedding had entered Rachel's nightmares several times now. Each time, a different person held the candlestick—sometimes it was her, sometimes Tully, sometimes Heather, sometimes Fiona Arthur. Sometimes Dad wasn't hit immediately, and he fell to his knees first to beg for mercy.

She stepped farther into Mum's room. "Okay if we come in for a visit? This is my friend Darcy."

It was the third time Rachel had brought Darcy along to visit Mum. Rachel hadn't encouraged it—she hadn't even suggested it—but Darcy had insisted.

("I'm not missing the chance to meet my girlfriend's mum," he'd said.

"She's not going to know who you are, Darcy," Rachel told him. "Most likely, she won't even know who *I* am."

"Maybe not," he said. "But I'll get to see who *she* is.")

Darcy was fantastic with Mum. He had a calm, easy manner about him that relaxed and engaged her. It was hardly surprising; it had the same effect on everyone.

"How are you today, Pam?" he asked her.

Mum's eyes moved to Rachel and widened a little.

"Where'd you find him?" she asked.

She'd asked the exact same question the last time Rachel had brought Darcy to visit.

"Cup of tea, Pam?" he said. "White with one sugar, right?"

"How did you know?" Mum cried, delighted.

Mum used to love it when Tully brought boyfriends home. She'd been particularly enamored of Sonny when she first met him, and maneuvered herself into the seat beside him at Christmas, where she demanded to know everything about him. It was funny how some parts of her remained, even after her memory was gone.

While Darcy busied himself making tea, Mum looked at Rachel meaningfully.

"Where'd you find him?" she asked again.

She'd asked Rachel that about seventeen times during their last visit. Rachel was starting to feel insulted.

"He works for me," she said.

"Works for you?" Mum said. "What is it that you do?"

"I'm a baker," Rachel replied. "I've got some pictures of my cakes. Would you like to see?"

Mum nodded enthusiastically, and Rachel got out her phone and flicked to a picture of a cake she'd made recently for a christening. Mum always enjoyed looking at pictures of cakes.

"I also brought in some other pictures," Rachel said, reaching into the canvas bag she'd brought with her. "I thought you might like to look through them."

"All right," Mum said, as Darcy placed a cup of tea in front of her.

Rachel pulled some framed pictures from the bag. There were some family photos, Tully's graduation picture, a photo of Mum and Dad's wedding. In Mum's early days in care, she had found that while Mum didn't always recognize the people in the photos Rachel showed her, they usually caused a lift in her mood.

Rachel held up a picture of Tully at her debutante ball.

"Isn't she pretty?" Mum said.

Rachel held up one of Christmas just a few years back.

Mum didn't even pretend to look at it. Instead she stared at Darcy. "Where'd you find him?" she asked.

"This is a nice one," Rachel said, finding the photo she'd really wanted to show Pam. It was the earliest picture she had of Mum and Dad together. According to legend, it was taken on their third date, when they'd played lawn bowls. Mum always laughed about the fact that she wore heels because she'd thought they were going out to dinner. Rachel held her breath as Mum frowned at the photo. Was that a glimmer of recognition in her eyes? Rachel waited for her to say something. Anything. Pam didn't. Instead, she lifted the frame to her face and pressed her lips to the glass, right where Dad's face was.

66

TULLY

A hundred hours of community service. That was Tully's sentence for her theft from the hardware store. She had to admit, it was quite exciting fronting up to court. She felt like she was on one of those TV crime shows. The magistrates' court wasn't quite as exciting as the ones shown in *Law & Order: SVU*—it was mostly just traffic offenses and some quite entertaining drunk-and-disorderlies—but she'd been reasonably entertained until her name had been called.

The matter had been dealt with in a matter of minutes. The magistrate and her lawyer both seemed somewhat bored as they spoke, and Tully hadn't had to do much other than state her full name for the record. Her lawyer had been apologetic afterward; he'd tried to get her off without any punishment at all. But community service wasn't too bad. She'd been assigned to cleaning graffiti from local tennis courts and neighborhood community centers. A couple of the areas were quite close to Tully's house, and she found the exercise quite gratifying. That graffiti had been bothering her for a while.

"Come on, girls!" Tully yelled. "Elbow grease!"

She liked to think she'd taken on a bit of a leadership role in her community service group. Honestly, some of them didn't know the first thing about stain removal. Yesterday she'd gone to Bunnings—the scene of the crime—and bought better rubber gloves for everyone. The full circle of this delighted her. As she went up to the cashier to pay for the gloves, she contemplated telling the young man the story, but she suspected he wouldn't appreciate it. Youths could be so self-absorbed these days. Didn't know a good story if it came up and bit them. And so she just paid her money and took the gloves. That in itself was no small victory.

She enjoyed the banter between the ladies as they scrubbed the walls. Valerie—a woman about Tully's age whose proudest achievements were her son and the fact that she'd never paid a parking fine in her life—was one of her favorites.

"My son Carlin did this one," Valerie said, pointing to an eagle sprayed on a corner of the wall. "He knew I was cleaning down here today. Rascal." She laughed.

Tully looked at the eagle. It wasn't half bad.

"How old is Carlin?" she asked.

"Fourteen."

Tully looked at the picture again. "He's got talent."

"Yeah. Talent at making stress for his mama."

"He should go to art school," Tully said.

"I can barely get him to show up to his supermarket job. How do you think I'm gonna get him signed up to art school?"

Tully shrugged. But she made a mental note to make some inquiries about scholarships for art school anyway.

She'd invited the girls back to her house for lunch afterward, an offer only three people accepted. But three was better than none, which was the reception she'd got the first time she offered. Progress not perfection, she always said. She'd made a round of chicken sandwiches, some lemonade, and a chocolate sponge cake. It wasn't to Rachel's standards—nowhere near—but over the past few months, when ordering catering was out of the question, Tully had grown quite adept at cooking basic things. She understood why Rachel and Mum loved the art of casual dining now. There was something soul-affirming about it.

The urge to steal hadn't gone away like she'd hoped. In fact, Tully often found herself standing in the supermarket, wondering if she could just drop a small packet of herbs or a ballpoint pen into her pocket so that she could breathe properly again. Those times, she'd learned to abandon the shopping cart and return home without the things they needed. Online shopping helped a lot with this, and Sonny went to the store in her place when she was having a particularly anxious day. But she'd noticed it was getting easier. Once again, progress, not perfection.

Sonny had been working hard, trying to make back the money they had lost. In the meantime, they enjoyed living in a smaller house. Tully no longer had a cleaner, and she found it rather satisfying to do the cleaning herself. The boys were doing fewer hours at their community preschool than they'd done at their private one, and Miles was loving having more time with her. That, combined with the therapy he had every week, had resulted in a huge change in him. He'd slept in his big-boy bed every night since they moved house.

She still thought about Dad a lot. She missed his face, his throaty laugh, his intelligent perspective on things. She missed hearing him on the phone with the boys, listening with delight to whatever nonsense they decided to tell him. She missed the way he used to listen to her, too. Like he was interested. Like a father listened. The hardest part, though, was the special occasions. They'd made it through Father's Day, but Christmas was coming up soon. She hadn't told Rachel how much she missed him. It felt like a betrayal to Mum. And yet she couldn't shake the feeling that he wasn't *all* bad. Perhaps the very worst people still had some good in them. And perhaps the very best had some bad.

67

HEATHER

It was the Christmas Heather had always dreamed of. In her big, beautiful home, the light sparkling off the pool, with children playing on the grass. Rachel and Tully had provided most of the food, but Heather had bought a ham. Before lunch they'd all exchanged exquisitely wrapped gifts, then embarked on a hilarious game of Stealing Santa, where they all opened a "silly gift" and then fought over one or two of them. The whole thing was magnificent.

Stephen should be here, she thought, not for the first time. Over the past few months, every time they got together as a family, she thought it. He would have loved to see them all coming together like this. It felt so wrong that *she* was here, with his family, when he wasn't. Still, she didn't take the privilege for granted, even for a second.

She refilled her glass of champagne, which helped a little. She'd been drinking a lot more lately, but she supposed that was understandable. She was a grieving widow, after all.

"Can we go in the pool, Hevva?" Locky asked.

Behind him, Miles sat on the floor, already nude, slipping an inflatable floatie onto his wrist.

"Sure," Heather said, sipping her champagne, "if it's okay with your mum and dad."

"I'll take you in, buddy," Darcy said, appearing in his board shorts.

Heather had to admit, she felt a pulse of something at the sight of Darcy's pectoral muscles. Then again, she supposed he was a good match for Rachel, who looked particularly stunning today in a floor-length bohemian sundress with a low-cut neckline. Her curves were truly out-of-this-world. Heather had always worked hard to maintain her slim figure but there was something about seeing Rachel that made her want to have a second helping of lunch. Rachel, ironically, hadn't eaten much at all today, perhaps too distracted by the lovely man on her arm, and the family around her.

Sonny appeared then, also in board shorts and carrying a giant inflated swan. "Ready, boys?"

"Wait," Tully said, "I have to put sunscreen on them."

The older men disappeared outside, and Tully clasped Locky between her knees, smearing sunscreen over his scrunched-up face. Heather squatted down next to Miles—who was much more accommodating—and did the same to him. He'd been much calmer these past few months, Heather had noticed. Perhaps it was having Tully around more? Or perhaps it was the fact that, since Stephen's death, everyone was a lot calmer.

Pam had passed away a month ago of pneumonia. It was a common way for people with dementia to die, but it had still come as a shock. They'd got the news that she was ill on a Wednesday, and by Saturday she was gone. The funeral had been small but lovely. Heather had attended, but remained at the back of the room.

"It feels quieter without Mum and Dad, doesn't it?" Tully said.

The boys ran outside, leaving Heather, Tully, and Rachel to clean up.

"You know what I wish?" Tully said as they loaded up the dishwasher. "I wish we'd been able to confront Dad. I still have so many questions I want to ask him."

"Me too," Rachel said. She was holding a tea towel and drying a large salad bowl. "I just wish we'd been able to hear him admit it."

"Just because he didn't admit it doesn't mean it isn't true," Heather said.

"But what if it isn't?" Rachel said, putting down the bowl. "What if we got confused somehow?"

Heather could tell by the way Tully nodded, that she was plagued by similar doubts. It caused a physical reaction in Heather. It felt vaguely matriarchal, which was comical, given she was the youngest of the women, and certainly not their mother.

"We didn't get confused," she said firmly. Stephen had spent so long gaslighting her, but she trusted herself now. She needed Tully and Rachel to trust themselves too. "Remember what we felt the moment Stephen grabbed Pam? We all felt it. Our instincts are there for a reason."

Tully opened her mouth, but Heather held up a hand, stopping her.

"Listen. I know how it feels to doubt myself. But I'm done with that. And, honestly? I think the money in the hot water bottle meant Pam was done doubting herself too."

She was getting through to them now, Heather could feel it.

"The last thing your mother would've wanted was to pass on her doubt to you two."

"She's right," Rachel said. "Mum would hate us feeling like this."

"It's time to start trusting ourselves," Tully agreed.

Heather nodded.

What choice did they have? It wasn't as if they could ask Pam.

Epilogue

Pamela

Pamela counted out the money. Ninety-seven thousand three hundred and seventy-two dollars.

"Thanks, Mum," she said out loud.

Obviously her mother couldn't hear her. Two days ago, Pam had got the phone call from her in the hospital. A suspected heart attack, Mum had said gravely, explaining that she'd been taken by ambulance to the hospital. Pam was fumbling for her keys, ready to drive to the hospital, when her mother added, "Oh, Pammy? Can you swing by my place and grab my hot-water bottle on the way?"

Pam hesitated. "I can probably find a hot-water bottle here somewhere. . . ."

"No," her mother said firmly. "I need *my* hot-water bottle. It's important, Pammy."

Her mother provided instructions for where she would find it.

At the back of the wardrobe, behind the shoes. When Pam brought it to her mother's bedside, her mother showed her its contents.

"A hundred thousand dollars?" Pam cried. "Mum, where did you get a hundred thousand dollars?"

Mum explained that for years she'd been withdrawing her pension money each week and hiding the cash in the hot-water bottle. When Pam asked why, she explained that if the government saw she wasn't spending it all, they'd reduce the amount she received. Turned out her mother was quite the pension fraudster.

"What if you'd died and never told me?" Pam asked.

"Then the people cleaning out the house would have got a nice surprise."

Pam had brought the hot-water bottle home and put it in her bedside drawer for safekeeping until her mum got out of hospital. But her mother had died that morning of another heart attack. Now, she supposed, the money was hers.

Pam wondered what she would do with all this money. What would Mum have wanted her to do?

Mum was always telling Pam that she needed to get away, unwind, take a break from her life. Perhaps she and Stephen could go to one of those health retreats? One with facials and massages. She could use a massage. Lately her body hurt all the time. One too many falls, she suspected. She was always tripping here, or stumbling there.

A few weeks ago, at book club, she'd commented on her aches and pains, and all the ladies had agreed. Old age, they said. Menopause, someone else chimed in. But afterward, as she helped herself to Mary's Black Forest cake, Diana Rothschild had made a comment that rankled Pam.

"Do you find that you are more likely to injure yourself while Stephen is around?"

Pam had been mortified. What was she insinuating? Stephen would never lay a hand on her. He was a doctor. Do no harm! She'd shrugged the question off and avoided Diana ever since. But she couldn't stop thinking about it. Because as upsetting as Diana's comment was, Pam *did* find that she was more likely to injure herself while Stephen was around. One hundred percent more likely.

But then, that made sense, didn't it? When she was with Stephen she was more likely to be distracted and stumble or slip. There had only been one incident, a few years back, that was harder to explain. She and Stephen had been in the middle of an argument, when suddenly, he'd wrapped his hands around her throat. In a way, it had been a relief. At least now, she knew. But the next day, Stephen denied anything had happened, and without so much as a bruise on her neck, she'd been forced to conclude that she was losing her mind. But what if she wasn't? What if his experience as a doctor had allowed him to leave her unmarked somehow? What if?

What if?

It got her thinking about something Fiona Arthur had said to her, years ago, right after Stephen left her. "He's not who you think he is."

A strange comment, admittedly, but given the situation, Pam had written it off as sour grapes. And yet . . . what if it was more than that? What if Fiona also had unexplained falls? What if she'd also spent her marriage wondering if she was going crazy when something more sinister was at play?

Maybe Pam would reach out to Fiona? After all, now she had

this money, she had options. Maybe it was finally time to ask questions?

Pam got out a notepad and a pen. These days, with her memory issues, if she didn't write things down, they didn't happen. She wrote down Fiona Arthur's name. Then she wrote down Tully's name. If she got the news she feared, she'd need to pack, find a new place to live. There'd be a lot of paperwork. Her daughter may have had her troubles but if there was one role Tully was born for, it was this.

Pam heard Stephen's car pull into the driveway. She tore the page out of the notepad, folded it in half, and stuffed it inside the hot-water bottle. It was as good a hiding place as anywhere.

"Pam?" Stephen called.

"Coming!" she said, shoving the hot-water bottle into the back of the closet. She'd come back to this later, when she remembered.

Acknowledgments

A couple of years ago I received a phone call from my beloved Great Aunty Gwen. She'd had a fall and been taken to the hospital, but that was, as far as she was concerned, unimportant. What was important, she told me, was that I drop everything and drive directly to her home to retrieve her hot-water bottle. Odd request, I thought, but who was I to argue? The heart wants what it wants. Alas, Gwen's house was not on my route to the hospital, and in my eagerness to get to her, I offered to bring my own hot-water bottle instead. When my offer was swiftly declined, I offered to purchase her a new one. But none of my suggestions would do.

Finally, I agreed to collect the hot-water bottle. It could be located, Gwen said, behind the set of drawers in the cupboard of the spare room, under a pile of old newspapers. And just like that, the hot-water bottle became a lot more interesting.

As I drove to Gwen's house, I theorized as to what could be in the bottle. Body parts seemed the most likely option. Bones, or organs—perhaps a human heart? It made sense. After all, Gwen is a strong, savvy ninety-three-year-old single woman—surely there had been a scorned lover or two in her lifetime? And how wonderfully perverse it would be if she yearned to keep a piece of that lover close in what might have been her final moments!

Regrettably, it wasn't body parts. Rather, it was tens of thousands of dollars, wrapped in plastic bands. Not as good as a human heart, but on balance, not completely uninteresting.

Inside the hospital I accosted Gwen's wheelie-bed as she cruised toward her x-ray scans.

"What's going on, Gwen?" I demanded. "Have you robbed a bank? Stolen money from an ex-lover? Become a granny drug dealer?"

The explanation was considerably less exciting. A pension payment and a healthy distrust of banks. By that point, though, a book idea had started to form in my mind. It became *The Younger Wife*.

And this brings me to the thank-yous.

I'll start with my publisher. You'll have to bear with me here, because it's going to get weird. St. Martin's Press published my first book, *The Secrets of Midwives*, and they've published every book since. On our first phone call, Jen Enderlin told me that she was excited not just about that book, but about all my future books. A nice thing to say, but in a world where we're constantly told that editors don't take chances on new authors, or that they don't give authors the time they need to find their stride, I didn't know if I could trust it. Fast-forward six books—and let's be real, some of my books have been what we might generously call "a disappointment"—Jen has remained excited about my future books, and backed it up by continuing to offer me contracts. Is she the exception to the rule? I don't know. But Jen Enderlin is the reason I'll never be cynical about publishing. As for the rest of the gang—Lisa Senz, Brant Janeway,

Erica Martirano, Katie Bassel, Jessica Zimmerman—what an amazing, talented bunch of humans. I am obsessed with you all.

This brings me to my beloved Pan Macmillan Australia team, who have also continued to hang around since book one. There must have been times you wanted to jump ship. Thanks for staying aboard. I'd like to extend particular thanks to Alex Lloyd who, despite his youthful looks (and, it must be said, excellent hair) has two of the best editorial eyes in the business. Also to Cate Paterson for her continued (unfounded) belief in me, and to Sammy Manson, the most innovative of marketing people. I am a lucky lady.

To Rob Weisbach, who has to wear so many hats in his role as my literary agent. Next I'm going to make you wear a beret. You will look fabulous in a beret. (Read: I can't find the words for how great you are, so I'm talking about hats instead. You get that, right?)

To Andrew Bailey and Patrick Lyttleton for always giving me legal advice for my characters. The fact that you never bat an eye when I ask how one would divorce someone with dementia or get away with murder speaks volumes about all of us.

To Kerryn Merrett, as always, for providing police expertise.

To Meagan Ruse, for sliding into my DMs and helping me with a tricky part of this manuscript.

To Mia Freedman and Kena Roach, my very helpful early readers.

To Mum, for always gleefully pointing out when I'm (confidently) using a word incorrectly—there will never be enough time to absorb your English language pedantry, but our heated discussions about whether the proof is, in fact, in the pudding will always remain among my fondest memories of us.

Finally, to my favorite bunch of weirdos—Christian, Oscar, Eloise and Clementine. Life has its challenges, but there's one thing I know for sure: weirdos will one day take their rightful place on the throne. While you're waiting for that day, go read a book.